The Backdoor Curve

by Jerry Beebe

D1445749

Printed in the United States of America

First Printing, 2017

ISBN: Paperback Edition 9781521586648

Dedication

This book is dedicated to MY angel, my daughter Jenny. My first reader and my biggest supporter. Without her help, this book would never have been possible.

I love you, Angel…

Chapter 1

"Nick Danno?" Karen asked, shaking her head in disbelief.

"Yep."

"That butthead from Clinton Heights?"

"I believe his official title is Mayor of Clinton Heights."

"The union guy who stole that money?"

"He's the treasurer of the plumber's local," I said. "He was never charged with any crime. An internal investigation by the union determined that it was an accounting error."

"Right. And he's looking for you?"

"He called the office twice today. Said it's very important that I get back to him."

"What does he want?"

"I don't know. That's the question."

"Do you owe him money?"

"NO," I said, laughing. "Do you really think I would borrow money from Nick Danno?"

"He wants a favor then," Karen said. "He's not the type to just call to see how you're doing."

She was right, of course. He wanted something. The question of what occupied my mind as I looked out over the rusty chain link fence at the Dorchester Little League baseball diamond. I hadn't been to this field in years. The place where my brother Jimmy and I spent our childhood summer days from sun up to sundown, or until our mother would drag us home by the ears. This very spot was where I first decided that I would become a professional baseball player.

It seemed smaller than I remembered.

Jimmy and Karen's little boy had just started tee ball. My nephew Gene was not a natural athlete like his dad, but he was the biggest kid on his team, and that counts for a lot when you are six. Gene was guarding first base as if it was a bag of Halloween candy filled with the international gold standard of confectionary treats, Reese's Cups. Not the "fun" size either, the JUMBO ones. Sporting a crimson Cardinals jersey emblazoned with the team sponsor logo "Sullivan's Riverside Tavern" on the back, Gene looked grim and determined as he guarded first base.

"Hey, Gene," I called out. "Looking good out there."

"Thanks, Uncle Skip,"

"You like first base?"

"It's is my favorite position," he said, never taking his eyes off the batter approaching home plate.

"Why is that?"

"'Cause there's shade," he said, motioning with his glove hand toward a big tree overhanging that side of the field.

I had to admire the logic.

The spring of 2008 had been a lot like the winter of 2007. March came in like a lion and went out like a lion. So did April. But with the changing of the calendar to May, the weather changed, and warm temperatures beckoned everyone outdoors. Under the new green leaves of the ancient maples surrounding the field, I stood with a dozen dads as they shouted instructions to their children, convinced they were watching the very first baseball moments of the next Mike Trout. Behind them, moms were doing their best to keep control of the out of control siblings, impatient and bored, swatting gnats and begging for treats from the snack stand.

Karen was watching her three year old daughter Allison toddling around the bleachers. The girl stopped and bent over, picked something up and immediately stuck it in her mouth. Karen was on her in an instant. She pried open the child's jaws and extracted a soggy brown glob.

"What is it?"

"I think it's a wood chip," Karen said, studying the evidence.

I looked around at the other parents. I knew many of them. Dorchester is a small town. A few were my age but most were younger, in their early thirties. I had no children, no current love interest and no immediate possibilities. I always blamed it on my job. I'm a sports writer for the *Philadelphia Bulletin*, and I cover the Phillies. Hard to be a responsible husband and father when seven months of the year you are flying across the country covering baseball games. Anyway, that was my official excuse.

"Maybe something to do with the paper," Karen said. "Publicity?"

"I was thinking maybe he wants Phillies tickets," I said.

"Could be. Has he every asked you for tickets before?"

"Well, no. Actually he's never asked me for tickets."

"Something's up," she said. "I tell you, he needs a favor. That has to be it."

Back on the field, Coach Jimmy made a last walk around with his clipboard roster, pulling his son from his position straddling first base to a spot a couple of steps toward second base. Behind the plate, the opposing team coach wearing a Yankees hat walked up to the tee with a yellow rubber ball in his hand.

"Look alive, everybody," Jimmy shouted back at his team.

The Yankee's coach was Jimmy's friend Max Hirsch. There were more kids this year who wanted to play than there were coaches, so Jimmy asked Max to volunteer. Surprisingly, Max had said yes he would be happy to get involved. Did Jimmy's description of the many 'hot team moms' play a minor role in this decision? Possibly. But in the interest of community service, Max was all in and took a very active role as manager.

Perhaps, too active.

As the next player approached home plate, Karen leaned over and gave me a nudge with her elbow. "This is the kid I was telling you about."

"He's huge," I said. "He towers over the other kids. Are you sure he's only six?"

"No one knows for sure. He's not in Gene's class in school. He doesn't even go to school here in Dorchester. Max says he's homeschooled. He added him to the roster after the tryouts."

Butch Bukowski had been a source of controversy in the Dorchester Tee Ball League. His sudden appearance in a Yankee uniform had spawned shocking rumors around the league. Among those, that payments of ice cream, candy and other assorted treats had been offered for services rendered, but those allegations had never been conclusively proven.

"What about a birth certificate?" I asked.

"Lost in a house fire. But Max says he will vouch for him."

"Is that supposed to be an endorsement?"

"Max says he would swear it on a stack of Bibles," Karen said with a sarcastic smile.

"Max hasn't seen the inside of a church since the fourth grade, when he got kicked out of Sunday School for stealing change out of the collection plate," I said.

Coach Hirsch looked around suspiciously, then bent back the tee hard and balanced the ball on top. Bending the tee was technically not illegal, but it was certainly less than ethical. Bending the tee would allow a child to swing up at the ball better, making the hit a fly ball rather than a ground ball. Max walked around behind home plate, smiled and nodded to Jimmy, who shook his head. The big boy took his position behind home plate, at the back of the batter's box. Then, nodding to his coach, he took two giant crow hops forward and let loose with a ferocious swing.

The ball soared into the sky, well over heads of the infielders. It rolled through the outfield dandelions, past the left and center fielders, who were on their knees digging for a worm in left center. By the time they realized that a ball had been hit in their direction, the batter had barreled around first and was headed for second.

"Hey," Jimmy yelled to the outfielders, "wake up out there."

Startled by the coach yelling at them, the left and centerfielders got up and saw the ball rolling past. Almost in unison, they then motioned to the right fielder, the smallest boy on the team and ordered him to get the ball, which by this time had stopped at the base of the outfield fence. Meanwhile, Butch rounded third and made his way panting and gasping across home plate and into the arms of his teammates celebrating yet another home run.

I had lost track of the score. Karen was trying to watch her son on the field and their daughter playing under the bleachers. Alongside her was a mottled neighborhood dog scavenging for dropped food.

"Was that seven?" I asked her.

"Nine I think," Karen said, looking at her watch. "One more run and that's it. Ten run mercy rule."
She looked down at her daughter. "Allison," she yelled, "don't eat that. It was in the dirt."

I looked under the steel treads. "Looks sort of like a Snickers bar," I said.

"Yeah, but I don't see a wrapper." Karen shot me a horrified look. She vaulted off the seat and under the bleachers to intercept the next mouthful.

The phone in my pocket began to vibrate. I walked away from the bleachers. It was the paper.

"Sorry to bother you, Skip," the receptionist said, "but you got another call from that guy Nick Danno. It's the third time he's called today. He said it was very important and to call as soon as possible."

His honor had been elected the new mayor of Clinton Heights, Pennsylvania last November. It was a larger and much more affluent town directly across the Delaware River from my hometown, Dorchester, New Jersey. Clinton Heights and Dorchester, although in different states, were linked by one of the only bridges across the river for twenty miles in either direction, so they shared some commonality. But they were as different as two towns could possibly be.

Clinton Heights was clean and polished, orderly and modern, middle upper class and thoroughly yuppie centric in every detail from their brand new state of the art regional medical center to their three Starbucks. Conversely, Dorchester was not any of the above. It was old school central Jersey, well-worn and broken down in spots, a stark melding of urban and suburban lower middle class, blue collar at the core. Gritty would be a kind description.

I've known Nick Danno ever since high school. The last time I talked to him was at the Clinton Heights hospital fundraiser in January. I decided to get it over with and find out what he wanted. I walked away from the stands to a quiet area out along right field and punched in the number.

"Nick, it's Skip McCann."

"Skip, it's been years. Great to talk to you again."

"Well, actually I saw you in January," I started.

"Listen, Skip," he interrupted, "I don't have much time here; I'm off to another city council meeting, but I wanted to run something by you."

I knew it. He wanted something.

"You know," he began, "at the Fourth of July parade this year, our guest of honor will be Brad Cole. Remember Brad? This year is our twentieth high school reunion. And for you too, right old man? Now, this isn't for public knowledge yet, but at the meeting we got talking and thought about how great it would be to have a rematch of our big game in '88. Like a three-inning

12

exhibition. And maybe Brad could make an appearance too, if it's okay with his manager. Wouldn't that be great, just for old time's sake? How's that sound?"

In the last forty years, only one Dorchester High School baseball team had ever beaten Clinton Heights High School. That was in 1988, my senior year. To this day, that victory is a major irritation to the town fathers of Clinton Heights.

Brad Cole and I were the best players on our teams. Brad was drafted by the Los Angeles Dodgers straight out of high school that year and was starting third baseman and National League Rookie of the Year for the big club when he was twenty-one years old. Now, with three MVP awards he would probably make the Hall of Fame when he retired.

Meanwhile, I decided that I wanted a college education, so I accepted a very generous full baseball scholarship from USC. My future was secure. That is until my senior year, when I tore my ACL sliding into second base. And like a sudden thunderstorm on an otherwise sunny day, everything changed. It was a crushing blow. All I ever wanted was to be a professional baseball player. My lifelong dream was over, just like that.

I would rather have gotten him Phillies tickets.

"Ah, gee, Nick, I don't know," I stalled. "Most of the guys are gone. I don't know if we can even field a team. I'll have to get back to you."

"I know you haven't played ball in a long time, Skip. I hope you're not scared to play," he said, with a cackling laugh at the end. "Hey, if you don't want to play, you can be the manager. You don't have to take the field. You can ride the bench."

Nick Danno had a gift for being able to push people's buttons. He was always able to get whatever he wanted by subtle and not so subtle threat and manipulation. I guess that's why he was a rising political star.

"No, it's not that, Nick. It's just ah, logistics."

"Well, then, I'm sure you'll round up nine," Danno said. "So, it's all settled. We'll pencil it in on the calendar for the afternoon of the 4th."

"Like I said, I don't know for sure,"

"Sorry, Skip," Danno said quickly. "Gotta run here. I'll have my secretary call you and work out the details."

"Let me check first before. . . ."

With that, the line disconnected.

I stood there for a while, just staring at my phone. A rematch of the 1988 Cross River series game. It had been a miracle win all those years ago. But, to do it again? With Brad Cole back in the lineup. Very unlikely. This would not be good.

Although I still loved baseball, I had not played since my injury. Didn't really want to. Threw my college baseball gear away in the dorm dumpster. Depression? Sure. Post traumatic stress? I don't know. Whatever you call it when you realize that you will never, ever get the one thing you want most in your life. After that, I had absolutely no desire to ever take the field again.

That is until that May afternoon at the tee ball field in May 2008. Even though I thought the whole thing was a bad idea for Dorchester, and despite the fact that it had been years since I held a baseball bat with the intention of hitting something, I knew I absolutely had to be on the field for that game.

I heard a roar from the Yankees side of the field. They had scored the game's final run. The Yankees had ten runned the Cardinals. Now, kids and parents exited the field at a great pace and were piling into minivans and SUVs. After a tee ball game in Dorchester, everyone headed down the street to a local baseball tradition, Custard King.

Custard King was located on the main road into town out past the high school. The single two-lane highway into Dorchester had seen better economic days. Among the urban decay of a dozen closed and abandoned businesses, the colorful flashing neon lights of Custard King made the old ice cream stand look like a casino on the Vegas strip. Out by the road, a large faded electric sign from the late 1960s featured the image of the famed Custard King himself, including his golden neon jewel encrusted crown. Now, forty years later, his majesty's weathered likeness resembled a disturbing cross between Queen Elizabeth II and Snoop Dog.

Max was at the head of one of the lines. He got his order through the window, and I saw him present a Custard King Kitchen Sink Double Fudge Sundae Royale, with wet nuts and whipped cream, served in a bowl the size of a hub cap to Butch Bukowski. Karen and Jimmy and their kids were in the other line.

"Good game, Coach," I said to Jimmy.

He shook his head. "Pathetic. The only thing good was that it was short, that's about it."

"Max has that team on fire. He's got some great players."

"Yeah, the best players ice cream can buy," he said.

"You're the one who got him coaching," Karen said, shaking her head. "You knew what he was like."

"Yeah, I know. Don't remind me."

"Oh, by the way," I said. "What are you doing Fourth of July?"

"What do we always do Fourth of July? Drink beer, the Dorchester parade, drink some more beer, do the barbecue and fair at the football field, drink some more beer and tailgate in the parking lot, then watch the fireworks and stagger home. It's a tradition."

"Maybe not this year."

"What's going on?" he asked.

"You wanna play a baseball game?"

Jimmy gave me a funny look. Although we talked Phillies all the time, I never, ever brought up the idea of playing the game again. It was sore spot between us. He had asked me countless times to join his teams, and I always said no.

"On the Fourth of July?" he asked.

"Yep."

"With who?"

"The Clinton Heights 1988 team."

Jimmy's eyes widened. "Are you kidding me? A rematch of the Cross River series game?"

"Yeah, Nick Danno called me about it."

"Skip," Jimmy said, "a few of those guys are still playing in the over-35 league, and they're beasts."

"So, you're not interested?"

"The hell I'm not. I'm about the only one still playing league ball."

"What about Billy and Kyle?" I said. Billy Harper and Kyle Larkin were former Dorchester baseball team members who played with Jimmy in the over 35-year-old baseball league.

"They'll play. Will Brad Cole be there?"

"Yeah," I said. "He'll be there."

"Good Lord," Jimmy said, shaking his head. "We are going to get our asses kicked. He's a major leaguer. We need some ringers." He looked me straight in the eyes. "How about you?"

"I'm no ringer. Not anymore," I said. "I haven't been on a field in years and I'm way out of practice."

"You were the best baseball player this town ever saw."

"A long time ago maybe, before I got hurt."

"You may still be. You wouldn't know, would you?"

I had no answer to that question.

"So," Jimmy said, folding his arms and looking up at the sky with a questioning expression. "A rematch of the '88 Cross River series game. Biggest game of our lives. Are you in?"

"Yes," I said. "I am in."

Jimmy looked dumbfounded. I guess he thought I was kidding him. He looked at me through narrowed eyes. "Now don't shit me, Bro," he said. "For years I've asked you to come back on the field with me and you always turn me down. Now I'm serious. Are you really in this time?"

"Yes. I'm really in."

"You are in? You will play? You're sure?"

"I'm positive."

"You haven't picked up your glove since college."

"I'm not quite sure where it is."

"I know where it is," he said. "It's in your old bat bag in the attic, along with a bunch of other stuff that Pop saved."

"Guess I'll have to dig through it," I said.

"Good Lord," he said slowly, shaking his head, "I never thought I would live to see the day." He took off his Cardinals cap and wiped his forehead. "My big brother going back on the field."

"Don't get too emotional yet little brother. I haven't played in years. I may suck."

"No," he said. "You won't suck. Not you. No way. When it came to baseball, you were the always the best. You were scary good, Skip. And everybody who ever saw you play knew it."

"That was a long time ago. We will see."

"So what do we have," he said, "maybe five or six guys? This game is only a month and a half away, we don't even have a full team and we haven't practiced together in 20 years. We're playing a team that's lead by one of the best players in Major League Baseball." He shook his head, but with a grin from ear to ear. "I don't know, Skip. This could end up being a freakin disaster."

"Yes it could," I said. "Another in a long line of humiliating disappointments for the town of Dorchester. A monumental mistake that we might regret for the rest of our lives. So, how about it?"

"The McCann brothers, back on the field together for the first time in 20 years?" He asked. "Skip, I wouldn't miss it for all the ice cream at Custard King."

I sat in my car for a while with my small twist sugar cone dripping onto my hand, pondering two important questions. First, how we would put together a competitive baseball team when most of the original players were gone, scattered across the country. Second, would the chocolate ice cream that had dripped all over my shirt leave a stain.

I finished the cone, wiped my shirt with a napkin as best as was possible and drove back to my apartment. Around the building on the Front Street side was my usual last minute dinner choice, Lee's Best Food in Town Chinese restaurant. I ate there at least two or three nights a week outside of baseball season. The delivery cars were both on the road that night, but the dining room was nearly empty save for one couple in the first booth on the right. Mrs. Lee smiled at me when I came in, wrote down my take out order for orange chicken, and told me it would be ten minutes.

I looked over at the couple in the booth. The woman was facing my direction. She was a cute, petite redhead with a small upturned nose and a great smile. She looked maybe 25 or 26 with big green eyes, wearing blue nurses' scrubs and laughing at her companion. He had his back to me, but I knew his voice.

Best Food had a monster fish tank behind the counter in the waiting area with gold fish swimming back and forth. I walked over to the fish tank behind the couple and eavesdropped by the partition.

"And the guy in the sombrero says, 'Badgers? We don't need no stinking Badgers!'"

The cute nurse looked awkwardly sideways, stifling a snorting laugh. "Oh Tony, that was really bad."

"I know. I've built my reputation telling the worst possible jokes I can."

"Well, then you have two reputations," she said smiling.

"What's the other? Super doctor perhaps?"

"How about super-lecherous doctor?"

"What? Lecherous? Who told you that?"

"Practically every other nurse at the hospital."

"Really?" Tony said, as if in disbelief. "Come on now, haven't I been the perfect gentleman tonight?"

"Yes, actually you have," she said.

"Disappointed?"

"Maybe a little," she laughed.

"And despite my alleged 'reputation' you still agreed to go to dinner with me?"

"Well," she started. "I was curious."

Tony signaled to Mrs. Lee for the check. "I'm curious about my fortune. How about you?"

Mrs. Lee came over with the check. She reached in her left pocket and gave a fortune cookie to Tony. Then she reached into her right pocket and gave one to the nurse, who picked up the cookie, and cracked it open.

Tony read his fortune and then looked up and took a deep audible breath. "Okay, here goes," he said with a shrug, holding the fortune cookie up in front of him.

21

"Kristen, I would hate to ruin my bad reputation. I really enjoyed having dinner with you, and the last thing I want is to see you disappointed. So, how about we go back to my place for a little while? I live right upstairs. There's a great deck on the roof with big comfy chairs overlooking the river. It's a beautiful night. I've got a wonderful Loire Valley Sauvignon Blanc in the fridge I've been saving for a special occasion, like this. What do you say?"

He passed his fortune across the table. Kristen read it out loud.

"Destiny awaits! Speak your heart's utmost desire."

She looked up at him, eyes wide. "I'd like to accept your proposition," she said, flashing that great smile, and read him her fortune cookie.

"Accept the next proposition you hear."

He laughed. "Oh my God, It must be fate."

"I'll just be a minute," she said, grabbing her pocketbook and headed off to the ladies room.

As she disappeared around the corner, I leaned forward and spoke from behind the fish tank. "And another one in the win column for starting pitcher Dr. Tony Adamo."

"Hmmm," he said, turning his head and smiling. "Why, it's either a big mouthed talking carp or maybe famed Philly sportswriter and dating strikeout leader Skip McCann, with what looks like a chocolate ice cream stain on his shirt."

Dr. Tony Adamo and I had been neighbors and best friends ever since kindergarten. He played second base and I played shortstop on every baseball team from tee ball to varsity high school. He even lived with my family when his parents died. After medical school he bought this building, which also housed his medical practice and the town's much needed urgent care facility, and two apartments on the top floor.

"How DO you do it, Doctor?" I asked, smiling.

He slid out of the booth and handed his check to Mrs. Lee at the counter. "You assume that I'm out here trying to take advantage of a beautiful young nurse who just moved to the area. Nothing could be further from the truth. I'm just a concerned, helpful colleague, trying to ease her acclimation to a new town. I have nothing but the purest, most altruistic thoughts."

"Thank you, Doctor Tony," Mrs. Lee said, handing back his change. "Oh, and Jonny say we getting low on your 'accept next proposition' fortune cookies that you bought. You used them up fast. He order more for you." She hurried back to the kitchen.

"You rigged the fortune cookies?" I asked.

"Change of subject if you please," Tony said. "What are you doing around here tonight? I've got dibs on the roof."

"Phillies are idle. I was at my nephew's tee ball game. You'll never guess who I got a call from."

"Miss America?"

"Guess again."

"Mr. America?"

"Nick Danno."

"Close."

"You'll never guess what he wanted."

"Probably the baseball game rematch on the Fourth of July."

I stood there dumbfounded. "How do you know about that? He just called me this afternoon. It's supposed to be a secret."

"It is a secret," he said, popping a mint into his mouth. "That's why half the town is talking about it. He let it leak at a city council meeting last night. It was all over the hospital today."

"How are we going to field a team?"

"We? Are you coming out of retirement?"

"Yeah," I said. "I think I will."

"Really?" he said, looking at me in disbelief.

"Really."

His look of shock turned to a broad smile, and he leaned in and grabbed my shoulders in a bear hug, giving me a big slap on the back. "Pinch me, I must be dreaming! Me at second and you at short," he said. "The greatest double play combo in the history of Dorchester baseball, back on the field. Damn, Skip. It's about time."

"I was injured. I tore up my leg. I couldn't play."

"You are trying to bullshit a medical doctor. Don't even try. Your leg

24

was fine 18 months after the surgery. Sure, you lost a couple of steps, but then again you were always twice as fast as everyone else on the field anyway. The problem was not your ACL, it was in your head."

"Thanks for the diagnosis, Dr. Freud."

"Don't mention it. I'll bill your insurance company. Anyway, count me in. God, who else is left? I guess there's Woody, that is if he can make it around the bases without having a heart attack."

"I talked to Jimmy, and he's in. Billy Harper and Kyle Larkin play on his over-35 team. They'll probably play."

"John Stone?" Tony asked?

"I wouldn't count on it," I said. John Stone was the home run leader on the 1988 squad. He was beaned in the head in the Clinton Heights game by Brad Cole. The ninety plus mile per hour fastball actually cracked his batting helmet. Suffered a severe concussion and spent a week in the hospital. "I think John's done with baseball," I said.

"So were you," Tony said.

"Yeah. I was, until today. But you know what I always say. Never say never. Life can be a funny thing sometimes."

"Yes, it certainly can," Tony said. "Well, that's six at least. I can get a current list of alumni addresses and phone numbers. I think a lot of them will be coming in for the Fourth this year."

"Let's hope so. We need bodies."

He looked out of the corner of his eye, and then grabbed my hand and began shaking it. "It's no problem at all, I'd be happy to volunteer my time. Oh, there you are, Kristen," he said, as the nurse walked up. "This is Skip McCann, a volunteer candy striper and bedpan emptier over at the retirement home in Florence. They want me to come by and give a talk to the seniors on the dangers of calcium deficiency and bone loss. Call my secretary tomorrow, Skip, and she'll work out the details."

"Oh, that's so nice of you, Tony," Kristen said with a sweet smile.

"Bless you doctor, you're an inspiration," I said, returning the handshake.

"A little cold water will get that stain out," Tony said, pointing a finger at the offending brown splash. "And I'd get that shirt into the washer, pronto." He smiled and turned to the pretty nurse. "Now, if you'll excuse us. I have a date with destiny."

Chapter 2

The next morning, I was in my cubicle at the paper, the cleanest, neatest and most organized cubicle in the news room. That's because I only go in to the office a couple of days a week at the most, so I don't do enough work there to get it messy. I do most of my writing for the games in the press box at the ballpark or at the apartment. I love technology.

My editor Stan sat on the corner of my desk skimming my latest Phillies column. He had been the Phillies beat reporter when I came on board ten years ago. Now he was the boss.

"I can't believe you think the Phillies have a shot," he said, shaking his head. "They look awful."

"I think they're coming around. I don't know, I just have a feeling."

"Yeah, right. I have a feeling, too," he said. "I have a feeling that you're trying to kiss ass with the Phillies front office. What's in it for you? Open bar in the executive dining room?"

"Oh for God's sake, Stan, this isn't my first rodeo. I've been watching the Phillies since I was a kid. I've seen them at their worst. I remember the acres of empty yellow seats in the 700 section of the Vet. They were terrible. But, I'm telling you, this year will be different. Call me crazy, but they showed me something this spring."

"You are crazy. They lost every one of the five games I saw in Clearwater."

"I sat right next to you in the press box," I said. "You weren't watching the players. Every time I looked you were checking out the Hooter's girls sitting down by the foul lines."

"There was more raw talent with those girls shagging foul balls than with the players on the field."

"You know spring training," I said. "The starters play only a few innings. They're sizing up young talent. It's not meant to be competitive."

"I'm telling you, Skip, I've got them maybe third place. No better. I've been watching the Phillies for fifty years. I remember 1964. Trust me, I know. If you think they're going anywhere in the playoffs, you are sadly mistaken."

From across the busy room a voice called out, "Skip, call for you on line five." I punched it up.

"*Bulletin*, sports desk."

"Skip McCann?" the voice was tentative, and it quavered a bit.

"Speaking?"

"Skip, it's Kim. Kim Gundersen. Remember, from USC?"

I remembered.

I met Kim on my first day in class as a college freshman at USC in August 1988. I remember watching out of the corner of my eye as she came in the doorway, stood for a minute and looked around. Attractive, her Asian features were framed by long black straight hair pulled back into a pony tail that trailed down her back. She was wearing a yellow sun dress with thin straps over her brown shoulders. Her body was toned; she was lean and muscular. She looked and moved like an athlete. I immediately thought that she was in the wrong class.

She looked around, frowning. Then with a shrug, she walked around to the back row of the class and took the seat next to me.

I looked over at her. "Hi," I said.

She looked back and smiled. "Hi," she answered.

"Are you in the right class?"

"I think so." She looked at her class schedule. "C16, Radio Production 101?"

"You're in the right class," I said. "It's just that you kinda stick out like a sore thumb."

"What do you mean?"

"Look around," I said. "Radio Production 101 is not the where you will find the bold and the beautiful. The room is full of nerdy looking radio geeks."

"Yeah, I see that," she said, looking straight at me.

"Are you looking at me?"

"No."

"Yes, you were. You were looking at me."

"I was looking in your direction."

"Are you sure?"

"Yes. I wasn't looking at you. You look sort of normal."

"Thank you, I think."

"You're welcome."

At that moment, a very large, scruffy looking guy with wild disheveled hair, five-day beard and bloodshot eyes stumbled in. He was dressed all in black, wearing a very wrinkled Sex Pistols tee shirt with a chain for a belt and listening to a Walkman playing very loud punk music. Kim and I looked at each other at the same time. She raised her eyebrows and motioned toward him with her eyes. He walked up to us and looked at the empty seat on the other side of Kim. Her bag was hanging on the back.

"Is this taken?"

"Yes," she said.

"Oh," he replied, looking around. "Are you sure?"

"Absolutely."

"Okay," he said, and with his music still audible he ambled down the row and took a seat near the front of the class.

I was looking at her. "I take it you're not a big Sex Pistols fan?"

"No," she said, never looking up and thumbing through the paper syllabus on the desk.

I sat there for a minute, processing what had just gone down. Kim was looking intently at the paper.

"You just lied to that guy," I said, shaking my head. "Not good. I may have to report this violation of the student code to the administration."

The corners of her mouth began to twitch. She looked over at me with a very mischievous grin.

"I wasn't lying," she said.

"But there isn't anyone sitting in that seat."

"I didn't say there was. All I said was that it was taken."

"By who?"

"Whom," she answered.

"Okay. By whom?"

"By my bag."

I had to admire the logic.

"What's your name?" I asked.

"My name is Kim. You can call me, ah, Kim."

"Okay, ah-Kim. And I'm Skip. But, you can call me Johnny Rotten."

"Okay, Skip," she said.

"Skip, I hope you remember me?" she said over the phone, jolting me back into the present.

"Of course I remember you, Kim. I'm in shock."

"It's been a long time."

"Yes, it has. Like years."

"How are you?" she asked.

"I'm doing great."

"So, you're a sports writer? You always said that if you couldn't play, then that would be your dream job."

"Ten years in. I love it. How about you?"

"I work for a marketing company in San Francisco."

"And I heard you got married?"

"Yes, I did. You remember Roger?"

"Yes," I said. Roger was her on again off again semi steady boyfriend who came around when he wasn't hanging with his law school buddies.

"I tried to call you when I got back to Jersey," I said, "but you disappeared on me. I couldn't reach your mom or dad either."

"I tried to call you too, but I kept missing you," she said. "That first year after college was crazy. My parents ended up moving to Washington when my

Dad got a job with Microsoft. I moved to San Francisco and got married. I heard you got married, too."

"Yes, I did," I said. There was a moment of awkward silence in my mind as I recalled by brief and unsuccessful attempt at marital bliss.

"Kids?" she asked, almost tentatively.

"Not that lucky. How about you?"

There was a pause. "I have one. A girl."

I hadn't talked to Kim in sixteen years, but I remembered her well enough that I could recognize a nervous edge in her voice.

"Listen, Skip," she continued, "the reason I'm calling is because I'm going to be in Philadelphia next week, and I was hoping to get the chance to see you. Are you free on Tuesday? Maybe we can have lunch."

"Absolutely, Kim. I'd love to see you again. I've wondered for years what happened to you."

"Good. Because I need to talk to you about something." There was an uncomfortable silence. I almost started to talk again when she blurted out, "I need to ask a pretty big favor."

"Okay," I said.

"Thanks, Skip. It means a lot."

I gave her my cell number and told her to call me when she got into town.

My mind raced as I hung up the clunky black handset. Kim had vanished after graduation. And now, after what, sixteen years without a word she was suddenly reaching out.

'A pretty big favor.' Hmmm. Probably not Phillies tickets.

I got back to my place shortly after five. It was a typical late Friday afternoon down at Sullivan's Riverside Tavern, right across the street from my apartment. In some of the more gentrified old towns along the Pennsylvania side of the Delaware River, the trés chic eateries on the water featured cozy outside tables for two with brightly covered umbrellas and a matching striped awning. Waiters wearing crisp white shirts would greet you warmly with fake nondescript accents and tell you about the sushi offerings and the chef's Lemongrass Curry with Kale and Tofu blackboard special. But not here. This was Jersey. Dorchester was decidedly not gentrified and Sullivan's was as far from trés chic as you could possibly get.

The decor was an interior designer's worst nightmare. The room was lit with the multicolored glow of a dozen neon beer signs, advertising forgotten brews like Ortlieb and Ballantine that had disappeared from the taps eons ago. The faded knotty pine walls were covered with old sports memorabilia and posters, framed photos yellowed with age and cigarette smoke. In the center of the facing wall hung an ancient black and gold dart board so worn with puncture marks that you could barely make out the numbers. A battered Seeburg Firestar jukebox in the corner played a mix of classic rock and country

34

records. And mounted above it hung a dusty old deer head proudly wearing a 1980 Phillies World Series cap on it's horns. Sullivan's was an unabashed oasis of old manhood from a time long ago, set in today's contemporary sea of mixed gender blandness.

The after work crowd was beginning to assemble along the bar. The customers talked about their jobs, their money troubles or problems with their wives and girlfriends. Meanwhile, they kept an eye on the television just in case something exciting flashed on, like a sport highlight, a Victoria's Secret commercial, or the attractive TV weather girl.

One thing about Sullivan's - they have the absolute best hot dogs I have ever tasted. Hot dogs are my thing. I'm not ashamed to say that I love hot dogs and consider myself a hot dog connoisseur. As a sportswriter I have sampled enough ballpark food to write a book about the quintessential American summertime treat. I've tried them all, from New York's Hebrew National to Chicago's Vienna Beef to LA's DodgerDog, from Bratwurst to Mettwurst to Rippers, but my favorite dogs were to be found in Dorchester. Sullivan's dogs are plump and flavorful, with a hint of garlic but not too salty. They have a nice snap to them when you bite into one. Perfect. The bar owner, my uncle Harry, gets his dogs fresh from a guy who sells them out of a cooler in the back of his pickup truck. Says they are made from a secret recipe by Amish farmers,

"Too many holes in this Phillies team, Skip. I don't think they've got what it takes to win the NL East again."

35

Sitting next to me was perhaps the biggest man in Dorchester. Brenton Walter Wood stood six feet six inches tall and almost half as wide. He cut a very imposing figure, taking up nearly two barstools. His voice was as big as his frame. Woody had been the biggest kid in my kindergarten class, and no one ever got close.

"Don't count them out yet," I said, with a shrug, taking a bite of my jumbo hot dog with Pennsylvania Dutch sauerkraut. "This team has, I don't know, something. They're struggling now, but I think they've got a real shot this season."

"Naw, too inconsistent. The pitchers need help and Charlie looks like a lost dog managing in that dugout."

"Hamels is young, but he's got good stuff. Moyer is old, but he's smart. And Manuel may look dazed and confused sometimes on TV, but I gotta tell you he really knows this game inside and out. And I'll bet in September this team starts to gel."

"What about this Fourth of July game with Clinton Heights? How could you agree to a rematch with those ass hats? We don't even have a full team?"

"I never agreed to anything. Chief ass hat Mayor Nick Danno dreamed this whole thing up."

"Am I on the team?"

"Of course you are. What kind of a question is that? You were our starting first base man."

"Well, I'm sure you haven't noticed, but I'm not in the best physical condition any more."

"Woody, you were never in the best physical condition. Even in Little League when you hit a home run you'd be out of breath trotting around the bases."

"That was asthma."

"Bullshit. That was Custard King."

"I just hope I can make it to first base," he said. "Ninety feet. That's like six times to the refrigerator and back, a lot for a guy my age."

"You're thirty-eight, same as me."

"I've had a hard life."

"If you say so."

"Maybe some of other guys will come back for the Fourth," he said. "What about Flash Gordon? Man, he could flat out fly."

"Tony's working on it," I said, finishing my dog. "He probably has his entire office staff calling around."

The Phillies lost that night 5-3 to the Astros. I got home at my usual time, a little past midnight and a knock came at the door. Tony poked his head in.

"You have company?"

"Do I ever?"

37

"Miracles happen. Maybe a ball girl, a security guard or a peanut vendor?" He walked in and dropped onto the couch.

"No action tonight?" I asked.

"No, tonight is an off night," he said with a sigh. "I'm on tomorrow with a nurse anesthetist from Lambertville. Off Sunday, and then on Monday and Tuesday."

"Monday AND Tuesday? Twins?"

"Friends of girls in the office."

"What about that cute nurse last night?"

"Kristen?" He had a far off look and made a faint smile. "I cannot lie to you, Skip. She was fun. I may ask her out again."

"Ah, the exciting life of a rich successful doctor. You're a lucky man."

"Lucky in cardiology, unlucky in love," Tony said.

I knew where this was going.

"Really, Tony," I said, "of the hundreds of women you've dated. . . ."

"Thousands."

"Okay, of the 'thousands' of women you have dated, not even one gives you an irregular heart beat?"

"There will only be one woman who could cause me arrhythmia. And she's gone. Forever."

"For God's sake, Tony, that was almost twenty years ago."

"You never forget being left at the altar."

"It wasn't the altar; it was the high school prom."

"Thanks for reminding me," he said.

Her name was Angelina, and she was Tony's first and only true love. Incredibly built, flowing dark hair, olive complexion and Sicilian beautiful. And she knew it. They had gone out on a couple of dates and Tony asked her to the prom. It was going to be the biggest night of his life. Unfortunately, the lovely Angelina was not at her house when he went to pick her up. Her father said she had already left. When Tony got to the prom, she was already there and in the arms of her new boyfriend, Curt Miller, whose dad owned the construction company doing the turnpike bridge resurfacing. An upgrade in her eyes over the not so rich orphan Tony Adamo. She married and moved out of the area a year after graduation, but Tony had never forgotten her. She was the gold standard by which all the other women in his life were measured. And no one ever came close.

I decided to change the subject. "You want to catch the Phillies on Sunday? Press box?"

"Who are they playing?"

"The Dodgers and our good friend Brad Cole."

"Mr. Wonderful? Sure, I'm in."

"Any luck with the Fourth of July game?"

He shook his head. "I had the office call everyone on the '88 roster. Most have moved away. Only one definite. Winston Marshall. Still in New

Jersey, playing over-35 ball in the Toms River league."

"Well, that makes seven."

"I'd really like to have Flash Gordon in center field," he said. "That guy could flat out FLY."

"We have to have at least one practice, too."

"Ya think so? You are smarter than you look. I always thought you had managerial potential."

"Tony, we need more guys."

"I put my collections people on it," he said. "Offered a five hundred dollar bounty for every former player they get to come back. Those guys will get a phone call and a letter from my staff every day until they cave in."

Most Saturdays when the weather cooperated and whenever I wasn't on the road with the team, I would pick up a dozen fresh bagels from Sunrise bakery on the corner of Main and First and walk the six blocks to the big old three-story house where I grew up. Jimmy, Karen and their two kids moved in to take care of our mother after she was diagnosed with lung cancer.

This particular Saturday, the Dorchester spring town yard sale was in progress. The sun was bright, it was already warm. As I walked along, I glanced at the usual assortment of clothes, housewares and curios lining the sidewalk.

As I walked along, something unusual for a yard sale caught my eye. A huge stuffed and mounted sailfish. Tony had a sailfish on the wall in his apartment that he had actually caught himself on a fishing trip in Cabo. This one was bigger. I ended up buying it for seventy-five dollars, just to see the expression on Tony's face the next time he came into my apartment and saw this enormous beast over the mantle. It was awkward and difficult to handle, but I tucked it under my arm as best I could trying not to stab other shoppers. I continued down the sidewalk.

The house where I grew up was on Sixth Street about half a block from the school. As I turned the corner of Sixth Street, I passed Tony's old house. Another family had moved in over the winter. They had a small table with some assorted items, more kids toys and a couple of pieces of old furniture. One of the pieces was a coat tree; hanging from one peg was an old faded baseball hat.

It was a Dorchester Little League all-star team hat. This particular hat was green with "Dorchester" on the front in script and underlining the letters a row of gold stars. That particular design had only been used one year. I set down the bagels and the sailfish on the lawn and picked up the hat. On the underside of the brim the initials "TA" were faintly legible.

"Where did you find this hat?" I asked the woman at the table.

"Oh, it was buried in the attic, down along the eaves," she said. "It must be twenty years old."

"It's twenty-seven years old. How much?"

She gave me a funny look. "How do you know that?"

"This is a special hat. It was from the Dorchester Little League 1982 season, the year we went to the state championship. I was on that team. A good friend of mine lived here at the time. These are his initials," I said, handing her the hat and showing her the underside of the brim.

"Is he still around?"

"He's the town doctor. He runs the medical urgent care practice over on Front Street."

"Dr. Adamo? Really? I took my daughter there last week. She had strep throat. He was great. And cheap, too."

"Dorchester residents don't pay retail with Tony," I said. "The people of this town helped to put him through med school. It's his way of giving back."

"Do you see him often?"

"Actually I live next door to him."

She handed me the hat. "This is his. Make sure he gets this back."

"Thanks. I will. This will really make him happy," I said, sliding the hat into my back pocket.

Out on the lawn at the house where I grew up, Karen and the kids were manning the table with the money. Jimmy and his friends Max and Wayne were carrying treasures down from the attic. Jimmy and Wayne were fighting a large round coffee table out the door while Max stood and shouted instructions.

"How's business?" I asked.

"Not bad," Karen said. "We might just make enough to pay the electric bill this month." She looked at the sailfish under my arm. "Early morning fishing trip?"

"Yep, what do you think?"

"Already stuffed and mounted. Convenient."

I dropped the sailfish down and put the brown paper bag of bagels on the card table. "I'm impressed," I said. "You've got the 'A' team up early this morning." I said, gesturing toward the crew of movers.

She reached down to take something out of her daughter's mouth. "Allison, don't eat that; it was in the dirt."

"Is that a worm?" I said.

"Hard to tell now," she said, looking closely at the mangled bit of soggy gel.

"Hey there, Skip," Max said walking up to the table and grabbing a bagel from the bag. "You're just in time. Got some hungry working men here."

"You're hands look empty, Max."

"I'm the foreman today. Back's acting up again. Don't want to push it."

It was common knowledge that Max had been collecting disability for what seemed like forever from a mysterious accident. He had been working a whole four weeks for the city of Clinton Heights as an assistant for his uncle at the public works department. The day after his thirty day city employee probationary period ended, walking out to his car, he tripped over a rogue pine cone in the parking lot. His mother's brother-in-law's cousin was a doctor in Perth Amboy whose professional medical opinion was that Max's resulting injury was severe enough to preclude him from returning to work in the office. Despite the fact that the insurance company had video surveillance of Max bowling, waterskiing on the Delaware River and riding his ATV.

Jimmy and Wayne were setting down the unwieldy coffee table at the curb. "Take five, boys," Max said, mouth full of bagel. "It's break time."

"YES, cinnamon and raisin," Jimmy said, snatching a bagel from the bag. "Thanks, Bro."

He looked down at the sailfish sitting on the lawn. "Dinner?" he asked.

"Redecorating."

"Your place can use it," he said. "Now you can take down that day-glow velvet picture of Elvis."

"Wayne," Karen said, "how about a bagel?"

Wayne Towne was about ten years younger than the rest of us. Like Jimmy, he joined the plumber's union right out of high school, and they had become fast friends. At first glance, the best way to describe Wayne Towne was "impossibly beautiful." Tall and muscular, flowing blond curls framing ice blue eyes. Romance novel cover material. But despite the Adonis physique and supermodel looks, Wayne Towne had the mind of an eight-year old. It's not that he was mentally disabled, at least not completely. He had picked up the plumbing trade quickly and was good with his hands. But, mentally and socially he was like a child, a big sweet naive child.

"Thanks a lot, Mrs. McCann," he said, gingerly reaching in for a French toast bagel.

"Two more trips and I think that will do it," Jimmy said.

"That's good," Wayne said. "I promised my neighbor I would fix her shower later this morning."

"Who is that?" Karen said.

"She's new in town. Her name is Mrs. Hopkins."

"What about 'Mister' Hopkins?" Jimmy asked.

"I don't think there is a 'Mister' Hopkins," he said, chewing his bagel. "She lives by herself two doors down from me. It's so strange. I've tightened that shower head twice now, but for some reason it keeps coming loose. It almost looks like there are wrench scratch marks on the fitting. You ever hear of anything like that Jimmy?"

Jimmy pursed his lips, his brow furrowed in thought. "Sounds like maybe her, um, fitting has been loosened and tightened so much that maybe it's just worn out."

I looked at Karen. Her eyebrows were up, and she stifled a giggle.

"I think she wants your body, Hose," Max said, reaching for another bagel.

Max never called Wayne by his real name, instead calling him "Hose." Wayne's father was the town fire marshal, and his entire family was part of the volunteer fire company. Many people thought the nickname was a reference to his firefighting family. However, most of the friends he had grown up with in Dorchester, both male and female, knew that it actually sprang from a high school classmate seized with horror in the freshman gym class shower room. The first time Wayne joined the other kids without his towel, it was clear that in one major regard, he was truly a man among boys. The words "epic" and "legendary" were used when describing him, especially among his girlfriends.

"No, I don't think so," Wayne said. "She's really nice. She always tells me how sorry she is for having to call me whenever there's a problem, and that it's great to have a real man around to help her when she's in trouble. She makes me cookies whenever I fix something for her."

"How are her cookies?" Jimmy asked.

"Pretty good. And they're homemade, not that refrigerated stuff. Chocolate chip. I love chocolate chip. Anyway, I think what happens is she gets into the shower and sees the shower head dripping and then calls me up 'cause she knows I'm a plumber. She just stays in her robe the whole time 'cause she wants to take a shower after I fix it. That's all."

"Yeah, I'm sure you're right," Jimmy said with a smile.

"I'm not a plumber," I said, "but maybe the best thing here is a new shower head."

"That's probably her idea all along," Karen said, trying and failing to hold in a giggle.

"Yeah, why didn't I think of that," Wayne said. "That old fitting just wore out. A new one will fix her up in no time!" A snort came from Karen's side of the table.

"I think we need to get the rest of that junk out to the curb," Jimmy said, shooting a disapproving look at his wife. "It's already hot in that attic."

"Okay, let's do it," Wayne said, turning for the house.

"Listen, Wayne," Karen called to him. "I'll bet it's over a hundred degrees in that attic now. Why don't you take off your tee shirt so it doesn't get so sweaty?"

"Oh yeah, you're right, good idea," he agreed, pulling off his tee to reveal a rippling muscular body already glistening from the morning's work. "Hey, thanks, Mrs. McCann."

"It's MY pleasure, Wayne," she grinned, shooting a wink and a smile at Jimmy.

Before heading up to the press box for the afternoon game, I grabbed a basket of crabby fries and watched batting practice from one of the stand up tables in the concourse overlooking the field. An older couple named Bob and Hilda came up and asked to join me. As they split a jumbo barbecue sandwich from Bull's BBQ, we made small talk.

"So," I asked, "what do you think of the Phillies chances this year?"

"Call me crazy, but I think they have a shot," Bob said.

"Everybody thinks he's crazy," Hilda added.

"I've seen a lot of bad Phillies baseball, so I know not to get my hopes up," he continued. "But there's something about this year that reminds me of 1980. These guys want it, bad."

"That's what I think too, Bob," I said. "I saw something this year at spring training. I like their chances."

"Bob and I went down to Clearwater for some games," Hilda said. "He said the same thing."

"One morning during spring training we were eating breakfast at Lenny's," Bob said. "You know Lenny's, right?"

"Next to the ballpark. Sure do," I said. "Love their breakfasts."

"Anyway, we are sitting there at a booth about to place our order and in walks five or six players. Sat right down at the table next to ours. I even forget who was there."

"Chooch was there," Hilda said.

"That's right, Ruiz was one of them." Bob went on. "Well, what impressed me about those guys was the closeness. The camaraderie. I'm telling you, sitting around that table they looked and acted like a team, not just a group of athletes thrown together by a front office GM."

"It's all about team play," I said.

"That's right. Baseball is a team sport, Bob said. "I've seen a lot of games won by guys who played as a team, beating other guys who may have been better athletes, but they were all individual prima donnas. You win baseball games by playing as a team."

"I think he got blueberry pancakes," Hilda said.

Bob looked at her. "Who?"

"Chooch."

I pondered Bob's comments and made mental note to ask Ruiz about the blueberry pancakes at Lenny's as I watched the Phillies beat the Nationals that afternoon 4-1. Moyer threw a gem, allowing just one run and four hits over seven innings. Lidge got the save.

Sullivan's was crowded for a Saturday night without a game on TV. The bar stools were all taken, and pockets of guys stood around behind them. From the jukebox, Bob Seger was reminiscing about his 'Night Moves.' Jimmy and Max were seated along the wall. As I walked up to Jimmy, a green pony bottle of Rolling Rock magically appeared on the bar in front of me.

"I'm telling ya," Max said to Jimmy, "the problem is that transformer."

"What transformer?" I asked, squeezing in beside them.

"Max here," Jimmy said tilting his head, "thinks that the reason my electric bills are so high this year is because the transformer in the substation behind the house is bad."

"When transformers are going bad, they don't put out enough voltage. The lower the voltage, the more electric you get charged for," Max said. "You said that sometimes the lights dim down for no reason, right? That could be the transformer."

"How high is your bill?"

"Twice as much as last year this time. And sometimes, the lights in the house will just dim down for no reason. West Jersey Power sent someone out, and he said nothing was wrong on their end."

"Well, no shit, of course they're gonna say that," Max said in disgust. "They're making extra money off you. Why would they want to fix that problem?"

Pete the bartender was pouring a Yuengling draft behind the bar. "You know, Jimmy," he said, "my cousin lives in a row house in Upper Darby. One month his electric bill doubled. Couldn't figure it out. He had an electrician look it over and found that the neighbor had tapped into his box when he wired up his new hot tub. My cousin was paying to heat this guy's hot tub. And you want to know the worst thing?"

"What was that?"

"He never even got an invite."

"That's harsh," Max said, shaking his head. He took a long pull on his beer. "Real harsh."

"I'm not in a row house," Jimmy said. "You'd have to tunnel under my lawn to get to my electric box."

"You don't have anything new that uses power?" I asked.

"Nothing really. Karen got a new hair dryer, but come on, how much hair drying do you do in a day?"

"Stove, water heater?"

"No, they're all still gas. Gas clothes dryer. Got some air conditioners but we've only used them once this year."

"I read an article on those things they call 'wall warts,' the little bricks that provide power to your computers and the new TVs. Even though you turn off the computer, they're still working, using power," Pete said.

"Maybe," Jimmy said shaking his head. "We've got a computer, and the flat screen I got for Christmas has one of those power bricks. But jeez, three hundred seventy-five dollars worth? I still think that's too much."

"Transformer?" I said, thinking about it. "I don't know, could be. God knows it's probably the same one that was feeding the house when Pop bought the place. That old electrical substation behind the house looks so old, it could have been installed by Thomas Edison. Max is right, they won't replace it unless it just out and out fails."

"Yeah," Max said, "when it stops working. You know, I have an idea."

"I don't know if I want to hear this," Jimmy said.

"The thing is like fifty years old, right? It's beat. Maybe, just maybe we 'help' it along to the transformer graveyard, you know what I mean?"

"I know I don't want to hear about this," I said, sliding a bill across the bar to Pete.

"I need to talk to an electrician friend of mine," Max said.

"In the meantime, I would look for something new that maybe is using up all this power," I said.

"Maybe Karen bought something that uses electricity that you don't know about," Pete said, sliding my change back.

"Besides the hair dryer, has she made any big purchases?"

"She spent a hundred and fifty bucks at a sexy lingerie party some girl in the office was hosting."

"Maybe she bought something at the sexy lingerie party that uses electricity," I said, looking at Max.

"That could be why sometimes the lights dim in the house," Max said.

Chapter 3

I wanted to get to the ballpark by 11:30 Sunday morning to catch batting practice. I knew Tony had been out last night and I thought I might have to leave a pass for him at the gate, but he surprised me at 8:30 with breakfast sandwiches and coffee.

"Just getting home?"

"Yep. Thought I'd pick up breakfast. You can buy my lunch."

"How did it go with the nurse anesthetist?"

"She put me to sleep," he said, opening the bag. He stopped, eyes wide with wonder at the sailfish hanging over my mantle.

"Whoa, look at that," he said.

"It put up one hell of a fight."

He looked at me with a skeptical grin.

"In the elevator that is," I continued. "Wouldn't fit inside. Had to bring it up the stairs."

"It's bigger than mine," he said.

"Sounds like a personal problem."

"You're always trying to compensate," he said, taking a bite of his sandwich. "Next thing I know, you'll be getting a Porsche."

"Don't you own a Porsche?"

"Oh yeah, the convertible. I almost forgot."

"I've got something for you," I said, pulling out the Little League cap.

Tony gasped, speechless. He put his sandwich down, reached out his hands and took the old cap, holding it carefully as if it were a Fabergé egg. He stared at it for a long time, looking under the brim at his initials.

"The new people who moved into your old place found it in the attic."

"The year was 1982, the year we went to the Little League State finals."

"That was a hell of a game," I said.

"You scored in the top of the sixth on the suicide squeeze."

"You laid down the perfect bunt."

"Yeah, and then they scored twice in the bottom of the inning to beat us," he said. "Seems like 100 years ago."

"Twenty-six years this summer, to be exact."

"The summer of 1982," Tony said. "Now that was a great year."

"We had a great run," I said.

"Remember that field?"

"Yeah, Bernardsville, wasn't it? After our crummy gravel infield, it was like playing in Yankee Stadium."

"We played up like five steps in the infield because the ball came off the grass so slow."

"The stands were beautiful. They had individual folding seats. That field was nicer than a lot of the college fields I played on at USC."

"You know, the thing I remember most about that game was after it was all over," Tony said, "my Dad came up to me and gave me a hug. He had the biggest smile on his face. I asked him why he was smiling because we had just lost. He said to me that years from now when I think of this game, I won't think of the final score. I'll think about all the fun and good times I had this summer just getting there. 'Life is not about the destination,' he said. 'It's all about the ride. Never forget to enjoy the ride.' And he was right. That is what I remember most. All of us guys, the tournament games, the summer practices, hanging out at the Custard King, goofing off down by the river and then going out and playing ball. It was the best. We had a great ride."

There was silence as we both stared at that old baseball cap, for a brief moment reliving in our minds the magic of our twelfth summer.

"Why don't you drive us over to ballpark today?" I said. "It's a nice morning. I want to enjoy the ride with the top down in that Porsche of yours."

We got to Citizens Bank Park and watched batting practice from behind the cage, chatting it up with some of the players and coaches. You get more of the good material for your column from these informal bull sessions then you do in any organized interview. Then we headed up the concourse behind section 140 for lunch. "The Schmitter," a huge sandwich with grilled steak, salami, fried onions and tomatoes, with their special sauce and dripping with plastic cheese was my current favorite Citizens Bank Park menu selection. Tony called it a "heart attack on a bun" and instead he got the chicken cheesesteak. As we ate our sandwiches at a standing table looking down the third base line, we were joined by a guy about our age wearing a Phillies hat and his young teenage daughter wearing a Dodgers hat. They were trying out the Philly dogs.

"A Phillies fan and Dodgers fan?" Tony said.

"I'm originally from New Jersey. I lived on the West coast for the last fifteen years," the dad said. "My wife and I split up, and I moved back home to Haddonfield. My daughter, Ashley is visiting from LA."

I knew lots of split families, but just the way he said it made me feel terribly sad. Couples get together and fully intend on living the rest of their lives with each other. But sometimes, life has other plans. People never stay the same, and many times the person you fall in love with is not the same person ten years later. And neither are you. But, your child? Even though your child will change as much or more than you, they will always be your child. They will always be part of you. I didn't have children, but I could not imagine having a child, and then leaving them for a new life on the other side of the country. I don't think I could do it.

"Who's your favorite player?" Tony asked the girl.

"Brad Cole," she said in a matter of fact way as if to say, who else would there be.

"Really," Tony said. "Did you know Brad Cole grew up near here?"

"No, I didn't," she said.

"And when he was in high school, Skip and I played baseball against his team."

"Really?"

"Brad Cole pitched. He struck me out twice. But Skip here," he said pointing at me, "hit a home run off him and won the game."

"I still don't think he's completely forgiven me for that," I said.

"Oh wow," she said, looking at me with new respect. "I tried to get his autograph, but he didn't come over with the other guys."

"Brad doesn't sign autographs before the game," I said. "He has a strange pregame ritual. He won't talk to anyone, even his manager. He just sits there and stares out at the field, getting himself mentally prepared."

"I've always wanted to get his autograph," she said.

"Do you have a business card?" I asked the dad. He nodded and fished one out of his wallet.

"I'm a sports writer for the *Bulletin*," I said. "I may get the chance to see him after the game. If he's in a good mood, I may be able to get an autograph for you."

"Really?" she said. She looked at her dad, the excitement on her face. "That would be so awesome. Thank you so much."

"That would really make her very happy," the dad said. "Brad Cole is her favorite player. I owe you one. Thanks!"

Brad Cole did not disappoint his fans that day. He put on a show that afternoon going three for four, with two doubles and a home run in the top of the ninth, which won the game for the Dodgers 8-6. Cole always tore up the Phillies. He had been pretty vocal when during the 1988 baseball amateur draft the Phillies passed him up. He had imagined himself as the heir apparent to Mike Schmidt at third for the Phillies. Cole always said that the Phillies would regret not choosing him, and he would always do his best to make them sorry for their oversight. In retrospect, he had been true to his word.

I grabbed an extra press pass for Tony, and we made our way down to the Dodgers locker room after the game. I always tried to say hi at least once to Brad whenever the Dodgers came to town. As expected, he was surrounded by reporters, giving details about his game winning homer. He was in a particularly good mood, sitting on a folding chair like a king on his throne, tossing out sound bites. He spotted me at the back of the crowd and stood up.

"Well, look here," he said, wading through the throng of reporters. "Skip McCann, how the hell are you?"

"I'm good, Brad," I said shaking his hand, "but not as good as you. I haven't hit any game winning homers lately."

"Not since 1988. Hey, guys," he said turning to the crowd, "did you know that Skip here hit a game winning home run off me in high school? Our only loss that season."

"Brad, I saw the strangest sight here at the ballpark today."

"Lots of strange looking characters here in Philly," he said. "That's why I live in Los Angeles." The crowd of reporters laughed.

"In a sea of red Phillies hats, I saw one lone girl wearing a blue Dodgers cap."

"A rose among the scrubs, you could say."

"She told me that nothing would make her happier than a Brad Cole autographed ball."

"Was she hot?"

"Well, I guess so. If you like fourteen year olds."

That got a laugh from the press corps. Brad was in an unusually good mood. He grabbed a practice ball from his bag. "What's her name?"

"Ashley."

He scribbled his autograph and tossed the ball to me. "And who's this?" he asked looking to my side. "Don't tell me, Doctor Tony Adamo."

"Good to see you again, Brad,"

"The guys in Clinton Heights on the hospital board speak very highly of you."

"They speak highly of you, too."

"Yeah, well they better. They like it when you donate a few million to the hospital building fund. Hey, speaking of Clinton Heights, I guess you're on for the Fourth of July game?"

"You'll see me out there," I said.

"We heard you'll be there. Are you throwing out the first ball?" Tony asked.

"Fuck that, I'm playing."

"I thought the Dodgers were in New York that weekend," I said.

"I already cleared it with Joe. I'm the Clinton Heights Fourth of July parade grand marshal. It's a big deal for the town, me, a big famous celebrity coming back and all, so he's giving me the day off."

"So, you'll be playing. Wow, that's, that's just great news," Tony said looking at me, rolling his eyes.

"And I'm still pissed about that home run, Skip," Cole said. "Good thing the doc here will be on hand because if I pitch an inning, don't be surprised if a little chin music comes your way."

"Thanks, Brad, that'll be something to look forward to," I said.

"Hey, whatever happened to that other slugger you guys had, the right fielder? Big kid, hit a bunch of home runs during the season?"

"The guy you beaned? He went to the hospital with a concussion."

"He was crowding the plate. I just hate it when somebody tries to crowd the plate. I get so pissed. Makes me want to throw at them."

60

"John Stone," Tony said. "He was all right, pretty shook up though. He still lives in town. If he shows up, you can apologize."

"I never apologize. Apologies are for losers," Cole said. "Oh, what the hell, maybe I'll sign a ball for him."

The next morning, I had a radio interview. Since the late 1940's, a small day timer station at AM 1340, WDCR had called Dorchester home. In the early 1970's, the current owner Murray White had come to work right out of college. He wanted to get into radio because it was common knowledge that radio jocks make a lot of money and get a lot of girls. Unfortunately, neither worked out for him, but he did grow to love the town of Dorchester so much that he ended up buying the radio station at a great price from the old owners, who were convinced that AM radio would soon die off and only FM radio would remain. Murray had a friendly, engaging personality, along with a deep, smooth voice, and the community loved him. Nearly everybody listened to Murray in the Morning for local Dorchester news and gossip you couldn't get anywhere else. Murray White was the voice of Dorchester.

I had known Murray since high school. I was always interested in radio, and Murray hired me to do some producing, mostly operating the control board for some of the brokered local programming. After college I did some sports shows and live games.

Murray had asked me to come over early that morning to the studio and go on the air with him. As a Philly sportswriter, he wanted to hear my current take on the Phillies team. I walked into the empty lobby area and straight through into the hallway to the air studios. The red ON AIR light was on, and Murray was behind the ancient console. He saw me through the window, and continuing to talk, he motioned for me to come in. I quietly opened the door, the familiar smell of almost seventy years of cigarette smoke imbedded in the acoustic wall tiles greeting me.

"You're listening to the Voice of Dorchester, AM 1340 WDCR, I'm Murray White. Coming up next at eight o'clock it's ABC National News, brought to you by Bob Fare Chrysler Dodge on Main Street. You'll always get a fair deal at Bob Fare Chrysler Dodge. And then when we come back here at Good Morning Dorchester, we'll be talking with hometown hero Skip McCann, a sportswriter covering the Phillies for the *Bulletin*. We'll see what he thinks the Phillies chances are this year in the National League East. And, we'll also talk to him about the big game coming up right here in Dorchester on July Fourth. The baseball rematch of the century. Stay tuned." Murray hit a button and turned one of the big round knobs. The red ON AIR light went out, and Murray pulled off his headphones.

"Skip," he said, reaching over and shaking my hand. "How's it going?"

"Going great, Murray. How's life in the fast lane at WDCR?"

"Going about twenty-five miles an hour in the left lane with its turn signal on."

62

"You're sounding good."

"I better," he said, getting up and walking over to the coffee pot. "This year is my thirty year anniversary of owning the station. I don't know where the time has gone. It slips by so fast. Seems like yesterday you were wearing a Dorchester Wildcats baseball uniform. Coffee?"

I nodded. He poured some into a styrofoam cup for me and refilled his ancient AM 1340 WDCR mug. Murray never washed his studio coffee mug. The inside had a dark chocolate brown patina that he swore made each successive cup taste better and better.

He came back, gave me my coffee and sat back down in the studio chair. "How's Tony?" has asked.

"Tony's good. He's busy."

"He does a good thing there with his urgent care practice. The town needed it. It's nice when somebody gives back to the community."

"You were a big part of that," I said. During our senior year of high school, Tony's parents were killed in a car crash on the turnpike. He lived with my family the last six months until graduation. He had no money and no where to go. More than anything, he wanted to become a doctor. One thing led to another, and then Murray stepped in and broadcast a radio-thon for donations from the townspeople and local businesses. He raised thousands of dollars for Tony's college fund. And Tony would never forget.

"I'm just a big mouth," he said. "It was the community that made it

63

happen."

"I guess it worked out well for everyone."

"I'm told he's Dorchester's most eligible bachelor. I'm surprised some pretty young girl hasn't snapped him up yet."

"Not for lack of trying. Tony's just not interested."

"Gay, is he?"

"Gay as a French horn, Murray."

He gave me a serious look, then threw his head back and laughed loud. "You liar! He's the biggest horn dog in town. Even worse than me, and that's saying something."

"He's just into equal opportunity for women," I said.

"Me too. What about you, Skip? You ever going to take that ride again?"

"I don't know, Murray. My last ride was a bumpy one. Been there, done that. I guess we'll have to wait and see what good things life has in store for me."

"From your lips to God's ears, my friend," he said. Then, he put on his headphones and hit the microphone button.

"AM 1340 WDCR, welcome back to Good Morning Dorchester, I'm Murray White. This portion of the show is brought to you by Walt's Main Street Hardware. Don't be a nut. Don't screw around with the big chain stores. Bolt on over to Walt's Main Street Hardware and tell them Murray White sent you. With me in the studio this morning is someone who, if you grew up here in Dorchester, you probably already know. Born and raised here, and the captain of the 1988 Dorchester High School baseball team that beat Clinton Heights. Now, a sports writer for the *Philadelphia Bulletin*, Skip McCann; welcome to Good Morning Dorchester."

We talked Phillies. I told him I thought they had a shot and advised him not to make any vacation plans in September or October because the Phillies could be in the playoffs. We took some phone calls. People were optimistic about the Phillies chances. He went to another commercial break, and then we were back.

"AM 1340 WDCR, welcome back to Good Morning Dorchester, I'm Murray White. Without a doubt, the number one thing people in this town are talking about today is the big baseball game rematch between the 1988 Dorchester Wildcats and Clinton Heights Bombers. Now, the original game took place twenty years ago, and yes folks, I was there as we covered it live. For those of you who were not around then, let me tell you about the biggest baseball game in Dorchester history."

"For twenty years," he started, "Clinton Heights had dominated the Cross River Annual Series; they never lost. They were ranked in the top ten of all high school baseball teams in the country. But in 1988 they were not facing the normal group of high schoolers from the little town of Dorchester. They were playing the single greatest baseball team this town has ever assembled.

We knew something was special about these kids when they went to the Little League State championships in 1982. They had won the New Jersey Group One high school state title the week before, but now they were facing the biggest game of their lives, the much feared, nationally ranked Clinton Heights Bombers, featuring a very young Brad Cole. That's right, the same Brad Cole you know today as a three-time National League MVP third baseman for the Los Angeles Dodgers.

But we had our own secret weapon. The man who is sitting here in the studio with me, the team captain and on field leader, Skip McCann. In his senior year, he set school records for most doubles, triples, steals, on base percentage and batting average, a whopping .688! He even pitched, nine wins, no losses and was selected first team All New Jersey State shortstop, which won him a full scholarship to play college baseball for the nationally ranked University of Southern California Trojans. He remains in my opinion, the single best baseball player that has ever come out of Dorchester. He was our best, facing their best. It was a match up for the ages."

"Brad Cole pitched for Clinton Heights," he continued. "A classic power pitcher with the

best fastball I've ever seen in thirty years of covering high school baseball. Skip pitched for Dorchester. A great fastball, an outstanding slider and a knee buckling changeup. We knew it would be a pitchers' duel and sure enough, six innings later it was 0-0. Seventh inning. Skip mows down the top of the order, including Brad Cole who went 0 for 3 that day. It was his first game without a hit in three seasons. Then, Dorchester gets up in the bottom of the inning. Our best home run hitter was out, hit in the head earlier in the game by a wild pitch. Brad Cole dusted off the first two and up comes Skip McCann, the pride of Dorchester. Last inning, 0-0, two outs, the game is on the line. It all came down to our best against their best. The count goes to three and two. And then. Well, rather than me tell you, since we have Skip McCann with us in the studio, I'll let him tell you what happened next."

I was shocked back to reality, not fully ready to jump into the conversation and kind of embarrassed by the accolades being heaped upon me.

"Well, Murray," I said, "the count was three and two. He had been missing with his curve all day, and I didn't think he would trust it. I knew he wouldn't walk me, he was too cocky and wanted to strike me out again. He needed to throw a strike to end it, so I was looking fastball all the way. He was getting tired. His other pitches that inning were definitely slower than they were the first time I was up. I saw him rear back and fire extra hard, thinking that he was going to try and give this pitch extra gas to get it by me. He had kept the other two strikes low around my knees, very hard to hit. But I guess maybe trying to throw this one harder, it made the pitch rise in the zone. It came in about letter height. I was out in front and I got lucky."

"And what Skip McCann means, ladies and gentlemen, by getting lucky is that he hit a towering walk off home run, and for the first time in twenty years Dorchester beat Clinton Heights by a score of 1-0. And in the twenty years since, it remains the only win Dorchester has ever had against Clinton Heights. And coming up on the Fourth of July, these two teams will meet again, twenty years later, at the same baseball field, for a rematch of that game back in 1988. And, in uniform for Clinton Heights will be none other than Los Angeles Dodgers star Brad Cole himself. He's the grand marshal of the Clinton Heights Fourth of July parade this year. This Fourth of July game will be broadcast live right here on AM 1340 WDCR and brought to you in part by Logan Family Pharmacy, your Dorchester drug connection at 210 Main Street. Don't forget, yours truly Murray White will be in the same broadcast booth just as I was twenty years ago. The big question is, can these guys from the '88 team still play? Tell us Skip, how's the team shaping up?"

"Right now we are still figuring out who is available to play. The whole team is scattered across the country, but it seems everybody comes back for Fourth of July in Dorchester. So, I guess we'll see what happens."

"How about that center fielder you had, Flash Gordon," He asked. "I don't think I've ever seen a high school kid cover as much ground in the outfield as he did. Boy, could he fly."

"We're working on him, Murray." I said.

"And John Stone, the kid who set the home run record that year. How about him?"

"We haven't talked to John yet, but you can be sure he's on our short list."

Sometimes you don't see someone for a while, and then you talk about them and all of a sudden they show up. I promised Jimmy that after the early morning radio interview I would help him and Wayne cart all the unsold furniture and junk from the yard sale out to the county landfill.

"Busy morning," Jimmy said, looking at the line of trucks ahead of him waiting to back up to the unloading area.

"Maybe they all had yard sales," Wayne theorized.

"Landfill's closed on the weekends," I said.

"That could be it too," Wayne said.

When it was our turn, Wayne backed up to the edge of the guardrail. Beyond it, about twenty feet down was a line of large open tractor trailer containers. We started muscling the bulky furniture first and then grabbed the smaller boxes of trinkets.

"Nothing hazardous or chemical in those boxes?" John Stone's voice called out.

John Stone looked much as he did twenty years ago. Maybe a little less hair and little bigger belly. Tall and powerfully built and still in great shape. All these years doing physical work for the county had made him even more muscular than he was in high school.

"Big John," I said, stepping off the pickup and shaking his hand.

"Skip," he said, flashing that familiar grin that took me right back to senior year in high school. "It has been a while, hasn't it?"

"I think last year Fourth of July. You were working the barbecue stand for the fire company," I said.

"John, how's it going?" Jimmy said walking up.

"Life is good. God is great! Hey, Skip, I just heard you on the radio talking about the old baseball team."

"Yeah," I said. "And speaking of baseball, I heard that your boy is playing ball for the high school." I said. "They call him Junior."

"He loves the game," John said.

"They say he's good. He hits the long ball like you did."

"He's better than I was,"

"I don't know about that. We had some good times," I said.

And as soon as I had said those words, I winced. Everyone knew that the beaning he took in the big game with Clinton Heights had stopped whatever career he had in athletics cold. After spending a week in the hospital, he complained of headaches and bright flashing lights. His first practice at the university he couldn't even stay in the cage without bailing out in terror of being hit again. Within three weeks, he was washed out.

"So you played on the '88 team with Skip and Jimmy?" Wayne said.

"Yeah, I did, Wayne."

"Are you coming out for the big rematch with Clinton Heights?"

"Oh, I'll be there," he said. "Not on the field, but I'll be there in the stands, watching."

"Why not on the field?" Wayne asked. "You were on the 1988 team."

"Well, to be honest, I got whacked pretty hard in the head. I don't think I want to go back and try that again."

"Jimmy says you were really good. You got a scholarship."

"Yeah, that's true. I had some success."

"So, you didn't like it?"

"Wayne, I loved it. More than anything. But when God knocked me down that day, it was because he had other plans for my life. My future would be bigger than just being an athlete. Besides my job with the county, I volunteer in town with your Dad at the fire department. I'm a lay preacher at my church. I work with kids in Camden who don't have a dad or sometimes even a mom. I may not be a millionaire baseball player, but my life is rich. I'm dedicated to the Lord's service, and I couldn't be happier. Besides," he added. "I'm thirty-eight years old. I'm really out of shape. I can't run around the bases anymore. I shag some balls with my son but my athlete days are long gone."

"Well, gosh," Wayne said with a glance at Jimmy and me. "Look at Skip and Jimmy. They're not athletes anymore either,"

"Thanks, Wayne," Jimmy said.

"Oh, sorry, Jimmy. What I mean is. . . ."

"We know what you mean, Wayne," I said. "Listen, John, we'd love to have you on the field with us. But, even if you'd rather not play, make sure to stop by. Some of the guys are coming back."

"How about Flash Gordon? That guy could really fly in center."

"Tony's checking up on him. It would be great to have you in the dugout with all of us," I said.

"It would be nice to see the guys again," John said. "It was a great year, until that last day. Yeah, I will be there cheering you on. God bless you, Skip. God bless all of you."

Tuesday morning the phone rang at 9:30. It was Kim Gundersen.

"Did I wake you?"

The Phillies and Dodgers had gone extra innings last night before the Phils won it 4-3. I got home around 3 a. m.

"Late night at the ballpark, but that's all right. I needed to be up anyway," I said. "When did you get in?"

"Late Sunday night," she said. "I visited with friends in Bryn Mawr yesterday. Can we get together today? Maybe for lunch?"

"Today for lunch would be perfect. I have a long day tomorrow and then I'll be on the road with the team for ten days. Where are you staying?"

"I'm at the Crowne Plaza," she said. "Do you know where that is?"

"Yeah, it's on Market Street, west of City Hall. How does one o'clock in the lobby sound?"

"It sounds great. See you at one."

The weather was nice, so I drove over to Florence and caught the River Line light rail down to Camden, took PATCO across the Ben Franklin Bridge to City Hall. I came up the stairs to a sunny crisp blue sky day. The food trucks were in full deployment, an international bazaar of ethnic food creations lining Market Street. Local office workers were camped out on the steps and benches eating their brown bag lunches and enjoying the warm late spring sunshine. I walked the three blocks to the Crowne Plaza.

Kim was waiting in the lobby, standing by the check in counter. She was facing the other entrance and didn't see me come in. I stopped for a moment to look at her. Seeing her standing there after all those years made my heart ache.

The first thing I noticed was her hair. In college she had long hair, but always wore it up or tied back. Now her hair was shorter, not even reaching her shoulders. As a track athlete, she was in great physical shape in college, but today she looked thin and somewhat fragile. Maybe tired would be a better description. She didn't look twenty-one anymore, but she could still easily pass for thirty. The other thing I noticed were her clothes. A brightly colored print top and very casual striped loose fit slacks that looked more like pajamas than pants. Very Asian in style, I thought. Not the standard midwestern wardrobe that she brought from Minnesota to college. Time had changed Kim Gundersen's appearance. But she still looked good to my eyes.

73

After a moment I continued into the lobby. She saw me out of the corner of her eye walking up. She turned and looked at me, a wide smile breaking out on her face.

"Skip," she said. She put her arms around me and held me tightly for what seemed like an eternity.

"It's been a long time," she said softly in my ear, releasing me and stepping back for a closer look.

"Yes, it has. You cut your hair."

"So did you."

"You've lost weight," I said.

"You've gained weight," she said.

We both laughed at the same time.

"It's good to see you," she said.

"It's good to see you, too. You look great."

"You look great, too," she said, looking me up and down.

There was an awkward moment of silence. We just stared at each other.

"Well, I haven't eaten anything and I'm starving," I finally said.

"Some things never change," she said, rolling her eyes.

"What's your pleasure?"

"I'm up for anything," she said. "Someplace quiet. I don't want to go far though. I'm catching a flight home tonight."

"There's a pub right here at the Crowne. How's that sound?"

"Sounds great."

The little restaurant in the hotel was deserted except for the staff. We got a booth by the window overlooking the street.

"I read your column in the *Bulletin* this morning," she said. "I loved the blueberry pancake story. You're a good writer."

"Thanks."

"A sportswriter in your home town and covering your favorite baseball team. You did pretty well for yourself, McCann."

I told her the story of how I got the job at the paper. It came at an all-time low period in my life, 1998, when I lost my dad and my mom got her bad medical news. My marriage to my high school sweetheart Beth was over. She had moved out, and we were getting a divorce. I was working part time at AM 1340 WDCR and bartending at Sullivan's. I felt like I had hit rock bottom, the end of the road. At my Dad's funeral of all places I met an old friend of his who knew the sports editor at the *Bulletin,* Joe McGarvey. He got me in the door for an interview. Joe remembered me as an athlete from high school, as he was covering local sports at the time. He liked my writing and by chance had caught one of my football broadcasts on WDCR. He decided to give me a shot. It was the break I was looking for.

"How is your knee? Did it heal?" she asked.

"Eventually. It feels fine now. No pain."

"Do you still run?"

75

"Not as much as I would like to."

"Me neither," she said. "I ran a lot until a few years ago when I got sick. I'm better now but I haven't gotten back into the habit. I always enjoyed running. I remember all those times we ran on the beach."

"So, how's Roger," I asked.

"Um, he's doing well. He's up in Sacramento all the time now. He's a state senator."

"Well, good for him."

"His district includes the Chinatown section of San Francisco. A great community. Nice people."

"So, your Mandarin came in handy."

"Yes, but hanging around Chinatown did more for my language skills than anything I learned at high school in Minnesota. I am very fluent now. I went back and got my masters in language education, and I'm very involved in the local community."

"And you're in marketing?"

"The company I work for specializes in marketing businesses to the Asian community. We do very well."

"And you're a mom."

A strange, almost uncomfortable look came to her face. "Yes, I am a mom. Her name is Janine."

"How old is she?"

A pause. "She turned fifteen in February," she said slowly. She studied my face, watching for my reaction.

The wheels began to turn in my mind. The server brought the beer and two pint glasses.

"Did you say fifteen?" I asked.

"Skip, I need to tell you something." I watched Kim take a deep breath and shake her head. "Something I should have told you a long time ago."

Here comes the bombshell, I thought. No, it cannot be possible.

"Do you remember that night?" she asked. "Our last night before you left?"

The bomb went off. The room was spinning.

Chapter 4

The night she was referring to, "that night" was Saturday May 17th, 1992. A little over 16 years ago, but who's counting?

It was my last day at USC in Los Angeles. And on the morning of that last day, the room was also spinning.

"Oh for Chrissakes, McCann, GET UP!"

Kim's face was a few inches above mine. She was screaming at the top of her lungs like a Marine drill sergeant.

"You are going to make us late," she said, hands on my shoulders, shaking me as hard as she could. "We have to be at the Santa Monica Pier by 10. We need to leave in 15 minutes. Now, get your ass out of bed, you idiot!"

"I'm up," I said weakly. My head was pounding.

"No, you're not. Jesus, you're hung over," she said, straightening up and rolling her eyes. "Open your eyes."

"They are open."

"What do you see?"

"I see a crazy hysterical woman with deep emotional problems screaming at me," I said.

"ARRGGGG." She said, stomping out of my bedroom.

That's how my last day at college started. Two days after graduation, I had been out the night before saying goodbye with some old baseball buddies. We made a few unscheduled stops and I got back very late and very inebriated. My roommate Sam, a theatre major, had moved out a few days before for a summer stock tour of the musical *Hair* so I was alone. I had some friends coming over later in the afternoon to get the rest of the furniture because I was leaving early the next morning for my long drive home to New Jersey. Kim and I had exchanged keys to our apartments a while ago, and she had used it when I did not answer the door.

I stumbled to the living room in the same clothes I had passed out in the night before. Kim was standing there, arms crossed, staring me down.

"I'm sorry, Kim," I started.

"Save it, McCann," she snapped. "Get in the shower and make it quick. Come on, let's move it."

"I don't have to take a shower."

"If you're riding in my car with me, you do. You stink of sweat and alcohol and God knows what else. Now MOVE IT!"

Fifteen minutes later we were flying down the Santa Monica freeway on our way to our last internship event. We were both working for radio station K-Earth 101 in Los Angeles, and today was the big K-Earth 101 "Happy Together" beach concert, featuring the 60s groups the Association and the Turtles. The free event on the beach was expected to draw over a hundred thousand people.

"I think we'll be there in plenty of time," I said, looking at my watch. It seemed blurry. I rubbed the dial face. It was still blurry.

She said nothing. She was staring out at the road, still seething. I felt I needed to say something to lighten the mood.

"You look particularly attractive today, Gundersen."

She gave me a sideward glance, still frowning, and then back to the road.

"You've got a little make up going on, a touch of eye shadow. I approve. Just enough without looking too slutty, like a valley tramp. And I love the lipstick. Is that a dusky peach?"

I saw the corners of her mouth begin to twitch.

"And that bun thing you did with your hair. I love it! It's got a *Star Wars* vibe, but kind of in the back instead of on the sides. I think they call that the Princess Leia cinnamon bun mullet look?"

Her hand shot off the steering wheel and whacked me across the arm.

"You're an ass, you know that, McCann," she said. Despite her best efforts, I could see the hint of a smile forming on her face.

80

We were promotions interns, and our jobs at the event were to cover the K-Earth prize tent, giving out Frisbees, beach balls and water bottles. We were selling the radio station limited edition tie dye concert tee shirts that we were modeling with proceeds going to a local children's charity. It was a carnival atmosphere; the beach was sunny and warm and mobbed with 40-something year old baby boomers and their families.

About two hours in Marty Martin, one of the weekend DJs, came over to the tent.

"Looks like it's my turn to man the tent," he said.

Kim and I looked at each other. "What about us?"

"I don't know," he said. "I guess go out and have some fun."

I grabbed a K-Earth 101 Frisbee and turned to Kim. "Come on. Let's see what kind of arm you have."

We kicked off our flip flops and headed down the beach to the edge of the water. I lobbed a soft underhand throw. She caught it easily and whipped it back to me so fast that I had to back up and jump to catch it. I fell over backward on to the sand at the edge of the water.

"Oh, shit," she said, running up and kneeling beside me. "I'm sorry, Skip. I wasn't thinking.
I forgot about your leg. Are you all right?"

I was still recovering from surgery for my torn ACL. I was fresh out of the brace and was

81

getting around fine, but the leg would still seize up on me sometimes if I pushed too hard.

"No problem," I said. "I still have one good leg. I can hop around."

With that, a lone ocean wave washed over both Kim and me. We sat there, soaked. Slowly we got up, looking at each other in shock, wringing the salt water out of our tee shirts.

"That's just great, little Miss Show Off," I said. "You decide to pull a 100 mph fastball on me, and now my ACL is probably torn again and if that's not enough, my underwear is wet. If I start chafing, it will be all your fault."

She walked over dripping, picked up the Frisbee, and walked back.

"You look like you're ready for a wet tee shirt contest," I said with a laugh.

She took the Frisbee and gave me a whack with it across the chest. I grabbed it out of her hands.

"Go long," I said.

She turned and sprinted down the beach, turning and stopping about 10 yards away.

"I said, GO LONG."

She turned again and began to run full speed down the beach. She was fast and ran like a gazelle. I twisted and fired a long, low throw. She was about 40 yards down the beach going at a full run when it caught up with her. At the last moment, she hurdled a big sand castle someone had built. As she landed, she catapulted back in the air and grabbed the Frisbee clean with one hand.

Behind me a group of boomers started clapping.

"Touchdown," I shouted, spinning around and raising my arms in the air. "McCann to Gundersen for six. Philadelphia Eagles win!"

She ran back up the beach, uncorking a low throw back. "You mean, Minnesota Vikings win."

We played Frisbee for a while. A young boy stood there watching us, and I lobbed one over to him. He threw it to Kim. Soon we were joined by other adults and kids. More Frisbees appeared. After a while it was a sea of Frisbees up and down the shoreline.

My knee was hurting. I limped up to her. "That's it for the knee for today. And, I'm hungry," I said. "Let's find something to eat."

"You're always hungry," she said.

Food trucks were selling a variety of ethnic treats. Whenever we would hang out, Kim almost always stuck with vegetarian fare. She was normally picky about what she ate, but today she was hungry and there was not much of a selection of healthy choices. We finally decided on one of the imitation Mexican trucks. I was surprised when she agreed to split some nachos.

"You are always eating these," she said.

"Breakfast of Champions," I answered.

She took a chip and poked around the container of processed cheese. "What is this?"

83

"It's plastic cheese," I said. "Haven't you ever had plastic cheese?"

"I try to put only healthy things in my body."

"What could be more natural than plastic cheese? It's the best kind."

"Constipation city," she said, dipping into the rubbery, gooey goodness. She put it in her mouth.

"It does taste pretty good," she finally said, shaking her head. "I like it. I'll probably pay for it tomorrow."

We finished the nachos. Then Kim surprised me by going back to the truck and getting a second order and we finished that. Then we walked around. Vendors were selling their own tie dye shirts, pipes, roach clips and 60s era beads and bags. I was looking at a tee shirt with a Woodstock graphic on it when Kim came up behind me.

"What do you think?" she said, her hands behinds the lobes of her ears. She was showing me the earrings she had just bought. They were peace signs set in the silver body of a butterfly with multicolor wings that glistened in the sunlight.

"They are so cool," I said. I leaned in to examine the intricate details and tilted the lobe of her ear out with my index finger for a better angle. As I was admiring the craftsmanship of the jewelry, I noticed that our faces were very close together, our lips almost touching. I could hear her breathing. It was short and shallow, nervous. She was shivering. Her eyes were open wide. She reached up and ran her fingers across my cheek.

"You need a shave, McCann," she said softly.

"I would have, except that SOMEBODY rushed me out the door before I had the chance."

"At least you got a shower."

"You know, one more thing would make this perfect," I took a pair of round John Lennon rose tinted sunglasses from the display on the counter and put them on her. I stood back and sized her up.

"You look extremely groovy, Gundersen," I said.

She laughed out loud. One of the things I always loved about Kim Gundersen was her laugh. She always had a great laugh. It was genuine. The kind that comes from deep inside, the kind you can't fake.

"I'm so glad you approve," she said.

"I do."

I paid for the sunglasses, and we continued walking around the concert grounds. We
gawked at the growing crowd, checking out the more bizarre baby boomers who were gathered for the show, dressed in the most outlandish outfits which probably were mainstream in the late 60s. We were young and they seemed so old at the time. But, it was a fun vibe and everyone was excited for the show.

"Kim, Skip." It was Rick the promotions director. He motioned us back to the tent.

"Ok, here's the deal," he said. "Pack up the boxes but don't leave the area. The Association is ready to start, and after them it's the Turtles. When the Turtles get going, come around backstage."

The Association started their set, and the crowd responded, singing, dancing and clapping. They played for almost forty minutes. Meanwhile, we packed up the radio station merchandise under the tent.

"Why do they want us to come backstage?" Kim said.

"I don't know," I said. "Maybe they need extra help loading stuff."

The Association finished their set. The roadies were setting up for the Turtles. We walked around to the back of the stage area as the band was being introduced, and all the radio station DJs were waiting. Rick pulled us aside.

"When the Turtles start playing their last song, 'Happy Together,' we're all going on stage to join them," he said.

I looked at Kim and she looked at me.

"In front of all those people?" she said.

"Oh my God, Kim, this is going to be so cool!" I said, grabbing her arm.

We very nervously waited backstage as they performed their other hits, and then the moment came. I took a deep breath as we all walked on stage for the encore in front of a hundred thousand screaming fans. It was stunning. The blue green Pacific ocean stretching to infinity to one side and the row of beachfront buildings to the other. And in between, a sea of faces stretched up the beach as far as you could see, hands in the air, beach balls bouncing randomly from place to place. The beach scene looked alive on its own.

The final song, "Happy Together" was one of the big anthem hits from 1967, the Summer of Love, and everyone knew the words. The roar from the enormous crowd gave me chills.

"Oh my God, look at all the people," Kim said. She was so nervous that she was shaking.

"Don't be nervous. They're not looking at you," I said. "They're all looking at me."

The panicked look on her face turned to a smile. She reached for my hand. I leaned past and slipped my arm around her waist. Flo and Eddie started playing. One hundred thousand voices strong, we started to sing. When we got to the chorus, I could hardly hear Kim singing next to me from the noise of the crowd.

With the final notes of 'Happy Together' the crowd went nuts. They just kept cheering. We bowed along with the group and the K-Earth DJs. The rush was fantastic.

Kim was standing there, eyes wide open, in shock from the excitement. "That was incredible!" she said. "All those people. It was insane."

"Not every day do we get to sing in front of a hundred thousand people," I laughed.

The K-Earth DJs thanked everyone for coming. As the crowd began to move off the beach, we made our way off the stage. I helped the guys carry the equipment back to the station van in the parking lot. I looked around for Kim, and I couldn't find her. I let some more of the crowd filter out, and then I headed back up toward the bandstand. The roadies had cleared the performer's equipment. There I saw Kim, sitting by herself on the edge of the stage, looking out over the beach. I walked back, hoisted myself up and sat beside her, our legs dangling over the edge.

"Waiting for your encore?" I asked.

Smiling, she leaned back and closed her eyes. It was late afternoon, the sun still had a few hours before it would set, but the LA smog was casting a warm red glow across her face and shining off her rose sunglasses. Little wisps of her hair were sparkling in the sunlight.

"I wish every day could be like today," she said, staring out at the empty beach.

"It's one I'll always remember," I said.

"A great way to end our senior year in college."

"So, you have any idea what you're going to do next?" I asked.

"Probably head back to my apartment."

"You know what I mean. After college."

"I've got some résumés out," she said, kicking her sandy feet back and forth. "If I can't find anything in Minnesota, then maybe I'll look around here. Or maybe San Francisco. They have a huge Chinese presence. I think I would like to do some kind of work in communications in the Asian community. How about you?"

"Now that the baseball thing is over for me I've been thinking about being a sportswriter. There's a radio station in my hometown. I could probably catch on there, but I think I would rather be a sportswriter. I like writing. I'm pretty good at it. Philadelphia is 20 minutes away; it's a big market."

"Who says your baseball career is over," she said. "You should try rehab. Build up your strength."

"Ever since I was a little boy, I had one dream. To be a major league baseball player. They say to make the big show you need a big arm and lots of speed. I still have the arm, but with this," I said, pointing down at my leg, "with this I will never be as fast as I was. I will never be fast enough to make it. No Kim, 'I' say my baseball career is over. It's time to move on."

She looked down at my knee. The sun had made the surgeon's scar a bright red jagged line. She reached over and traced her index finger along its length. I felt a chill.

"Does it hurt?" she asked.

"It does today. I haven't done much lately, and it got a workout. It's sore, but it's a good kind of sore, if that makes any sense."

"You'll have to start running again."

"I plan to. I miss it," I said.

"These last few months I've been running by myself," she said. "It's not the same. I miss running with you, Skip. I enjoyed that a lot."

I reached down and traced the scar with my own finger. "The sad thing is that I used to have great looking legs. Now they're scarred."

"Girls like scars," she said, laughing. She smacked my thigh with the back of her hand. "And you still have nice legs."

I looked down at her smooth tan muscular legs. "Not as nice as yours," I blurted out.

There was a moment of awkward silence. She looked at me, a curious expression on her face. "I never knew you even noticed my legs," she said quietly.

I had always put Kim in the "sister" category. We spent a lot of time together. She was supremely comfortable to be with. A close friend, but never anything more. One time, at the beginning of our sophomore year I made a drunken pass at her during a frat party. She shot me down like the Red Baron over southern France, and I never broached the subject again. I assumed I was in the friend zone until the end of my days. She had her boyfriends and I had my girlfriends, but we had never dated. We had spent many late nights discussing our hopes and dreams, but I had never talked to her like this before. Maybe something about the excitement of the day, the end of college and the uncertainty of was to come. Maybe the fact that I was leaving tomorrow. One of those things or all of those things. I don't know.

"I, uh, I think we should head back," I said. "They're getting ready to drop the stage."

I slipped off the stage onto the beach. Automatically, I reached around with both hands to help her down. She looked at me for a moment and then reached over and placed both her hands firmly on my shoulders and paused for a moment. Then, she slipped off and I was holding her in the air underneath her arms. She was light in my grasp, and I held her for a moment suspended in the air. I slowly turned and lowered her to the ground.

We walked back up the beach. She grabbed her bag out of the station van. We said goodbye to Rick, who thanked us again and promised if we ever needed a referral, he would be happy to write one. Kim's car was the only one in the lot.

When we got on the freeway, moving through the late afternoon traffic, I was deep in my thoughts when she looked over at me and blurted out, "I'm really sorry, Skip."

"What do mean?" I asked.

"For this morning," she said. "I was a total bitch this morning."

"You were a little bitchy, yes, but I wouldn't say you were a total bitch."

She didn't smile. "Yes, I was a total bitch. I woke up in a very strange mood, a sad mood, and I guess I let it get the best of me. I'm really sorry."

"What made you so sad?"

"This is your last day here. I wanted today to be great."

I put my hand on her arm and gave it a squeeze. "Today was awesome. I'll never forget it. We had so much fun. You almost killed me with a 100 mile an hour Frisbee bullet. Then my underwear got soaked with seawater, and now

I'm walking funny and I probably have a rash. And I finally got you to try plastic cheese. It was the best day ever. And not just because we got to sing with the Turtles in front of a hundred thousand people, either."

She smiled. "Thanks."

"And all this time I never realized what a great singing voice you have. You sang like an angel up there. You ever think about recording an album?"

"You ever think about getting your hearing checked?" she said.

As she parked the car she drove by my old piece of crap AMC Pacer, loaded with my stuff. "You really think it will make it back to New Jersey?"

"If it breaks down, I may call you for a ride."

We walked the sidewalk back to our apartments. "What are you doing tonight?" she asked.

"Nothing. As you probably know, I was out socializing last night and got in rather late. I want to leave at four in the morning tomorrow to beat the traffic so I'm going to sleep early. I want to make Vegas by two."

"Okay," she said. "I'm going to get a shower. I'll stop over in a little while to say goodbye. I won't be up at four."

My friends had come and removed the remaining furniture. I took the last few boxes of junk out to the car. The apartment was empty. I showered again, shaved and threw on an old well-worn Dorchester Wildcats baseball shirt and gym shorts. About the only things left in the apartment were my bag of clothes, an air mattress and a sleeping bag on the floor; everything else was out, packed and ready to go.

There was a knock at the door. Kim was wearing a pink USC tank top that came down almost covering her white shorts, and her hair was down, long and straight falling over the front of her face and shoulders down to middle of her back. We had hung out constantly over the last four years, but I had never seen her with her hair down like that before.

"Hi," she said, "last night in LA. Is this where the farewell party is?" She was holding a jug of cheap Carlo Rossi sangria, our favorite drink of choice on a college student's limited budget. We had spent many a night with Carlo, crying on each other's shoulders about bad grades, difficult friends, and lost loves over the past four years.

"Yeah, a crazy night here in my empty apartment."

"Want some company?" she asked.

"I would love some company."

She smiled and walked in. She had been in my place that morning, but now it was completely stripped and empty. "Nice place you have here. Who does your decorating?" she said, looking around at the bare walls and floors.

"Most of my stuff is on order, you know. Credit problems."

"Yeah, I see."

"How about we sit outside and enjoy the veranda?" I said. My fourth floor apartment had a small balcony which faced southwest with a nice view of the valley. I pulled the air mattress and sleeping bag out and I sat down. She sat

93

down close, leaning against me. We didn't speak for the longest time, our backs against the wall, our bare feet side by side against the black iron railing. We looked out at the horizon, the sun was just going down in a fiery hazy crimson ball. She tilted her head and rested it on my shoulder.

"I can't believe you'll be gone tomorrow," she said finally.

"Hard to believe it's all over."

"We've had some good times, haven't we?"

"Four great years. And a lot of memories."

"What will you remember the most?" she asked.

I leaned back and looked up at the sky. "Probably junior year, when we all moved out of the dorms and into the apartments. All those crazy trips we took, like the weekend in Tijuana. Throwing up on the roller coaster at Knottsberry Farm. Climbing on the Hollywood sign."

"How about when we got kicked out of Disneyland," Kim said, laughing.

"Who knew it was agains't park policy to jump out of the Jungle Cruise boat into the river?"

"Track was fun," she said. "I met a lot of great people."

I looked down at my scar, and rubbed it with my hand. "I'll remember baseball. It was a great ride, that is until I busted my knee."

She reached over for the Carlo Rossi. "And now, I can't believe that tomorrow you'll be gone. You are like my best friend in the whole world. I'm going to miss you so much."

"And I will miss you, too," I said.

"It's time for a toast," she said, unscrewing the top of the sangria jug.

"I'm currently out of wine glasses," I said.

"How about juice glasses?"

"Nope."

"Coffee mugs?"

"Nada."

"Dixie Cups?"

"Out of those, too," I said, shaking my head. "Hard times at Casa McCann."

She sat up and twisted around facing me from the side. Her one leg was curled underneath her, and the other she stretched out laying over the top of mine. "Ok then, forget the glasses," she said. "Here's to four great years, and goodbye to a friendship I will never forget."

With her eyes locked on mine, she slowly raised the jug to her lips and took a long drink, her tongue quickly licking her lips. She handed the jug of sangria to me.

"This friendship isn't over," I said, "even though we may be going in different directions. You know what I always say, 'Never say never. Life can be a funny thing sometimes.'" I lifted the bottle to my mouth and took a drink. I wasn't so graceful, and it squirted out and ran down my face, dripping off my chin onto my shirt.

"I think we have a defective bottle," I said. She laughed, and then leaning in, she softly kissed my chin where the wine had run down.

We had been study partners, running partners, platonic friends. We had told each other secrets that you only tell someone you really trust. There were times when I had wondered what it would be like to more than friends with Kim. But I was always in the "zone." I was always afraid to cross the line that exists between friends and lovers, and she had never seemed to want to take it any further herself.

But now our world had changed. She had kissed me.

I stared at her for a moment, half in surprise at her boldness. She looked different. Her eyes had a pleading expression, like someone who had just asked the biggest favor in the world, hopeful for a yes answer.

She looked, beautiful. And at that moment, I knew I wanted her more than anything in the world.

I reached around her neck, sliding my hand into her long black hair. She whimpered ever so slightly as I pulled her toward me, slowly and gently kissing her on her mouth, tasting the sangria on her soft wet lips.

I leaned back. Her body was frozen in the moment, her eyes wide open, as if in shock. I smiled. Then she closed her eyes for a moment, and the shocked look disappeared. It was replaced with a huge smile of her own. She put both hands behind my head and pulled me back to her.

We drank and kissed, and kissed and drank, and watched the sun set over the valley. We made love there on the balcony, a heated frantic lovemaking fueled with intense buried passion. When it was over we clung to each other for a long, long time, wrapped in the sleeping bag, saying nothing, not wanting it to end. The sun was down. It was dark.

"Let's go inside," she said.

We stood up. She grabbed the jug and our clothes. I took the air mattress and sleeping bag inside. I got down on my good knee to lay out the sleeping bag when she pushed her hip against my side, knocking me off balance. She rolled me right over on my back on the air mattress and quickly dropped down sitting on top of me. She grabbed my arms and pinned them back over my head, looking into my eyes. Her long straight black hair was hanging down over me like a curtain.

"Ah, I can't breathe under here," I said, trying to blow her hair out of my face.

She let go of my arms and sat on top, straddling my hips. She took her hair in her hands and pulled it together in a loose ponytail, and then let the end of it fall back on to my face.

"You're tickling my nose. I think I'm going to sneeze, and I'm out of tissues too," I said.

She looked down on me, laughing. Then she took the ponytail and began touching the end of her hair ever so lightly across my chest. It drew across, back and forth, circles, figure eights, teasing me. It took my breath away. I felt goosebumps rising on my chest. I felt something else rising. She felt it too because she looked down at me, twisted her hips and gave me a very naughty grin. I grabbed her ponytail and gently pulled her down and kissed her deeply. I felt her exhale and she gave a gentle sigh. I grabbed her hips and rolled her off the air mattress on to the carpet as I rolled on top of her. We began to make love again, slower and less frantic, less hurried, her long legs wrapping tightly around my waist.

We made love over and over, all night long. It was so incredibly exciting, making love with a person who was on one hand so familiar to me and previously unapproachable, and yet on the other hand so new and unknown. Finally, our bodies physically exhausted, we fell asleep wrapped together in the old sleeping bag.

I woke first, disoriented. Sunlight streaming through the sliding glass door. Then I saw her sleeping, curled up beside me.

So, it wasn't a dream, I thought. It had been real. I shivered. I got up quietly, took a shower and put on some clothes. When I came out, she was awake and wearing my Dorchester Wildcats baseball shirt.

"I love this shirt," she said. "It looks so good on you."

"It looks better on you," I said. "You can have it. Take care of it for me. Don't give it away."

"I won't do that, ever," she said.

"Promise?"

"Cross my heart."

"You missed your morning run today."

"Are you kidding me?" she said. "After last night, I'm having trouble just trying to walk."

I gathered the last of my stuff together to take out to the car. I had wanted to be on the road by four. We didn't fall asleep until nearly five.

We walked out of my apartment and locked the door. "So, what do we do now?" she asked.

"Well, I wanted to miss rush hour traffic. It's after 11 now, so I guess that won't be a problem."

She gave me a long look but said nothing. With no real sense of urgency we made our way out to my car.

"So, you're leaving?" she finally asked as I was putting my stuff away.

"Yeah, a little late, but I'm in no hurry."

"Do you really have to go? I'm missing you already."

I put my hand on her shoulders. "I'm just taking my stuff home to New Jersey, that's all. Where will you be in about a month?"

"I'm moving out of here at the end of the week. I'll be driving home. Probably Minnesota."

"I have your parents' number. This is not goodbye, Kim. I will be calling you."

"You had better. I have your number in New Jersey. If you don't, I'll be calling you," she said.

We kissed. It was brief; she turned her head and pulled away. I got in my car. I waved and she waved back. I drove off.

Heading east on the interstate I was thinking that after I got home I would call her. Maybe drive out to Minnesota, or she could come to New Jersey.

I was missing her already.

Never in my wildest dreams did I ever think that it would be 16 years before I would see her face again.

Chapter 5

I looked at her as we sat across from each other all those years later at the hotel pub in center city Philadelphia.

"Yes, I remember that night," I said.

She looked at me without speaking, as if searching for the words. They weren't coming easily.

"The day after you left," she finally began, "I started packing my things to go back home. I missed you so much. I was surprised when you left. I guess I thought that after we spent the night together you might change your mind and stay."

"Wait a minute," I started.

"No, no," she said, putting up her hands and cutting me off. "I've been putting this off for a long time, and I finally got the courage to come here and see you. Let me get this out."

She leaned back in the booth and looked up at the ceiling. "I was all packed," she continued, "and I was leaving for Minnesota the next day, and then, Roger called and asked me to come to San Francisco with him. To be honest, I was not so sure how I felt about him anymore. What happened that night between us, Skip, was something I always hoped might happen, but it wasn't something I had planned. I guess I thought you were never really interested in me that way. Seeing your empty apartment that night was it. That's when I realized that you were leaving, and I just knew I would never see you again. And my emotions just took over. I was caught completely by surprise."

"Me too," I said.

"You know I had been sort of seeing Roger for over a year, and I liked him a lot, but I was never head over heels in love with him. And he never seemed over the top about me, either. And now things had changed, so I was totally and completely confused. Eventually I decided, yes I would go to San Francisco for a few days and end things with Roger before I went home to Minnesota to start my new life. But, he was different. He had changed."

"How so?"

"Well, before he was all about his career. Passing the bar, getting a job with a good law firm. But that day he seemed really into me, into him and me. More than ever before. He showed me his new Chinatown apartment. He said there were some great job opportunities for me in San Francisco. Then he asked me to move in with him. At first I thought he was kidding, but he was serious. He didn't want me to leave. He literally begged me to stay. I was shocked. He had never been this eager for us to be together. I told him that I didn't know anymore, and then he reached into his pocket and pulled out an engagement ring. Right there, he asked me to marry him."

"My God, Kim."

"I said I needed time to think about it. I was hopelessly confused. Roger and I spent the weekend together in San Francisco," she continued. "He kept introducing me as his 'fiancée' and he was so very sweet and kind. I wanted to talk to you Skip, but you were on the road and I couldn't reach you yet. The weekend was great. I decided to stay in San Francisco for a few weeks with him and maybe look for a job. One thing led to another, and it was really nice. I decided that maybe I should give him another chance, just to make sure. But that night you and I spent together had opened a door to a part of me that I had always kept locked off. I had feelings for you and that worried me. I was unsure. I didn't think I could say yes to marriage with Roger. And I felt I needed to tell him about you, about us. I was trying to figure out a way to do this, when I found out I was pregnant."

"Pregnant?"

"Yes, I was out of my mind. Alone and pregnant. Scared to death. And who was the father? What had I done? I was always the one in control of my life. Not anymore. I had done what I always promised myself I would never do; let my emotions take over. Now, my life was forever changed; my dreams

103

were finished. I could never get an abortion, so now I would become a mother at 21. I would never give up my baby. You know I was adopted, and that my birth mother had to give me up. I could never do that to my child. I needed help. I couldn't find you, I couldn't talk to you. I needed someone. Roger was there. He was my rock." She put down the now shredded straw. "When I told Roger I was pregnant, he was thrilled."

"Why didn't you try to contact me?" I said.

"Why didn't you try to contact ME?" she said.

"I tried to call you, Kim, even before I got to New Jersey. The Pacer died in the mountains. Took two weeks just to get it fixed. My parents had to wire me money. I tried from Colorado and then again from Chicago. You had moved out, and your parents' phone number was disconnected. I didn't know how to reach you. You were just gone. I got home around the beginning of July and started calling all our old friends, but nobody knew where you were. After two weeks of constant searching I finally reached Sam who on the road with the show. He knew somebody in Roger's fraternity who told him the two of you had gotten married. I was stunned. I mean, I know that night we had was sudden and unplanned, but a month later you got married? I started to question everything that happened. The only answer possible was that you didn't want a relationship with me and that you had other plans."

"My parents never told me they were moving so soon," she said. And, for the record, I did call. I called about a hundred times. "The only number I had was your parents' house. I called right after I found out I was pregnant, but you weren't back yet. Your mom said she would tell you that I called. Naturally I didn't want to say what it was about. But I kept calling. Then, a couple of weeks later when I called, she said you had just got home but that you were out with your fiancée."

"Fiancée?"

"Yes, fiancée. I remember she repeated it three times. She wanted me to know that you were off the market. When I heard that, I was stunned. You told me about your old girlfriend from high school, but you never said anything about planning to marry her. Maybe you were still in love with her. Maybe when you got home and saw her again, you changed your mind. Anyway, when I heard that, I melted down. It was over, you were gone, and I was alone. And that's when I told Roger I would marry him. But I kept calling. I needed to at least speak with you, one last time. I called a week straight, every night, but your mother always said you were not at home, and I could tell that she was getting angry at me calling all the time. Finally, the night before I got married I tried one last time. I started to tell your mom how much I missed you and needed to talk to you, that it was very important. I was ready to tell her that I was pregnant and that you might be the father. But then she started in about how happy you were now that you were home, you were getting married to your high school sweetheart, everything was going so great, and if I was such a good friend who cared for you as much as I said I did, then I would let you be

105

happy, forget about you and never call again."

My heart sank. My mother always had the telephone at arm's length and monitored every call that came to the house. She never told me that Kim had ever called. My mother always loved my first wife, Beth. Beth's mother was my mom's best friend since elementary school and the two had schemed to get Beth and me married ever since we were kids. When I finally hooked up with Beth my senior year of high school, my mother was over the moon happy and immediately started wedding preparations with her friend. I had not proposed to Beth, wasn't really sure I wanted to marry her, but now that I was finished with school my mom was in full wedding mode and was sensing trouble with a potential romantic rival. She would not have allowed a strange woman from college to upset the biggest thrill of her life, a day she had dreamed about for years. It sounded exactly like something my mother would have said.

"Anyway when I heard that," Kim continued, "I decided that she was right. I needed to start taking care of me and my future. I needed to get back in control of my life. I had a baby to think about, and I was not about to have to give her up. I needed to forget about you and try to start a life with Roger. He was there, he wanted me, and he would support me and my baby. I didn't know for sure if you were the father anyway. I mean, it could only be Roger or you. Roger was with me and he said he wanted me more than anything, and you were engaged to someone else, so I assumed that for you, our last night together was just a one-night stand. So I dropped it. I married him. Janine was born, and I started my new life."

"You knew me better than anyone," I said. "You of all people should have known that I was not into one-night stands. Especially not with you. "

"And you should have known that I was never into one-night stands either. Especially not with you. You had to know how I felt about you."

"But you got married."

"You were engaged."

"I wasn't engaged."

She stared at me, almost not believing. "You weren't engaged?"

"No, I wasn't. Beth spent the summer after graduation with her grandparents on Cape Cod. I didn't even see her again until the fall."

"How was I to know that? It's what your mother told me. I didn't think she would lie to me."

So this was the reason I never heard from her after graduation. She thought I was engaged. She thought I had left her behind. And my mother, my sainted mother whom I adored had spun the whopper of all lies, to keep her dream of me and Beth safe. I sat there, silently cursing my headstrong mother and this terrible twist of fate.

"Tell me about Janine," I finally said.

"People say she's a lot like me. She looks like me, but she's much smarter and way more mature, more aware. She's kind and very loving. We are close, Janine and I. Her teachers call her a prodigy. She's in accelerated classes

107

in her school. She may graduate high school this year as a junior. She wants to be a doctor." She opened her purse and pulled out a photograph.

The image was of a young teenage version of the woman sitting across from me. Her eyes were slightly rounder, her skin was not as dark, but besides that they could be sisters.

"She's beautiful," I said.

"Three years ago I was diagnosed with cervical cancer. I had radiation, chemo and surgery. It was awful. My hair fell out. I lost so much weight; I still haven't gained it back. I had a nurse part time. Janine was only a child, but she took better care of me than the nurse did. She saved me," Kim said with an emotional choke in her voice, putting the photograph away.

"Pardon my asking, but where was your husband during all this?" I asked.

"Roger and I separated when Janine was six. Politics is his first love. Sometimes I think he was so insistent on marriage to me because he was living in Chinatown and he knew that having an Asian wife would make him a voter favorite. Anyway, it worked. He got elected. He lives full time in Sacramento now, and Janine and I still live in the Chinatown apartment. I asked him for a divorce, but he won't do it because he feels that getting a divorce from me, and with a child would not be good for his political career. It might alienate him from some of his constituents. I brought up divorce one time with him, and he told me that he would fight it, and because of his political and judicial connections he could get custody of Janine and take her away to Sacramento. He knows I could never live with that. So I dropped it. We have our separate lives. When necessary we put on our smiles and pose for family pictures at political events, and then we go our own way. He takes care of everything financially, but that's it. I do fine at my job, but I would not be able to afford to live where I do on my salary alone. And I would never be able to afford Janine's private school."

She was out of breath, and I was out of my mind. I waited to speak, trying to let her regain some of her composure. And I needed to regain mine. It was hard to think clearly. Was I this girl's father? Beth and I divorced after five very difficult years. We had no children. After I was hired by the paper, Tony came back from medical school and started his practice in Dorchester. That was when I took his offer and moved into the apartment in the old textile mill building he had just bought on Front Street. I had always wanted children, always knew I would love being a father. But after the divorce, relationships and kids were the last thing on my mind. As the new beat reporter for the Phillies I was traveling a lot. It was new and exciting and it took my mind off my failed marriage. I was on the road as much as I was home. A casual girlfriend with no strings attached was fine, but I had no time for things like a house in the suburbs with a wife and kids asking where Daddy was every weekend.

But now to find out that I might be a father. And that I had missed 15 years of my daughter's life.

"You should have tried to reach me, Kim. You had a child. It could be our child. I may be your daughter's father."

"I know, you're right" she said. "I became bitter and angry. The rejection hurt. The whole thing was very painful for me to think about. I needed to make the pain go away. So I shut it out, and the longer it went, the easier it was to put you out of my mind and forget you. As time went by, after it had gone on for so long, I felt too guilty to even try."

"So, why now, Kim? After all these years. Why now is it so very important that you fly out here to tell me this?"

She was looking down at the table, as if somewhere on the tablecloth there were the words to say. Our food and our beer sat there untouched.

"About a year ago," she said, "Janine started feeling tired. She's athletic and loves to run and she just didn't have her old stamina. I thought maybe it was hormones or puberty. I took her to the doctor who ran some tests." Her voice trailed away; she was lost in sadness.

"What did he say?"

"She has leukemia, Skip," she said, the tears coming to her eyes.

I had no words. We sat in silence as the traffic and the pedestrians passed by on the street outside our window.

"I didn't want to come here," she finally said. "And I never wanted to see you again. I wanted to forget you. Coming here is the last thing I ever wanted to do. But I had to, for my daughter's sake. And even though you have never met Janine, and despite the fact that I have shut you out of our lives for all these years, I have come to ask you, to beg you, to do whatever it takes to get you to take a blood test and see if you are a compatible bone marrow donor for my little girl. Because without a donor, her doctors say she only has a month to live."

That night I sat in Tony's private office downstairs. He was the first person I called after I left Kim. I gave him the information she had given me, and he told me to meet him at the office.

"I spoke with her doctor in Los Angeles," Tony said. "Turns out it's Rich Hostler. We did our residency together at Penn. Hell of a nice guy. A surfing nut. He used to run down to Long Beach Island whenever the waves were big."

"Is he good? Would you want him if you were her?"

"Skip, he's head of oncology at Cedars Sinai in Los Angeles. He's one of the three or four best in the world. And he's handling this personally."

"So, what's the story?"

"The story is that Janine Bateman is one very sick girl. VERY sick."

"So, she has cancer, then?"

"Leukemia isn't just one cancer," Tony said "It's a term we use for a variety of cancers of the blood. Some cancers are more lethal than others." He

111

walked around the big cherry desk and picked up a file on the side table. "Unfortunately, this girl has one of the most lethal forms of blood cancer we've ever seen. It's unusually aggressive, and deadly. 98% of patients with this type of cancer die within the first 12 months. It just overwhelms them. It consumes them. Eats them up. Her prognosis is not good."

"So, she's going to die?"

"We're all going to die." He shrugged, closed the file and tossed it on his desk. "I'm not a fortune teller; I'm a doctor. I hate to say that situations are hopeless until we've tried every possible course of treatment. But you need to know this; the odds are not in her favor. Overwhelmingly not in her favor. Don't get your hopes up, Skip. This girl is very sick. It's late in the game, and her treatment options are extremely limited. It will take a miracle."

I know Tony like a brother. He is one of the most optimistic, 'we can do anything' kind of guys you will ever meet. So to hear him say those words, I was shocked. It was bad. The cancer would take her. This girl, so young and with so much of life left to live.

A girl who just might be my daughter.

We sat in silence for a while, finally I lifted my head.

"Okay, how am I important in all this?"

He sat down behind the desk. "If you are the biological father, and that of course is still a big if here. But if you are her father, then you might, and I stress again, might be able to donate biological material for treatment. Material

112

that, in this case must come from a suitable donor."

"What about Kim? Isn't she compatible? She's her mother."

"Kim underwent treatment for cervical cancer three years ago. She cannot be a donor. The risk of contamination and reinfection is too great. If just one microscopic cancer cell has survived in her body and gets into the girl, in her present condition, it's all over."

"Relatives?"

"Kim was adopted. There is no available information about her birth mother, other than she was a student from Taiwan. After she gave birth, she disappeared. The birth family cannot be located."

"Isn't there a donor organization?"

"Yes, and they do a great job in matching up donors and recipients. However, in this case the girl has a very rare blood type and they do not have anyone in the system who is compatible with her."

I guess I am her only hope, I thought.

Tony leaned over the desk. "Now, before I begin I need to ask you some personal questions."

"I think you know everything there is to know about me, Tony."

"Not quite. Question one. Did you have sexual intercourse with the patient's mother, Kim Gundersen-Bateman?"

My last night in LA was a subject I had never spoken to anyone about, not even Tony.

"Yes, I did. You know we were close. Best friends, really. It was my last night at USC. We were drinking, one thing led to another."

"Been there, done that," he said. "And I'm assuming you did not use a condom?"

"No. It just happened. Neither one of us was planning this. You remember Kim from when you came out to see me that last summer."

"Yes, I do remember Kim. And to tell you the truth, I was jealous as hell."

"Really? Why? As I recall you were busy almost every night you were out there."

"I was jealous of your friendship. How close you guys were and you weren't even dating. You just seemed like a couple, you would finish each other's sentences. I always thought you two might settle down together after college. I was surprised when you came home from school alone and took up with Beth again."

"I never knew you felt that way," I said. "And you were my best man."

"The best man's job is to show up at the wedding sober with a ring, and to organize the bachelor party, which I might add was one of the most awesome incredible events of pure debauchery I ever participated in," he said with a dreamy smile. "Anyway, it wasn't my job to talk you out of marrying Beth. It was none of my business."

"And I probably wouldn't have listened anyway."

"You're right. Okay, next question. The night you slept with Kim, do remember how many times you had intercourse?"

I paused for a minute.

"One or two? Ballpark?" he asked.

"I think it was four. Maybe five."

"What? FIVE? Come on, get serious here, Skip."

"I am being serious. I don't remember the exact number, but it went on over the course of nine or ten hours. Then we were exhausted, and we just fell asleep."

"Good God, man, you were a freakin' stallion," he said, shaking his head. "That poor girl."

"I think she liked it. She said she did."

"Ah, to be 21 again," Tony said. He was writing in the file.

"I assume that since Kim is asking me to take a blood test; does that mean her husband is not suitable?" I asked.

Tony looked at a paper in the file and shook his head. "He wasn't a match."

"Must have been a shock for him."

"I'm sure he was disappointed, but not every parent is a suitable donor for this type of treatment."

"What do you mean?"

"For this type of procedure, siblings match up best. Only about 30 percent of parents end up being suitable donors."

I sat up. "So, you're saying that he really could be this girl's father after all?"

"I'm saying that not matching as a donor does not preclude one from being a biological father."

I knew Tony well enough to know when he was dancing around an issue. "You're holding something back here, Tony. Out with it."

"I take doctor/patient confidentiality very seriously, Skip."

"Good. And I am your patient. Janine is not."

"Okay, that's fair. But before I go on, we need to have an understanding."

"Shoot."

"Now, don't get mad."

"What?"

Tony looked up at the ceiling. "Once I draw these blood samples and submit them for testing, we have passed the point of no return. You have one last chance right now to back out and walk away. You can say no. You haven't seen or heard from Kim in years, you do not know this girl and there has been no evidence presented that her legal father is not her biological father as well. I think I know the answer to this question. I HOPE I know the answer to this question. But I am required to ask it."

"No way, Tony," I said. "I've got to know for sure if I am her father."

"And for the record we will not definitively know the answer to that question from these preliminary tests. But if we proceed with this, there will be further testing, and you will know for sure. And if it turns out you are her biological father, we will be opening up an extra-large jumbo size can of serious shit with huge emotional ramifications for you, Kim, her husband, and the girl."

"And if I don't, she dies. And I might be losing my child. It could be my only chance ever to be a father. It could be her only chance to survive."

"Let us suppose for a moment that you are a suitable donor for this girl, but it also turns out that you are NOT the girl's biological father."

I hadn't thought of that, and the question stopped me for a moment. Tony sat there, staring at me.

"For Christ's sake, Tony," I finally said, standing up and leaning over the desk at him. "Of course I would do whatever I could to help her. After all these years we've known each other I can't believe you would ask that."

"I ask because it's my job. I have to ask. And I know that in the 30 years we've been best friends, you've never lied to me. And you better believe that I will hold you to your word on this."

"Why in God's name would I not be willing to help in any way I could?"

"Some people might have second thoughts if they found out that the recipient was not the person they thought they were."

"Absolutely not."

"And, the donor process is, well, to put it honestly, it's very painful," he said. "The pain can last for weeks after the procedure."

"Do you really think I would back out on this girl, knowing that I might be able to save her life?"

"No, but I still needed to hear you say it." He stood up behind the desk. "Sit down in the chair before you have a stroke. You're no good to us dead."

I sat down. He walked around to a lab table and selected some syringes and tubes. "First things first, let's get your blood samples. We need to find out if you are even in the ballpark."

"You never answered my question. You saw the blood tests. Is her father also her biological father?"

"Determining parentage requires a DNA test. It's a different process. You can't be absolutely sure without performing the correct test, and even then in some cases it can subject to interpretation. The results can be inconclusive."

"How about from the blood tests? If you had to guess from the information you do have, what do you think are the odds."

Tony took a while to respond. He was taking an extra-long time getting his syringes out. I was getting ready to ask again, when he spoke.

"If I were to guess, and it's only a wild unscientific guess, based solely on the advanced blood screening results and comments in her file that Rich sent me, I would say the chances of her legal father also being her biological father are about one in ten million," he said.

Neither one of us spoke for a moment. I could hear the sound of clinking as he put his implements on a metal tray and carried them over to my chair.

"No shit, Tony. One in ten million? Really?"

"Really really." He pulled up a stool. "Stick out your arm."

Silently he drew out four vials of blood from my arm, then stuck on an adhesive bandage.

"Now, open your mouth."

"Should I say, ahhh?"

"Shut up. Wider."

He took a small strip and swabbed the inside of my mouth.

"I can't help but wonder what a guy must be thinking," I said, when he had finished. "Knowing that the girl you raised as a daughter might not be your biological daughter. Obviously you don't love them any less, but still."

"He doesn't know that."

"How can he not know?"

"Because he was told that he is not a suitable donor in this case. That's all that we really know. There was no DNA test performed. It never got that far along in the screening process. He just thinks he's not a match."

"But the odds are mighty long from the blood test. Their doctors are probably thinking the same thing. Why didn't they tell him?"

"Doctor/patient confidentiality rules preclude us from discussing things

119

like that."

"But he's her father."

"You're exactly right. He's her FATHER. Do you realize what would happen if we did DNA tests and announced paternity results to every new father. The divorce rate would be astronomical. Kids would grow up without parents."

"So, this happens occasionally," I said.

"This happens much more than occasionally," Tony said, putting the vials into a medical shipping container.

"How much more?"

"I was shocked to find this out myself. In some parts of the country, it's estimated that as many as half of all married men have at least one child in their household who is not theirs."

"How can that happen?"

"Has it been that long, stallion?" he said. "Let me explain it to you. A boy and a girl get together. They have physical urges and longings. They hold hands, they start to sweat. Their pulse quickens and their pupils dilate. I'll get you a pamphlet."

"You know what I mean," I said.

"What happens? Shit happens. That's what happens. End of lecture," he said. "Now, it'll be a few days before we get the preliminary results, and then if you're still a possible then a few more days to determine your suitability. Then we'll do the full suite of tests, probably in Los Angeles. But let's not get ahead of ourselves. There are a lot of 'ifs' here to deal with. You're on the road with the team, so you can call me if you want after five on Friday. Or, you can wait and we'll get together when you're back in town."

"I'll call Friday."

"Good. And in the event of a match I'll follow up with Rich on a treatment date."

"Fifty percent," I said. "Wow. Talk about the lost generation."

"It's not a product of our generation. The same thing has been going on throughout history and in all cultures."

"Do you know anyone here in Dorchester?" I started.

"God damn you, Skip," he shouted. "You know how I feel about this. I only have three rules. One - do no harm. Two - provide care for people without considering their ability to pay. And three - never, never violate the doctor/patient confidentiality rule, NEVER!"

"Now who is going to have a stroke," I said, standing up and grabbing him by the shoulders. "Don't get your bowels in an uproar; it was only a passing thought, that's all. I can't help being curious. Besides, I know there have been times in the past when you've broken some of your own rules."

"Like when?"

"Like you always say you won't date patients. But last year, you hooked up with that girl from the travel agency who broke her ankle skiing."

121

"I will admit that on occasion, on a very few occasions, I have in the past stretched my own rules. When I saw that it would not be injurious or harmful to anyone, yes."

"Like Kristen, the nurse from the other night?"

"She's a colleague."

"And the volunteer candy striper from Clinton Heights."

"Well,"

"And the hospital security guard, the one with the handcuffs."

"Yeah," he said with a far off gaze.

"And the Mexican woman who runs the taco lunch truck on the street across from the hospital."

"Thank you, Mr. McCann. We'll be in touch," he said. "I am late for my date tonight. That will be $1500 dollars. We will bill your insurance company."

The Phillies were starting a ten game road trip with the Reds, Cubs and Pirates. I wanted to check in on my mother at the assisted living center before I flew out. Although I loved my mother and wanted to see her, I was uneasy about this visit in light of what Kim had told me.

Alma Sullivan McCann, stood just five feet tall, but she ran the house like Patton rolling through Germany. She was the epitome of the term "larger than life," and the master of her domain.

For almost 40 years my mother taught fourth grade at Dorchester

Elementary School, so she knew everything about everybody and never hesitated to jump into everyone's business. She was relentless, and usually got what she wanted by sheer will and never giving up. But she had a heart of gold. My mom was always first in line for organizing fundraisers and browbeating town residents to volunteer for her latest charity cause.

My Dad died in the spring of 1998, just a month after my mom was diagnosed with lung cancer. Doctors gave her 18 months to live, but they didn't know my mother. She had other plans. She successfully fought the illness for almost ten years, but the end was coming near. She was in the hospice section on oxygen and pain killers twenty-four hours a day. Some days she didn't recognize me. Tony said it would not be long. At least once a week I would check in on her.

She was out of bed, a sign that it was a good day, and sitting in her recliner, the oxygen machine purring along next to her on the floor. I decided not to bring up the Kim thing.

"I've got another new nurse, can you believe that?" she said.

"You really go through them."

"Three new nurses in three months. I finally get one trained the way I want them and they dump another new one on me. Ridiculous!"

"Do they quit?" I asked.

"No, they get moved around to another facility. The last one got another job in Philly I was told."

"How's the new nurse?"

"Dumb as a rock," she said, shaking her head.

"What else is new?"

"I heard that you have something coming up," she said.

"Oh yeah?"

"Karen stopped over yesterday. She told me that there's going to be a baseball game between your high school team and that team from Clinton Heights."

"It's our high school graduation twentieth anniversary. I guess the guys from Clinton Heights want a rematch."

"Karen says you are going to play."

My mother was giving me 'the look.' Narrow eyes, wrinkled brow, concentrating on my response. Growing up I saw that look many times when she demanded the truth about where I had been or what I had been doing.

"Yes, I am going to play."

She relaxed her gaze. "Well, it's about time," she said. "I always said you should have stayed with baseball. A lot of men recover from knee injuries and continue to play. You were good, Skip. Really good, you could have done it."

My mom had pestered me for years after my injury to get back into the game. It was the one thing I always defied her on.

"You were always happiest when you were out there on the baseball field," she continued. "You would play for hours and hours with Tony and Jimmy and the other guys."

"I enjoyed it, no question," I said. "Especially high school ball."

"Those were the best days," she said, staring off into space. "When you boys were in high school and Tony moved in. God, I loved those days. They came and went so fast. And then you were gone, off to college."

"But I came back."

"Yes, you did. And it was the happiest day of my life when you finally came home again." She sighed. "Anyway, I'm glad you are playing in that game. You may find that you missed playing baseball more than you know."

I flew out with the team early the next morning. I was hoping that being at work, doing something I loved would get my mind off the Kim situation.

It didn't.

I always liked road trips. Getting off the team plane in a new town. New sites, new experiences. Some guys hated the road trips because it took them away from their families. I had no family.

Or did I?

No, I did not. Even if I were the girl's biological father, her real father was still the man who gave her his last name. Nothing had changed.

125

Or had it?

Perhaps it was a result of growing older, but the thought of being a father and having children had been growing in my mind of late. I wanted to be the dad who coached my son in baseball and my daughter in softball. I wanted to run with them and chase them around the yard. I wanted to enjoy my children while I was still young enough to be involved in their lives, not watching from the sidelines like a tired old man. My twentieth high school anniversary was here. I felt that time was slipping away.

I felt that I was getting old, and that time was suddenly running out.

The Phillies took the first one in Cincinnati. Friday's game was a 7:05 p.m. start. I was restless, agitated. I left the media room, passed on the chili bowl, and grabbed a hot mettwurst. I walked around the rim of the Great American Ballpark eating the hot dog looking out at the Queen City skyline.

This encounter with Kim had stirred up a lot of long ignored feelings. And like it or not, the idea that I might have a 15-year-old daughter was consuming my every thought.

5:00 p. m. came. At 5:01 p. m. I called Tony.

"What do you know?" I asked.

"Okay, you passed round one. Round two is more complete. They are doing a more in-depth series of tests. I probably won't know anything for certain until you get back."

"I passed round one. What does that mean?"

"It means that based on your blood screening so far, you are a potential donor match. But more testing has to be performed to see the extent of your compatibility."

"Am I her father?"

"Jesus Christ, Skip, we've been through this. Blood types do not conclusively prove parentage. There is too great a margin for error. You can't be certain without a DNA test."

"Okay then," I said, raising my voice. "Based on the available blood test results, do you think there is a chance, just a chance that I am her father?"

"Well, of course there's a chance."

"How much of a chance?"

There was a pause on the phone.

"There is a strong possibility that you could be her father. Nothing is definite. Now, try and put that out of your mind for the time being."

"How strong a possibility?"

"A very strong possibility."

There was silence. I looked out over the city of Cincinnati.

"You know that you have a variant of type O negative blood," he finally said. "It's rare, not many people have it. Blood types are hereditary. They are passed genetically from your parents."

He stopped talking, as if he did not know what to say next. That was unusual for Tony.

127

"So then, what blood type is she?" I asked.

"Janine also has type O negative."

Chapter 6

The Phillies went six and four on their road trip. Not bad, but not great. And that's good for the Phillies. At least they weren't tanking. They were still in the hunt in the National League East. They lost the series finale with the Pirates, 9-8 in fourteen innings.

The team plane didn't land at Philadelphia International Airport until after three a.m. Tuesday was an off day; the hated Mets would come to town on Wednesday for a two-game set. Then we would take the train to Queens for a three-game series at Shea Stadium. It would be a busy week, so I slept late Tuesday, walked down to Sullivan's around two and grabbed a hot dog. No sooner had I sat down at the bar when I was jumped by a couple of retired guys getting an early start on happy hour.

"Skip, how's the '88 team looking?"

"You think you can do it again?"

They had a million questions. I told them the truth. I don't know, but we will be getting together soon and I guess we'll just have to see what happens.

Pete brought me a Rolling Rock. "This place is buzzing over the Fourth of July baseball game, Skip. It's the biggest thing to hit Dorchester in years," he said.

"And we don't even have enough guys for a full team yet," I said. "We'll be lucky to get nine."

"So I've heard. Somebody in Clinton Heights started a pool. You're heavy underdogs."

"What are the odds?"

"You really want to know?"

"Sure."

"Eight to one, against," Pete said.

"Ouch" I said.

"Yep."

"Are you in?"

Pete gave me a sheepish look. "Eight to one, are you kidding? They're great odds. Especially knowing that you will be back on the field. That's huge. Everybody I know is getting in on this. I'm in for $100.00, and I'm going to put more down."

I was a little disturbed at what Pete told me. It sounded as if someone in Clinton Heights was looking to take some money from Dorchester people who probably couldn't afford it. And with odds like that, it would be hard to pass up. What disturbed me most was Pete saying that since I was going to play, then that made it a must play bet. I hadn't taken the field in years. What if I wasn't good anymore? What if I sucked?

I left after one beer, took a drive and did some errands. I had a lot on my mind, and it was weighing heavily on me. I don't keep a lot of alcohol in my place, especially with Sullivan's across the street, but I was feeling the need for a drink. I go to a bar to be with people. When I feel the need for a drink I do it in private, by myself, with no interruption or distraction. On the way home I stopped at the chain liquor store on Route 130 near the turnpike. I browsed the bourbons and ryes but nothing was calling out to me. I grabbed a bottle of Jack but changed my mind and put it back on the shelf. What was I doing? I was in the wrong frame of mind to be in a liquor store. I decided to forget it and walked back toward the door through the cheap wine aisle, when I saw the old familiar face of Carlo Rossi. It startled me for a moment. My mind went right back to that apartment balcony in Los Angeles. I pulled a jug off the shelf. I looked into the eyes of Old Carlo.

"Well, well, we meet again," I said.

Carlo stared back at me in silence.

I was ready to put the jug back but changed my mind and took it to the register. When I got home I set it on the kitchen counter and prepared to crack the seal when I stopped myself. I knew that if I opened the bottle I would kill it, and a lot of old memories would come flooding back. I didn't want to spend my off day drunk and depressed. Common sense won the emotional debate and Carlo went in the refrigerator. Tonight I wanted some company. Tuesday night was Jimmy's bowling night, so around seven I headed over to one of Dorchester's most exciting night spots, D'Amico's Strikeout Lanes on the main drag into town.

It was a big old building with an arched roof that looked futuristic when it was built in the 50's. Renovated in the late 70's, it sported twenty-four lanes and a full service bar and lounge. The boys were all the way on the end, and I helped myself to a plastic cup and their pitcher of beer. Jimmy, Max, Wayne, and Woody's team, the "Plumber's Helpers," bowled fifty-two Tuesday nights a year. Most of the teams were made up of blue collar guys, construction workers, city and county employees. The "Plumber's Helpers" were actually pretty good; they won more than they lost. Jimmy and Wayne carried averages around 200.

Jimmy walked back down the lane after picking up his spare. "So, Karen wrote a letter to the West Jersey Power and Light, questioning our electrical usage. Today, a month later she gets a reply."

"What do they think?" I asked.

"They think he's full of shit," Max said, walking up to the ball carousel.

"They say that all their equipment is tested and accurate and the increased usage must be something we are doing," Jimmy said, sitting down on the hard plastic seat and reaching for his beer. "That's bullshit. They haven't tested anything."

"So, what are you going to do?"

"I don't know. Karen says she's going to write to the Board of Public Utilities. And Max says he knows somebody."

"My electrician friend knows this guy at the electric company," Max said. He's management. He'll get to the bottom of this; don't you worry."

"Having a friend of yours look into things is exactly why he should worry," Woody said, picking up his ball.

"Maybe you should get some of those energy efficient light bulbs," Wayne said. "I put some in my place. They're curly and white."

"Couldn't hurt," I said, signaling to the waitress for another pitcher.

Woody rolled another strike. That was three in a row. An animated picture of a turkey came up on the overhead scoring screen. Woody launched into his turkey trot, dancing back down the lane flapping his arms like the biggest bird you can imagine.

"You're hot tonight," I said.

"No stopping me now," he said. "I'm feeling 225, hell maybe 250!"

"You look more like 350," Max said.

"You're just jealous," Woody said. "Hey, when does the summer league start?"

"July 10th," Jimmy said.

"Don't forget, I'll be away that week."

"Where you going," I asked.

"Taking the family to Disney World."

"Again," said Max. "You go there every year."

"Where am I supposed to take five kids? Vegas?"

"Do you like going every year?" I asked.

"Actually, Skip, I do," he said. "We do the same rides, eat at the same places, stay at the same hotel, every time."

"Sounds boring," Max said.

"You would understand if you had kids," Woody said. "My oldest is going away to college in West Virginia next year. You only have them for a little while, and then they're gone." He took a long drink from his beer cup. "It's about the moments, Skip; it's about memories. We've gone every year for the last twelve years. This trip for us is our family time. Our lives are so busy these days - work, school, sports, music lessons, dance lessons. But that all stops when we are on vacation at Disney. That is family time. We have a lot of great memories of the vacations we've spent together. It's the look on their faces, seeing how happy they are. All of us together, as a family. Man, they are growing up so fast. I will miss it when they grow up."

It's about the memories, I thought. I drained the cup and reached for the pitcher.

"Hi, Wayne," a voice said from the top step behind the bowling team seats. Two girls considered to be very attractive for a bowling alley in

134

Dorchester were looking dreamily at Wayne.

"Oh, hi, Cathy," Wayne said with an innocent smile.

"This is my roommate Lori," Cathy said, motioning toward her companion. Both girls looked to be in their early twenties and were wearing ridiculously short shorts, which showed off their long legs very nicely.

"Hi, Lori," Wayne said.

Both girls stood silently, looking shyly down at their feet and then back at Wayne, waiting for him to make the next move.

Wayne had no moves.

"Hey, ladies, my name is Max. I'm Wayne's best friend." Max gave them a raised eyebrow and a wink.

"Tara told me you guys broke up," Cathy said quickly, looking away from Max and back to Wayne. "I'm really sorry."

"Yeah, me too," Wayne agreed. "She's a really nice girl, but she was always getting on me for spending too much time with the fire department and bowling and my friends and stuff. I thought it would be better if we were just friends."

"I would never do that," Lori blurted out. "I mean, a guy's gotta have his friends, right?"

"She's real sad," Cathy cut in, "but you're right. You've got a life."

"She's a great person," Wayne said. "I know she'll find somebody special."

135

"Listen, Wayne," Cathy said, "Tara told me you're a plumber. Lori and I share an apartment out past the school, Meadowview Apartments."

"I know where that is," Wayne said.

"Our shower drain keeps getting clogged. Do you think you could help out two girls, alone and on their own?"

"Well, I guess so. Don't the apartments have a maintenance man?"

They looked at each other, lowering their heads in an embarrassed gesture. "Well, yeah, but he's busy all the time," Lori said.

"A clogged drain? I may be able to take the trap apart. If that doesn't clear it up, I'll need to use a snake."

"Tara told me about your snake," Cathy said. The two girls giggled nervously.

"I don't have a plumber's snake," Wayne said, puzzled. "I don't know why Tara would say that. But I can borrow one from work. I could come by tomorrow, say around six?"

"Oh Wayne, you're our hero," Cathy said. "Come hungry, we'll make dinner."

"And dessert," Lori added.

"I love dessert," Wayne said with a smile. "Sometimes I just want to eat dessert first before anything else."

"I'm up for that," Lori said, looking at Cathy and giggling.

"Ok, I'll see you tomorrow night," Wayne said, and the girls walked away whispering to each other.

"Something tells me that there's more going on here than you know, Wayne," Woody said.

"Yeah, they want to see your snake in action," Max said, getting up to refill his beer.

"I don't know why Tara would tell them I have a snake," Wayne said. "I never did any plumbing work at her place." He took a sip of beer. "She never wanted to go anywhere or do anything. All she ever wanted was to have sex anyway. I mean, I like sex. It's fun. But when it happens all the time, it gets kinda boring."

"Oh, to be so bored," I said, raising my plastic cup in the air. "To Wayne and his boredom problem," I toasted.

The team raised their cups in Wayne's honor.

"So, Skip, what do you think I should do," Jimmy said. "Should I file a complaint with the BPU?"

"I told you, just don't pay the bill," Max said, sitting down. "Throw it in the trash."

"Then they'll cut off my power."

"No, they won't. I haven't paid my electric bill in years," Max said.

"How can that be?" I said. "If you don't pay, they give you a month or so, and then they shut you down."

"Not in the winter. They can't shut you down when it's cold out. State law."

"It's almost Memorial Day, Max. I don't think we're going to get anymore hard freezes this season," I said.

"How are you getting away with not paying your electric bill?" Jimmy said.

"You got to know what they can and cannot do," Max said, like an elementary school teacher lecturing a class on simple division. "For example, they cannot legally shut off the power to a place if there's a medical condition."

"And you have a medical condition?"

"Well, not me personally"

"You live alone," Jimmy said.

"They don't know that. My cousin, the doctor in Piscataway wrote a letter. He said I'm taking care of my mother, and she is on an oxygen machine life support. They won't disconnect the power if it could kill somebody."

"Max," I said, "your mother's been dead almost five years."

"Yeah. And I really miss her sometimes."

"My mother baked me a pie on Sunday," Wayne said. "My favorite kind, peach. I love my mother."

I woke up the next morning, the situation with Kim front and center in my mind. It was impossible to shake. It just wouldn't let go.

I wanted to get out of the apartment and it was a nice day, so I decided to do go for a run. I hadn't been running for a while. My knee had long since healed, and even though I would never run with the speed and stamina I possessed in high school and college, I was in pretty good shape for a guy in his late 30s who ate way too much ballpark food. Running always helped me clear my mind, and it felt good to get out and work up a sweat.

I ran along Front Street until it left town and turned into a narrow backwoods road along the river. The Delaware flowed by, as it always does, never ceasing. About a mile and a half down, I came to the six-lane turnpike bridge, towering high in the air overhead. I stopped for a breather and watched the traffic hurtling to and from the Pennsylvania side and hearing the roar as they passed on the big span. Swirling around the concrete bridge foundations, the river current was a little faster here.

Usually when I ran I would relax, unwind and my mental issues would fade away with each step. For the most part, I had stopped thinking about Kim a few months after I found out she was married. But this time, for the first time in years, I thought about times I would go running with her on the beach in Santa Monica. The foaming water around the bridge reminded me of the waves of the Pacific washing up around our feet. We would set an easy pace, talking the whole time. Every once in a while, she would stop to pick up a shell or a rock that interested her. She never had pockets in the shorts she wore, so I would stick the treasure in my pocket, and then forget to give it to her when we got back. I remembered the look on her face when I was cleaning out my apartment and brought over to her place a bucket full of shells and rocks that she had collected.

It was no use. My mind was out of control.

But, the memory made me smile.

The Mets were starting their series at Citizens Bank Park that night, always a sellout. I didn't have to be at the ballpark until four. Tony had left a message for me to meet him for lunch at Best Food. After the run I took a long hot shower and around noon I headed downstairs. I sat in the booth in the corner facing the door. There was a decent crowd, it was lunchtime and there were only two restaurant options in downtown Dorchester anymore. As usual, Tony was late.

"Sorry," Tony said as he hurried in, glancing at his watch.

"What it is with doctors always being late?" I said. "Is that something they teach in medical school?"

"Ok, maybe you think I should tell the eight-four year old woman with walking pneumonia to pop a cough drop? I'll be back in two hours after lunch?"

"All right, I get the picture."

Mrs. Lee brought my Udon noodles and Tony's usual. "First things first," he said, pulling a file from his messenger bag. "The lab work is finished, and all indications are that from these preliminary tests, you are a suitable donor." He leafed through the papers, studying them closely, then abruptly set them down. "Tell you the truth; it's remarkable. They searched for almost a year, but the markers are so varied that it's almost impossible to find someone compatible with this patient. They even tested Kim even though Rich did not want to use her because of her cancer experience. No one has come closer than you. From these tests, Rich says it looks like you could be an exceptionally suitable donor. He's amazed. Every single marker matched up. He says he never thought they could have found someone this close who wasn't a sibling."

"So what you're saying is,"

"What I'm saying is you could be an exceptionally suitable donor. That's it. Nothing more. Remember, parentage has little to do with donor compatibility. Kim wasn't compatible. Only thirty percent of parents are suitable donors. This does not mean you are the girl's father. This compatibility could be just a very fortunate coincidence for the girl."

"But our blood types match."

"Your blood types are rare, and there are similarities. There are plenty of people who share rare blood types who are not related."

"So it's just a coincidence that I'm compatible?"

"She could have just hit the lottery," Tony said.

"Do you really believe that?"

"Until I see more proof, yes. The question of paternity will drive you batshit crazy if you let it, so get it out of your head."

"Too late. I can't help it, Tony," I said, pushing away my noodles. "I

141

could be a father. That dying girl could be my daughter."

"You're killing yourself. You know this."

He looked at me for a long time across the table, neither of us saying anything. He finally picked up his chopsticks and grabbed a piece of chicken. "You COULD be her biological father. That's correct, but we don't know for certain. Here is all we DO know. There is a very sick girl who will not live another month unless she gets treatment. Right now, you are her only hope. There is a chance that you could save her life, and that's a very special thing. But that is all we know right now. That's it. Nothing more."

"I need to know more," I said. "I deserve to know more."

"And you shall, but that knowledge is not the priority here. The health and welfare of the girl is the priority. SHE is what's important." He put the chicken piece back on his plate. "Consider for a moment what happens to the parents and to the girl if it's suddenly revealed that you are her biological father? The parents are already stressed beyond belief at the thought of losing their daughter, and the girl is too sick to have to deal with the emotional baggage that the man whom she has been calling 'daddy' is not really her flesh and blood. Skip, despite your anxiety, you have to put this whole paternity question on the back burner while we try to save this girl's life. A shock like this could kill her. And as I keep trying to get through your thick skull, we do NOT know conclusively that you are indeed her father. And the way you're acting makes me very worried that if it turns out you are not her father, the

142

disappointment will kill you. So, once again I say, try to put it out of your mind and focus instead on what you CAN do."

I picked at my lunch. "So, I could be an exceptionally suitable donor. Now what?"

"Now, as your doctor I have to tell you about the procedure. In layman's terms it's called an 'accelerated bone marrow harvest.' Sort of a normal bone marrow transplant on steroids, so to speak. What they do is extract the soft bone marrow tissue using needles through your back from both of your pelvic bones, and then other material from other key parts of your body. It sounds like a lot of fun, but it's not. It hurts like a bitch. After the girl finishes this round of chemo, her blood cells are poisoned. She will be weak and extremely vulnerable to infection. They will race to implant your cells in her before that can happen. The cells need to be a biological match, or the body will reject them. Your cells multiply in her and replace the poisoned cells."

"Sounds simple."

"It's not. That's my kindergarten explanation for idiots like you. It's actually incredibly complex. And the procedure Rich will be doing is a combination of alternative treatments designed to supercharge the process. It's experimental and dangerous, but frankly it's revolutionary. If it works, she may live. He's had great results in other cases. This is his first attempt with a patient who has this type of extremely aggressive blood cancer."

"So, when does all this take place?"

143

"They've accelerated the timetable."

"What's that mean?"

"It means they're running out of time," Tony said, staring at his plate.

"Out of time?"

"She's too weak to continue with the chemo schedule. It's killing her. They need to to do this as soon as possible, before infection sets in or the cancer multiplies again. They will try one more chemo pump infusion next week. You will need to be in Los Angeles the first of June. Figure you'll be out of work for a while unless there are complications."

"Complications?"

"Skip," Tony said, pulling the bowl of noodles in front of him, "with anything of this nature there's always the risk of infection or a reaction to the anesthesia. You can never be certain. It could be a while before you can go back to very limited work."

"I guess I can get Bill to cover the games for me," I said. "Work shouldn't be a problem."

"One more thing," he said, slowly. "One more big thing." He set down his chop sticks and looked across the table at me very closely.

"This procedure, the harvest," he began, "is a big deal."

"Okay."

"For you," he continued. "This is a serious procedure. Very serious. It will be very painful for you, try to understand that. It's much more involved than a normal harvest. I'll do what I can to keep it under control with meds, but the best I can hope to do is dull the pain somewhat. In many cases, it lingers on for weeks or maybe even months. You will be worn out, tired beyond belief. You may hallucinate, see or hear things that aren't there. You will have zero energy to do anything. You will need to take it easy and rest. It will take time for your system to replenish the missing cells, as much as three or four months before you're really feeling yourself."

"I understand."

"Well then, understand this. If you agree to have this procedure, you need to know that you may not be able to play in the Fourth of July game.

That statement caught my full attention. "You're kidding," I said.

"No I'm not," he said, picking up the chopsticks.

"I'll be that weak?"

"You may be. I don't know for sure how your body will react. You are in excellent health and in pretty good shape considering all those damn hot dogs you eat. You may recover quickly. You might be able to take the field. But I know for a fact that you will definitely not be playing at 100 percent. No way."

"So, what do I do," I said. "I can't let that girl die. I won't let that girl die. I'm doing this, Tony."

"I just wanted you to know upfront what the costs might be," he said. "And the truth is, you playing at just 50 percent will still be better than any

145

other player on our team."

"I intend to practice with the team. I'm taking the attitude that I WILL be on that field."

"I think that's a good thing. But after the procedure, just take it slow. Ease your way back."

"And I don't want any of the guys to know this," I said. "Doctor/patient confidentiality."

"You got it," he said, finishing his noodles. "And I'll be watching you closely just in case there's a problem."

"You mean when I get back?"

"No, you idiot. The entire time."

"In California, too?"

"Of course in California," he said. "You didn't think I was going to let one of my patients go out there alone?"

"I'm a big boy."

"You're a bonehead and you need somebody to make sure you put your gown on straight without your ass hanging out the back. Besides, this is an incredible opportunity for me to see the latest experimental oncology treatments up close and personal. And Rich says he wants to take me to Malibu."

"Just what you need, beautiful tan girls in tiny bikinis."

"Not what one normally sees walking down Front Street in Dorchester."

146

"Who's covering your patients?"

"The new ER resident, Susan Koening. She covered for me in March when I went to Phillies spring training."

"With me as a question mark now for Fourth of July, what about other players?" I asked.

"We're stuck at seven. There are two possibles. Wes Kaminsky lives in North Carolina. He wasn't planning on coming up this year, but the girls are working on him,"

"What about Flash?"

"I'm ready to kill Flash," Tony said. "He's blocking our calls now. One of my collections girls was calling five times a day. He's a radio DJ in Tampa. They're calling the station during his show for song requests. They ask for 'Please Come to Dorchester' by the Wildcats."

I shook my head and laughed. "How is that working out?"

"Not too good. He tells them the Wildcats broke up, the song sucks and he won't play it. He's pissed because we're harassing him. I may have to try drastic measures."

"Like what?"

"You don't want to know. I can be ruthless when I want. However, I do have some good news."

"Brad Cole tore a hammy?"

"Better. While they were looking for former baseball team players to

147

harass, my collections people found Angelina."

"No shit. Where is she these days?"

"Arlington, Virginia. She split with that douche husband of hers. She's single."

"Tony," I said, "be careful with this one. You remember what happened last time."

"She apparently knows I am a doctor, and she told my collections girl that she might be coming to Dorchester for the Fourth to see her mom."

"Oh God. Just what we need, another distraction. Don't we have enough to deal with?"

"I've got everything under control," Tony said with a wink, grabbing the check.

Chapter 7

I was in the print media booth at Shea Stadium in Queens when I got a text from Tony. The first '88 team practice would be at ten Saturday morning of Memorial Day weekend. That was the day after tomorrow. Bring a glove and some baseball cleats. There would be seven of us.

I hadn't worn baseball cleats in years. I threw my old pair from college in the dumpster with my other college baseball stuff after I tore my ACL. Since I had some time before the nightcap game the next day, I took a cab to a mall near the team hotel.

"Most softball leagues require rubber cleats," the young blonde woman in the striped referee's shirt said as I slipped a pair of Adidas on. "These are more for college baseball."

"Well, actually this is for a baseball team," I said. "It's a twenty year high school reunion game and metal spikes are fine,"

I leaned over to tie the laces. I imagined I could hear her laughing under

149

her breath. What was an old man like him doing trying to play baseball? Maybe try softball, Pops! Or maybe wiffle ball. Baseball was for young men, the boys of summer in the prime of their lives. Not for old goats whom time had left behind.

"Twenty years? No way."

"Yes way."

"That would put you in your late 30s," she said, eying me up with her arms crossed. "You don't look in your late 30s. You look younger."

I wasn't sure if she was being sarcastic. She wasn't laughing, she looked serious.

I smiled. "Thanks. You just made my day. In fact, you just made my week."

"Did you play ball after high school?"

"Yeah, I played college ball."

"Where?"

"USC."

"Really?" Her eyes lit up. She took a step closer to me on the bench and leaned in. "Dedeaux Field?"

"You know the program?"

"I played softball at USC on an athletic scholarship."

"You must've been good. They have an outstanding softball program."

"All New York State first team pitcher my senior year," she said.

"I was all New Jersey first team shortstop my senior year in high school. It got me the full ride at USC. But I blew out my ACL senior year and that was it."

"I knew you were an athlete," she said.

"Why do you say that?"

"I see a lot of people come in here looking for athletic gear. I can tell, just by the way a person walks whether they're for real or not. I guess it sounds stupid, but it's true."

"No, it doesn't sound so stupid," I said. "I imagine you see all types in a store like this."

She looked down at the cleats on my feet. She bent over and squeezed the toe on one of the shoes.

"These fit you really well," she said motioning to my feet. "Walk around and see how they feel."

I did as she said, and she was right. They did fit well.

"You like working here," I asked, sitting back down and taking off the cleats.

"It's a paycheck, and it's close to home." she said. "I graduated in 2005. My degree is in television communications. It's hard to find a job. I sent out a million résumés. You have to know somebody just to get in the door for an interview."

"What's your name?"

"Kelli Johnson."

"I'm Skip McCann," I said. "Are you a Mets fan?"

"Are you kidding? My dad has been a Sunday season ticket holder for years. He took me to my first game at Shea Stadium when I was four. I bleed blue."

"What time do you get off from work?"

She paused, tilted her head and gave me a questioning look. She crossed her arms again, started to blush and then she looked down. "I get off at five," she said, looking back at me with a smile.

I wrote her name down on the back of the shoebox and took out one of my business cards and wrote another name on the back.

"Okay Kelli, here's the deal. There will be a press box pass waiting for you in your name at will call for tonight's Mets-Phillies game at Shea." I handed her the card. "The name of the guy I wrote down on the back of my business card, Steve Brody, is the executive producer of television operations for the Mets organization. He's also a USC grad and an old friend. I'm going to make a phone call. You head to the park after work. Change out of the referee shirt, put on something business professional and look him up. Show him my card and then blow him away with your fastball. He's always looking for good talent."

She held the card in her hand, her mouth open, her eyes wide, totally in shock. She stared at the name on the back of the card. "Thank you," she said

152

slowly. "Oh my God, thank you so much!" I stood up and she gave me a hug. "You don't know how much this means to me."

"Yes, I do. It wasn't so long ago when someone gave did me a favor and got me inside the door."

"That's all I need," she said.

"You've got the ball. Now, it's up to you. Go out and make it happen."

The Phillies manhandled the Mets 8-0 with Cole Hamels throwing a complete game shutout. My phone went off during the game. I never answer my phone during a game when I don't recognize the number. Afterward I listened to the message.

"Skip, it's Kim. I just heard from the doctors. You're a match! Oh my God. They've been so discouraging all along, telling me to prepare for the worst. Janine's blood type is too rare, we can't find anybody, all terrible news. And today I get a call saying we think we've got the miracle donor. This is the break we've been waiting for. We can save your daughter's life, but we have to act fast. She's finally got a chance. I'm so happy, you'll never know. I just knew that you. . . ." There was a conspicuous pause. "That you. . . ." A long tired exhale. "I just knew. I guess I always knew. I always knew. Anyway, thank you, Skip. Thank you, thank you thank you."

It was going on 2 am when the team's train pulled into 30th Street station. The digital clock by my bed read 3:50 when I finally got to sleep.

153

Promptly at 9:30 my cell phone rang with my complimentary wakeup call from Tony.

At 9:50 I stumbled out the door and met him at the car. He was waiting with a coffee and a banana.

"What, no Tastykakes?" I asked.

"After practice, if you're good you can have a Krimpet. Get in."

"Who made you the manager?"

"I guess I just assumed that since I brought the uniforms, rented the equipment and the field and took out the insurance policy, that I would also get to be the manager."

"Sounds logical."

"Get in."

"I don't have a glove."

"Jimmy's bringing one of your old ones."

"I don't have a hat either."

"I've got a box of them in the trunk," he said. "For God's sake, will you just get in the car? If we're late, we'll have to run laps."

The high school was across town, upriver near the old power plant. A chain link fence surrounded the athletic fields. Tony and I walked on to the field, stopped and looked around. Inside, the concrete block dugouts and gravel infield looked identical to what I remembered 20 years ago. It was as if time had forgotten this little square of Dorchester.

I felt eighteen again.

A group of older men and high school age boys were throwing baseballs around. The field was freshly lined, and a familiar figure was walking the chalk line machine back to the storage shed behind the backstop.

"All ready for you boys," John Stone said, smiling.

"Thanks, John," I said. "Looks great. How did you know we were practicing?"

"I got a call from the good doctor's office staff," he said, motioning toward Tony. "And my son is here. The high school team is going to be scrimmaging with you, kinda get you back into playing shape."

"That's great. I'm sure they have better things to be doing."

"The 88 team set the mark, beating Clinton Heights," he said, looking across the river at the Clinton Heights skyline. "Never been done, before or since. The boys want to see some of that magic one more time come Fourth of July."

"You're always welcome to join us, John. We could sure use you," I said.

"I'll be here to watch. Everybody will be here to watch."

"At least join us in the dugout, okay? We want to get a picture before the game."

"Sure thing, Skip. I'd like that," John said, pushing the cart back around the backstop.

I put my coffee on the bench in the dugout. Jimmy tossed me a glove. I stopped breathing for a moment and my heart skipped a beat.

It was my old high school glove.

There is nothing more precious to a ballplayer than his glove. You spend hours with it. You win, you lose, you laugh, you cry, and you share it all with that leather appendage. It molds itself to your hand, creating an individual bond. No other glove will ever feel the same. And after a while, it takes on your sweat, blood, skin and your DNA. The glove becomes you.

I got it in the spring of my sophomore year in high school, and for the next three years it was my constant companion. I drove my Dad crazy going to every sporting goods store in a 50-mile radius looking for the perfect glove. And then, one day I found it. The Rawlings Fastback Basketweb, Ozzie Smith edition.

I ran the tips of my fingers over the worn tan webbing, and then on the back hand side down the Edge-U-cated Heel, and the darkened indentation where my index finger would stick out behind the mitt. Along the side, barely legible was my last name written in permanent marker, conveniently next to the Rawling's slogan, "The Finest in the Field." I brought it to my nose and took a good long sniff of the leather. God, it smelled like baseball. It was the best glove I ever had.

"I thought this was lost forever," I said, looking over at Jimmy.

"Pop had it with his things," he said. "He kept it all those years. When he died, mom put it with her treasures. I found it when we cleaned out her closet. It was dry, so I put a little neatsfoot oil in the hinge. Needs to be worked in some more."

There were three or four kids standing on the field, waiting for me. A tall kid with a big well developed upper body brushed them aside. "He's mine," he said.

As they dispersed, he turned to me. "Warm up your arm, Mr. McCann?"

"Sounds like a plan."

"I'm John. Everybody calls me Junior. You were just talking to my dad over there."

He tossed the ball to me. It was scuffed and worn, colored an uneven mocha brown from being hit around the orange toned gravel infield. How many practice balls had I thrown around in my youth? Hundreds of thousands? I felt the seams, flipped it in the air a few times. It felt familiar. It felt good. Comforting. It had been a long, long time. Here goes nothing, I thought. I took a deep breath and tossed it back to him. I could feel the unused muscles in my arm beginning to stretch.

"My dad said that you were the best baseball player he ever saw," Junior said. "He told me that right here on this field in 1988 you and Brad Cole played, and everybody who was here knew you were the better player."

"I had a good game that day. Brad didn't."

"My dad said that you had a cannon for an arm and that you ran the

157

bases like a major leaguer. He said you never ever bothered to stop at first on an outfield hit, you just ran straight to second."

"That was before I blew out my knee," I said. "I'll be lucky to make it to first now."

"You still got that cannon though," he said. "I can feel it and we're only warming up."

"You remind me of your dad. He was built big, too."

"Yeah. I guess my dad was pretty good in high school."

"Your dad was unbelievable in high school," I said. "He led the league in home runs his senior year. I don't think that record's ever been broken."

"No, it hasn't. I came up four short this year."

"Well, maybe next year."

"This field was the last place my dad ever played baseball. Sometimes I wonder what he might have done if he had kept playing."

"I think we all wonder that."

"If he just hadn't given up. If he had taken one more chance. If he had faced that pitcher again, I'll bet he would have hit it out of the park. If only he hadn't quit," he said.

"Quit?" I said, shaking my head. "Is that what you call it?"

"Yeah."

"He was beaned in the head with fastball. He had a concussion. I'd call that seriously injured."

"I know that he says that God was calling him in a different direction and everything, but he just quit. He admitted to me he was too scared to go back."

I remembered the surgeon's words after my operation. It would be three months in a brace, and then six months of easy walking to begin to get it back in shape. Then, maybe after a year I could begin heavy training, but I probably wouldn't hit my peak for at least another year. And, he assured me that the best I could hope for would be average speed at best. The knee was that far gone. The days of my being the fastest player on the bases were behind me. I thought about staying with the game, but the reality of the slight chance of reaching single A minor league ball as a twenty-four year old, when faster prospects were coming in at eighteen and nineteen shocked me into reality. If everything went right, and it rarely did, I had a very slim chance of making the majors before I was thirty. And that was just too late. Professional baseball would not be in my future. Was it fear perhaps? Was I scared to find out that I wouldn't measure up anymore? Could I have handled that? I guess I'll never know.

"I tore my ACL in college and gave up baseball too," I said. "I decided to pursue other opportunities. Life is the result of the choices we make. I made what I thought was the best choice at the time based on the circumstances. Your dad did too. He's happy with his life, and that's what it's all about. Your dad chose well."

We threw in silence for a while.

"I didn't mean anything by that quitting thing," Junior said.

"I know, don't worry about it. Truth is, I often wonder myself what might have been if I had decided to give it one more try. And I'll bet your dad has had those thoughts, too, although he'll never admit it. Some things are best left unsaid."

"All right everybody in the dugout," Tony called out. "Team meeting."

We turned to walk over to the benches.

"Okay, guys," Tony started, "welcome back. You all know why we're here."

"To get our asses kicked?" Winston Marshall said, laughing.

"That's what we thought twenty years ago too, but it didn't turn out that way, did it?" Tony said.

The guys were quiet.

"We will try to get together a couple of times a week until the end of June. I know we are all grown up now. . . ."

"Speak for yourself," Woody said.

"And we all have a lot of commitments, so I'm not expecting to see everyone at every practice. But the more we practice, the better we'll get. And I want to say thank you to the current Dorchester Wildcats varsity team who will be working out with us and helping us get our games back."

The guys all looked around, acknowledging the boys in the dugout with nods of appreciation.

They all looked so young, I thought to myself.

"If you know you can't make a practice, just give my office a call. I have a live operator available to take your call twenty-four hours a day, seven days a week, so no excuse for not letting me know."

"Do we need a note from our mom?" Billy Harper said.

"No, but don't try the 'too sick to practice' excuse," Tony said. "I'll come over and make a house call."

"And then send a bill," I added.

"Okay, no more questions?" Tony said. "All right, infield outfield, let's go."

We knew for the most part where we were going to play. Woody at first, Tony at second, Larkin at third and me at short. As I ran out to my position for the first time in sixteen years, I felt my stomach churning. Even though I had done it a million times, I was actually nervous.

Junior began hitting some soft ground balls to warm us up. The first ball he hit to me was an easy bounder. I felt my chest tighten up and my heart started to race when I saw the first ball come off the bat in my direction. But, I had fielded so many baseballs in my time as a player that when the ball reached me, the muscle movement was automatic. Even after all the years away from the field, I moved with ease, pulling the ball up to my belt, pivoting and firing to Woody at first. After a few plays, it was almost as if I had never stopped. Tony and the others took a little longer, but they were by no means lost.

161

"Get two," Junior called out, and we started simulating double plays. In high school Tony and I had practiced double plays for hours on end, and as soon as we started, the old magic seemed to reappear. Tony took one, gave a shovel flip to the bag, which I barehanded, and then tiptoeing over the bag finished off to Woody at first. Some of the high school kids were standing along the third base line.

"Damn, he's smooth," one of them said.

"They're pretty good for old guys," said another.

I laughed to myself. Old guys.

Junior started hitting with more power, and the balls became harder to get to. This is where we showed out age. Balls I knew I could have gotten to twenty years ago flew by me out of reach. Junior hit one that split the infield between Larkin and me. Kyle reached for it, but playing in at third he had no shot. When I was twenty-one, I would have been on it with time to spare, but I was a lot slower now. I made a desperate stab and grabbed it deep in the hole. My baseball skills were running on auto pilot, muscle responses to situations I had practiced so many times over the years. I one fluid motion I pivoted, jumped and twisting and firing a rocket from deep short, which landed with a very loud smack in Woody's first base mitt.

"OWWW. Shit, Skip, I think you broke my hand," Woody said, taking off his glove and shaking his fingers.

Behind me along the third base line I heard one of the kids say, "Jesus,

162

did you see THAT?"

At the plate, Junior dropped his bat and started a round of applause.

We had two more practices before I had to leave for Los Angeles. The high school kids were great, and for a bunch of out of shape former players, we did better than I thought we would, but we were still a long way from being decent. I surprised myself with my arm strength, although I was sore as hell the next day. I was shocked at just how slow I was when I ran the bases. The mental adjustment was the hardest thing for me. None of us were as fast as we were in high school, but defensively we could still make the play if the ball was anywhere near us.

The thing that made the biggest impression was how much I loved it. I loved it so very much. It had been too long. I couldn't believe how excited and happy I felt to be running the bases again, even at half speed. It just felt so good. After all these years, I was home. This was where I belonged.

I stopped out at the bowling alley a few days before leaving for Los Angeles. With both Tony and me out of town for the next week, I had asked Jimmy to keep an eye on our place and get the mail for me.

"If you need to reach me, call Tony's cell," I said to Jimmy at the table. "I may not be able to answer my phone."

"Think you'll be okay for the Fourth of July?" he asked.

I paused for a moment. "Tony said I may not be 100 percent, but by then I should be able to play."

"Find any other players?"

"Looks like Kaminsky and Gordon are our only chances. Neither one will commit. Tony's working on them."

"Skip, if you die in LA, can I have your sailfish?" Max asked.

"No way, I want it," Woody said. "Skip, come on, pal, cut me in on the sailfish."

"Wayne," I called out, as he walked back from the lane. "If I die in Los Angeles, who should get my sailfish?"

"He's not interested in your trophy sailfish," Jimmy said. "Wayne's shopping for a girlfriend."

"I'm not shopping, Jimmy," he said. "She needs some help, that's all."

He unfolded a sheet of paper in his pocket. "I got this email, Skip," he said. "I almost didn't see it because it went to my spam folder. She sounds like she's in trouble." He handed it to me.

Subject: Hello from russia.

Hello have a good day,

I am not sure where to begin, it is first time I try to use internet to meet the man but the thing is, that I will work abroad I can choice USA, Canada or Europe and I would like to meet the man to share free evenings and be my guide. My friends helped me to send a few letters to different address and I do hope that I am lucky to meet good

and kind man. you should know that now I live in Russia and my goal

is to leave This country because it is impossible to live here for young

pretty woman. they tell I look well enough, I am blonde with blue

eyes, I am natural blonde. I will send a few photos if you reply.

if you don't have wife nor girlfriend, maybe we could try to meet? I

am free I have not children .and I have not boyfriend here. I am 25

years old, please write to me directly to my mail

Sasha@russiagirlz.net

See you soon, with great hope.

"Gee, Wayne, I don't know," I said. I didn't want to make him feel stupid. "An unsolicited spam email. I get these all the time. I think it may be a scam."

"I replied to her email, and she wrote back that she needed a thousand dollars to be able to come to America," he said.

"Sounds fishy to me," Woody said, shaking his head.

"It's a scam, Hose," Max added. "They just want your money."

"I don't think so, Max," Wayne said. "I already sent the money. She said she'll be getting her visa soon and she'll come to see me. And I sent a picture like she asked. She said I'm a 'beautiful man.' She sent me her picture, too." He pulled out another paper printed on his computer with an absolutely gorgeous blonde stunner in a tiny red bikini.

"I hope she doesn't wear that out in the snow in Russia," Woody said, looking at the photo. "She'll freeze to death."

"For Chris-sakes, Hose," Max said, "you are so gullible. You just threw away a thousand bucks. They email this letter to a million horny guys in hopes that one idiot will send some money. Mark my words, this is not real. You will never see this girl or your thousand bucks ever." He reached over, grabbed the picture from Woody and took a look.

"Wow," he said. "Hey, Hose, write her back and see if she'll send you some naked pictures."

The day before I left for LA I stopped to see my mom. I hadn't said anything about Kim or the possibility that I might be a father, but I wanted to say something. However, in her condition the question was when. And to what end. Did I really need to confront her over this, especially with the reality that she was not going to be with me very much longer. Did I want to say goodbye forever to my mother with this between us?

She was in bed. It was not a good day. Her eyes were glassy. She had trouble concentrating; they must have upped her pain medication. We made small talk. She was slow to respond. I had decided it was not the time to say anything when she suddenly spoke up.

"Karen says you are flying to Los Angeles," she said.

"Did she tell you why?" I asked.

"She said it was personal and that I should ask you about it."

"Okay," I started. "Well, it's like this. When I was at USC, I had a really close friend named Kim. Kim Gundersen. Do you remember?"

She thought for a moment. "Yes, I do remember. She lived in that same building you did. You showed me her picture. An oriental girl."

"Chinese, yes. Anyway, she has a daughter who is very sick. Leukemia. They need a bone marrow donor. She asked me to take a blood test, and it looks like I'm a match. So, I'm flying out tomorrow to do the procedure."

"Was this the friend you were always talking about? The girl from Minnesota?"

"Yes. We were very close. Especially at the end when I was leaving."

"Was she your girlfriend?"

"Sort of. She told me she called several times after I got back from USC, but I guess I was never around. Do you remember her calling the house?"

"I don't remember what I had for breakfast this morning, let alone a phone call from God knows when," she said sharply, turning away. My mother was suddenly uncomfortable, I sensed it. This subject had struck a nerve. Her answer told me everything I needed to know. I was going to drop it.

167

"How old is her daughter, Skip?" she finally asked.

"Fifteen."

My mother winced. She turned her head and stared out the window. "Fifteen?"

"Yes."

"Skip, is there a chance that you could be this girl's father?"

Despite the cloud of painkillers, my mother had got right to the heart of the matter. I paused for a moment, searching for the right words. "There's a chance," I said. "Kim and I were very close. But I don't know for sure. She said she tried to reach me but never got through. She married another guy about a month after I left."

My mother stared out the window silently. She closed her eyes.

"Anyway, Tony says that you can't be sure without a DNA test, so I really don't know either way," I said. "I know I'm a match, so if there is anything I can do to help this girl, I'll do it."

My mother reached out an old weathered hand. I took it in mine. The hand that had fed me, spanked me, and comforted me. Her grip was weak. She looked back at me, with a sad expression.

"You always do the right thing. Even as a child, you were always the fixer. You would try to make everything better for everybody you met. And you're doing the right thing now. Fly out there and save that girl's life."

168

"VO Manhattan, on the rocks and can you show a little love with the cherries?" Tony said to the flight attendant.

"And for you?" she said looking over at me in the seat next to the window. We were in the very first row in first class on United flight 401 to Los Angeles.

"Just water for him," Tony said, "he's only allowed to have water."

As the flight attendant walked forward to make the drinks, I leaned over to Tony. "I'm about to have what you admit is a very serious procedure. I think I'm entitled to a drink."

"Sorry, Charlie, no can do. I want to deliver you clean as a whistle and dry as a bone to Cedars Sinai tonight. Sooner you get it over with the sooner we can get home. When this is all over, you'll have earned your drink. Besides, I'm missing baseball practice for you."

"Something tells me you'll find something to occupy your time," I said. I grabbed a pillow and scrunched up against the window.

One benefit of flying around the country frequently was that I could fall asleep instantly on a plane. I closed my eyes. As I started to doze, I could hear Tony talking to the flight attendant.

"Is he okay?" she asked.

"As okay as can be expected. I'm his doctor. Tony Adamo. And you are?"

"I'm Nikki. If you need anything at all, Doctor Adamo, please don't hesitate to use the call button."

"I will, Nikki. And, it's Tony. I can't tell you HIS name," he said in an almost whisper. "If

word leaked out he was going into Betty Ford, the network would kill him."

"The network?"

"It's sad, really. They pay him all that money, he's adored by millions and in the end it all comes down to the bottle. But a couple of weeks in a top notch facility will fix him up as good as new. At least until the next time."

"That's so sad," she cooed.

"I love that pin you're wearing. Is that authentic jade?"

"Yes, it is. My grandmother gave it to me. She's one half Hopi Indian."

"Well, isn't that ironic. I spent a year after med school working at a free clinic on a Hopi reservation in New Mexico."

"Big Pine?"

"Yes, Big Pine, that was it."

"That's where my grandmother's family lived."

"It truly is a small world, isn't it, Nikki? Oh, I'm terribly sorry. I'm keeping you from the other passengers."

"They can wait."

I dozed off amid the chatter. Next thing I knew, Tony was elbowing me.

"Wake up, sleeping beauty. We're on the ground."

"Jeez, it only seemed like a few minutes," I said, rubbing my eyes.

"It seemed like five hours to me with all your snoring."

"I don't snore."

"The hell you don't," Tony said with frown. "Your uvula was vibrating like a jackhammer. I swear, if I hadn't sworn the Hippocratic Oath, I would have stuffed that pillow down your

throat."

"That wouldn't look so good on your record. Doctor suffocates patient "

"If the jury heard your snoring, they would call it justifiable homicide."

The plane taxied to the gate and the door opened. Nikki pulled our jackets out of the overhead compartment and handed them over, shooting me a strange knowing glance and then lingering on Tony with a smile. Two hours later I signed a thick stack of papers, was out of my clothes and into a hospital gown at Cedars Sinai.

"Looks like you're all set here," Tony said coming back into the room. "I'm checking into my hotel, grabbing room service and then hitting the sack early. Lots to do tomorrow. They have about a thousand tests they need to run on you. Be prepared to cough up a gallon or so of blood and some tissue samples from various parts of your body. And if everything goes well, then we will know if this thing is a go by day after tomorrow. If the tests confirm your suitability, and I assume they will, then the procedure will be within 48 hours. This is on the fast track. Time is critical; they need to do it right away."

"We can leave after that?"

"No, we can't leave that soon," Tony said, shaking his head with an impatient look. "I told you, you'll be here for at least a week. They will monitor you closely for any reaction and you'll be doped up for the pain. Just relax, you're not going anywhere for a while."

"Sounds like fun," I said to no one in particular.

"Listen, Skip," Tony said, sitting on the side of the bed. "It's going to hurt and you'll feel really sick and very tired for a while. If you're having second thoughts. . . ."

"Don't be ridiculous," I said, "there's no way I'm backing out of this."

"Just saying. This is a big deal. I'm glad you decided to go through with it. I think you would have regretted it if you passed." He looked at his watch. "And I would have felt guilty as hell having to drug you up like a zombie and drag you out here without your consent. But I would have done it." He got up and grabbed his jacket off the chair. A small scrap of notepaper fell out of the inside pocket onto the bed.

"What is that?" he said.

I picked it up, and as I was handling it over to him I saw writing in small cursive.

Tony,

Staying at the Ritz Carlton tonight. Call me when you dump off your mystery drunk guy and we'll get dinner, and dessert.

Nikki.

I handed it back to him. He read it, cocked an eyebrow and stuck it back into his jacket pocket.

"I think my dinner plans have changed," he said shooting back a knowing glance and walking out the door.

Chapter 8

"No more needles," I shouted, through clenched teeth. "I mean it. NO MORE NEEDLES."

"Relax, Skip," Tony said, looking through a thick folder. "All the testing is done. They're finishing up the results. Took a little longer than I thought. The procedure is scheduled for noon tomorrow."

"Do I have any blood left?"

"Don't be such a wuss. Skip, I've had four-year olds complain less than you."

"I'm starving, too. The food here is terrible. I think I'll order take out. Wonder if there's a good Thai place around here that delivers?"

"Thai food," Tony said, shaking his head. "That would be just great. That's the last thing you need going into a bone marrow procedure. You'd probably shit yourself on the exam table. Just think how embarrassed I would be. How about thinking of me for once instead of just yourself."

"Think of you? You've certainly had a rough time of it. In the time we've been here you've been surfing at Malibu, eating at Matsuhisa, partying at a TV producer's home in the hills, and you've been to bed with a flight attendant and a nurse."

"Two nurses. And I'm having dinner with a surf shop sales girl in 20 minutes. No Thai food for you. You start IVs and a liquid diet tonight. You'll thank me tomorrow. Believe me, food will be the last thing on your mind after the procedure."

"Thanks for cheering me up," I said, flopping back in my bed.

Tony headed for the door. "I'll come by around nine. Wear something sexy for me."

As he walked out the door, I heard him talking to someone in the hallway. He leaned his head back in. "Someone to see you, Skip."

It was Kim. She looked tired, worn out.

"Were you sleeping?" she asked, tentatively walking into the room.

"No, just talking with my doctor. You remember Tony?"

"Of course. I remember him from when he came out to visit you."

"He's still a great friend."

She came in and sat down in the chair next to my bed. "How are you feeling? I heard they ran a lot of tests today."

"Yeah, and I've got the needle marks to prove it. They say I'm a good match. I'm ready for action."

"Us too," she said.

"How is Janine?"

"She's in very good spirits. She's in isolation and just finished up the final round of chemo. Tired, but she's always tired."

"How about you?"

"Wired," she confessed. "Nervous. I was convinced this day would never come. We searched for over a year." She looked down. "You were my last hope, Skip."

"It will work."

"The doctors are very optimistic," she said smiling. "They were amazed at the compatibility."

There was an uncomfortable pause.

"Speaking of that." My tongue was sticking to the roof of my mouth. "The, um, compatibility. Have you told Janine anything about me, her donor? How we know each other?"

"No."

"She's not curious?"

"Of course she's curious," Kim said. "She has a million questions. She wants to meet you. Wants to know everything about you."

"What's so wrong about that?"

Kim sighed, slumped back in the chair. "Janine is exceptionally bright, very perceptive, very intuitive. She already knows you are not a random donor from the pool."

"Are you afraid of how she might react if she finds out her dad might not be her biological father?"

"No," she said. "As crazy as it sounds, Roger has always been like a stranger. We separated when she was young. They've never been close. He was always very distant, and she must have picked up on that. He ignored her. It broke my heart. The thing she wanted most was a father to love her, and she never got it."

"Then why not tell her?"

"It's not a subject I want to deal with right now," Kim spat out. "Not with the leukemia and everything else."

"What else?" I asked.

Silence.

"I think we have a lot of things to talk about, Kim. Things that have not been said. Secrets that are no longer secrets."

"Right now my mind is spinning and my head is ready to explode. All I can think about is my little girl. This is not the time, Skip."

Tony's words about putting my need to know on hold were in my head. The right thing to do would be to drop it. But I couldn't help myself.

"Once upon a time we used to do a lot of talking, you and me. You said it helped you make sense of things when you were able to talk about them. Remember? We would talk for hours about everything and nothing. If you want to talk, they took my clothes. I'm not going anywhere."

Kim got up and walked over to the window. "Roger is running for lieutenant governor. This morning, we finally had it out. Everything going on with Janine and now you. I told him that this charade is over, and I'm getting on with my life. He told me that if I wait until after the election in November, then he will agree to a divorce, a generous property settlement and he will give me sole custody of Janine. Right now, my whole life is upside down, completely out of control. I hate that feeling. It reminds me of where I was 16 years ago. And a big part of that is the fact that you are back in my head after all these years of trying to get you out of it. I can't take this on. Not now." She turned back and looked me in the eyes. "Please don't tell her about us."

"How can I tell her anything? I don't even know where she is."

"She may find you."

"If she does, I will just tell her the truth. A long time ago, we were good friends."

Kim looked down at the floor. "Yes. We were good friends," she said.

I took a deep breath. "After this procedure, and after she gets well, and she will get well, I would hope that we can be good friends once again."

There was an uncomfortable silence. Kim looked nervous and agitated. She walked past my bed straight to the door. She stopped at the threshold, took a deep breath and looked back at me.

"I came here today to say thank you in person, for what you are doing to try and save my daughter's life." She took a deep breath. "Please don't hate me, Skip. Don't think that I'm ungrateful for what you are doing, because it's the probably the greatest thing anyone has ever done for me. But I don't think I want try again with you. I don't want to go down that road again, I'm just too afraid," she said. "I really don't want to see you after this is all over. You just go your way and I'll go mine, like before all this."

"You can't really mean that?"

"Yes, I do. When you left, it was very hard for me. It took a long time, but I finally put the past behind me. I need to move on."

That statement caught me unaware. I had very mixed and confused emotions. On one hand I was angry and hurt that she had never contacted me. But being around her again had brought back old memories. Happy memories. I was conflicted, but I wasn't expecting her to say that.

"So, it's goodbye, hit the road. Thanks for the bone marrow, have a nice life?" I blurted out.

"Stop it, please," she said, leaning her head against the door. "You just don't understand."

"We were friends. Good friends."

"Yes, we were good friends. But nothing more in your mind, I guess. That wasn't the case for me."

"What do you mean?"

179

"Are you really that blind? Really, Skip?"

I didn't answer at first.

"Yes, I guess I am," I said.

She walked back in and stood next to my bed, bending over right in front of me.

"I loved you. I loved you so much. From the first day we met in college. You were cute and smart and funny and kind. And I wanted you in the worst way."

"But you never said anything. You dated other guys at school. Including Roger."

"Yeah, because you wouldn't touch me. You treated me like I was your sister. Your love was baseball. You had baseball on the brain. You always acted as if you weren't interested in anything more than just being friends with me. You may remember that I never lasted long with any guy. I hardly ever saw Roger. And meanwhile, the few times you weren't playing baseball you would bring your latest bimbo baseball groupie around, and then you'd come crying on my shoulder about how you couldn't find anyone right for you. And I was there all the time. It was as if you never even saw me. Like you never wanted me. I wasn't good enough. That's what I thought."

"That's not how I felt, Kim. I just didn't know you felt that way about me. I remember hitting on you at a frat party and you turned me down."

"You were drunk. I didn't want our first time to be a drunken romp with

180

you throwing up in my bed and passing out. Of course I said no."

"Well," I said. "I guess when you said no, I took it to mean you weren't interested in me that way. I thought YOU just wanted to be friends, nothing more."

"Did you think I just wanted to be friends when I attacked you on your balcony? Really, Skip? You always knew exactly what I was thinking, and you didn't know that?"

"I guess not. Not until that day."

"And then, we finally got together. For four years I had these dreams of what it might be like with you, to finally have you in my arms and love you the way a woman loves a man. And you know what? My dreams weren't even close. The real thing was so over the top mind blowing that I was totally overwhelmed. I was numb. It was the real thing, and it was fantastic. And for the first time in my life, I lost control of myself."

She walked back to the door. "And then the next morning, you left me and drove away," she said. "How could you do that to me after the night we spent together? I will never understand. Never."

"I told you it wasn't goodbye," I said. "I was taking my stuff back to New Jersey. You were the one who got married without even saying anything. You were the one who pulled away."

"You were engaged, at least that's what I was told. I needed you, and you were gone. I did what I had to do."

"Okay. It's over. I understand why you did what you did. I'm not happy about how this all worked out, but I understand. What I don't understand is why you want to shut the door on me again. It's a second chance. Do you hate me that much?"

"No, I don't hate you," she said. "When you drove away, I never felt so helpless, so powerless in all my life. It almost killed me. It was scary. You know I'm the kind of person who needs to be in control. Well, I was totally out of control. It took a hell of a long time for me to get it together. To be able to face each day without tears and sadness. To get on with my life. And now, here you come again, like a knight in shining armor, riding in here to save my daughter's life. Just like I always dreamed you would for me. And once again throwing my world into an emotional tailspin. Seeing you again, I feel my self-control slipping away. I won't let that happen. My emotions will not take over this time. I cannot lose control of myself ever again. I'm sorry, Skip. I mean it. This time, I'm driving away."

"Kim, wait. Please." I said.

"No. I've made up my mind," she said. "Please don't come after me. I don't want any contact with you. I don't want to see you. I don't want you around. I want you to leave me alone. This is goodbye, Skip."

She turned and walked away.

I didn't get any sleep. Around midnight, the duty nurses came in and

182

checked my vitals. I watched the clock by my bed tick off the minutes until they would wheel me down the hall.

Just before five a soft knock came at the door. Probably the night nurse doing her last rounds. I started to raise my bed to a sitting position.

It was not a nurse. It was a young girl. She shuffled slowly in towing her IV stand, a tube sticking out of the port on her chest and others in each arm. She looked gaunt and tired, and so very thin. So very fragile, like a porcelain doll. A fuzzy pink bathrobe was pulled over her hospital gown like a shawl and she was wearing Hello Kitty slippers. She wore a plain scarf around her bald head.

I'd heard it said that sometimes love hits like a lightning bolt. Well, believe it, because it's true. I was struck. My skin was electrified. It tingled from head to toe. Every nerve ending in my body was shocked instantly to life. I recognized her immediately from the photograph. And even though she looked awful, like death warmed over, she was still the most beautiful little angel I had ever seen.

"Are you Mr. McCann?"

"Yes, I am."

There was an uncomfortable silence. She stood there, silent. Her mouth was moving, but nothing was coming out. I could feel her searching for the words to say but finding none.

"If you're a doctor," I finally said, "I have to say that's the strangest outfit I've ever seen for a medical professional. Especially the slippers."

She tilted her head back and laughed out loud. I knew that laugh. It was a good laugh. Genuine. The kind that comes from deep inside. The kind you can't fake. It broke my heart, and it broke the ice. Her wide smile was beaming, contagious. I smiled back.

"This is California. We're a bit different here," she said.

"I guess so. Have a seat, Doctor."

She sat down in the chair next to my bed. "Actually my name is Janine Bateman. You came here to save my life."

"So, you're the person all this fuss is about. Well, it's nice to finally meet you, Janine. Please call me Skip. That's what my friends call me."

"Okay, Skip," she said, nodding her head. "You are not from around here, are you?"

"I'm from New Jersey,"

"New Jersey? A place called Dorchester?" she asked.

I wondered why she would ask that question. "Yes, that's where I grew up and went to high school."

"I see. That explains that," she said, as if she had made a discovery. "Dorchester. Is that near Philadelphia?"

"About twenty miles northeast."

"University of Pennsylvania is on my short list of schools," she said with a smile. "We have friends in Philadelphia, and last year I visited Penn. I

184

liked it."

"Penn is a great school. My doctor went there."

"Dr. Tony?" she gushed with excitement. "I just met him yesterday, he's awesome. I didn't know he went there."

"Undergrad and med school."

"Wow," she said. She paused for a moment and nodded. "Well, University of Pennsylvania has just moved to the top of my college list."

"It's a great school. Tony is on the alumni board."

"Anyway, I wanted to see you, and thank you for what you're doing for me. This is an incredible thing to do for a total stranger," she said.

She was looking at me closely. Her tone was questioning, tentative. Kim was right. She was very bright.

"I'm sure if our situations were reversed, you would do the same," I said.

She shrugged. "I'd like to think I would," she said.

I saw her look down at the IV tubes. She sighed. "I just hope this works," she said, head down, sounding thoroughly exhausted. The pain of the illness was all over her young face.

"From what the doctors say, you are quite a fighter."

"Yes, but I don't have much fight left in me. Sometimes I don't think I can go on. I feel myself starting to give up." She looked down again at the tubes in her arms. "I'm so tired of being sick. I just want the pain to go away.

And I'm so scared that I'm going die." She looked at me and said, "The doctors say you can make me better. Please, help me. Please don't let me die."

Her request hit me like a bare knuckle punch to the temples. I had never been so shaken, ever in my life. She looked so sad, so discouraged, and my heart melted. I was feeling her sickness and her pain inside of me. And her hopelessness.

I sat up, dropped the bed side rail and slid over to the edge near her chair. I reached over and took her hand. It was small with thin delicate fingers, but they were cold as ice.

"Janine, look at me," I said, "You are NOT going to die."

"I'm not?"

"Not from this. Not now."

"How can you be so sure?"

"Because you are not fighting this alone anymore. Today, you will be getting some of my cells. And my cells are strong and healthy. They are fighters and now they'll be fighting for you. And they will never quit. Your cells and my cells together will beat this cancer and make you well again."

She stared at me, her head nodding vaguely. Then, the puzzled unsure look on her young face began to change into a hopeful smile.

"Believe me, Janine," I said. "You will get better and the pain will go away. You will live. And one day this whole experience will be nothing more than a bad dream. I swear this to you. I promise you. And although we've never met before, there's one thing you need to know about me. I always keep my promise."

"Your hands are so warm," she said, softly. She took her other hand and covered my hands. Then she looked up and our eyes met. She smiled wide.

"If you say I will get better, Skip, then yes, I believe I will."

"Good. Believe it, because it's true. Don't ever lose hope, Janine. Never give up. Your best days are yet to come," I said.

"The doctors didn't think so. Not until you came here."

"Well, lets just say that I was unavoidably delayed. But, now I'm here, and today's a new day. The first day of the rest of your life. Your doctors are right. We will beat this together. You and me."

"Speaking of my doctors, the thing that's so amazing is that we're so close in compatibility," she said. "I overheard the doctors say that we're so close, we could be related. Our blood types are even the same. It's like a hundred million to one coincidence."

"Sometimes people hit the lottery," I said.

"Yeah, but still." She locked eyes with me. "Donor compatibility is largely based on heredity. You don't look Chinese and my mother has been acting very strange about this whole thing. I've been wondering."

"About your mother and me?"

"She tells me everything," Janine said. "You're not a random donor. She called on you, a mystery person out of her past and you came here just for me.

187

But she won't talk about you. That's not like her. We're best friends."

"I knew your mother from college," I said. "Before she married your father."

"Oh." she said. "Were you, her boyfriend?"

"Let's just say that we were very good friends. We spent almost all our free time together. We were very close. During our college years, WE were best friends."

"That is so strange," she said. "You were best friends, but yet my mom has never mentioned your name, not once, ever. I wonder why?"

That statement stopped me cold. I think she saw that.

"I don't know," I finally said. "I guess sometimes when you start a new life, you need to leave some parts of your old life behind."

"Perhaps, but I don't think that's it. I think there is something more going on here."

"You are very curious, you know that?" I said. "You ask a lot of questions."

"I've been told that before," she said, smiling.

"As for your questions about donor compatibility, that's a question for the doctors. As for any other questions about your mom and me, I think you are old enough and certainly bright enough to understand that those answers can only come from one person. Your mother. And if you really are best friends, then I'm sure you and your mom will be able to talk it out."

188

"I tried. She got weird on me."

"Ever have a person that you love more than anything else in the world, and one day something happens beyond your control and you think you might lose them forever?"

"Yes," she said, "three years ago, when my mom got cancer."

"Then you know there's a reason why she's getting so weird on you," I said. "Don't give up on her. She's an amazing person. Cut her some slack. If I know your mom, I bet she will find her strength and get it together. One day, all your questions will be answered."

She looked at me in that almost quizzical way, as if she was trying to figure me out. "There's just something about you, Skip. I don't know how to describe it. I don't know if I'm making any sense, but. . . ."

"Young lady," a cry came from the door. An older barrel shaped nurse with a very loud voice bellowed out. "You're supposed to be in isolation. You are restricted to your bed! What are you doing walking around? Everyone is looking for you! Come with me this instant!"

She turned and barked orders to another nurse for help. Janine squeezed my hands, and the nurses slid her into a wheelchair. They turned her around toward the door.

"Janine," I called. "Don't give up. You will beat this. You're not alone."

"I won't give up, not now, because I know I'm going to get better." she said as they wheeled her out. "And thank you, for everything. I'm feeling better

189

already."

Tony was there as they prepped me for the procedure. I would be under, so I wouldn't feel anything. Tony was describing what would happen, but my mind was far away. Finally, he stopped talking. I looked at him.

"Are you feeling okay?" he asked.

"Yeah."

"You don't seem okay."

"A lot on my mind."

"I think I understand," he said. "I heard you had a visitor this morning."

I said nothing.

"It will all be over soon," he said.

The last thing I remember as the anesthesia was being administered was Tony's face looking at me over the shoulder of the nurse.

It seemed like I slept a long time. The next thing I remember was a bright light in my eyes. I squinted and tried to turn my head.

"Get that light out of my eyes," I snapped. The light went out.

As my eyes adjusted, I looked up to see Tony looking down at me. He looked awful. It was as if he had aged ten years. His eyes were tired, dark circles underneath and bloodshot, and he was sporting an uncharacteristic three-day stubble on his face.

"Welcome back," he said, sporting a weak smile.

"You look like shit, Tony," I said.

"And it's all your fault. Jesus Christ, Skip, you gave me the biggest fucking scare I've ever had."

"What happened?"

"You've been in a coma for the last three days," he said.

"What?"

"You had an allergic reaction to the anesthesia. No way we could have known, and we were this close to losing you."

"Damn."

"You can say that again."

"Damn," I said again.

He laughed, relief beginning to bring the color back to his face. "How do you feel?"

"My back hurts like a bitch, and I'm kinda groggy, but other than that I feel okay."

"Great. We were flushing IV fluids through you like a firehose, trying to get that anesthesia out of your system. You rallied late yesterday. It was remarkable. It's as if someone flipped a switch, and you were back. Your vitals are fine, and now that you're awake we're home free. As a matter of fact, I'm checking you out today. We're going home."

"Checking me out? Is that a good idea?"

"Are you a doctor?"

"Why so soon?"

"Physically, you're okay to travel home. What you need more than anything is rest. Physically and mentally. I don't think you can get that here. Too many complications. Too many distractions. I think you'll do better in your own bed. Besides, you're right. The food here sucks. We need to get some good Dorchester food in your system. Some of Mrs. Lee's homemade wonton soup and sesame noodles."

"If you say so, Doctor," I said. "How's Janine?"

Tony paused, and looked away. My heart sank.

"She was doing great until last night," he said. "Your cells took amazingly well. Rich was very pleased. I saw her yesterday. She was worried about you. She knew about your reaction to the anesthesia. And then later last night she started to slip. A major infection. Rich said thank God he did the procedure when he did. If your cells were not in her, we might have lost her this morning."

"Is she going to make it?"

"I don't know, Skip. I just don't know."

"I can't leave now. I have to stay with her."

"No, we have to leave. Today. Before it's too late."

"What are you talking about?"

Tony stood up and paced around the room. He looked over at me.

"There's another reason why we need to get home. Your mom took a

192

turn for the worse. She's in intensive care. I talked to her doctor. They don't think she'll make it to the weekend. This will be your last chance to see her."

"Help me up," I said.

I got out of bed. A wave of dizziness hit me and I sagged back onto the bed. "I'm a little lightheaded, and I'm sore but other than that I'm good," I said.

"Okay then, you sit right here and don't move. Let your head clear up a little bit. I'll send the nurses in to take out your catheter and IV. Your clothes are in that drawer. They'll help you get dressed, but be careful. You've been out for a while, and you're going to feel dizzy and lightheaded for a while. I managed to get us on the afternoon flight. I have to sign a hundred papers, and then you will sign a hundred papers. We can leave after that. I'll be back in an hour."

The nurses were in almost immediately and yanked out the catheter and IV. After they dressed me and gathered up my stuff. Tony came back with an administrator, who brought with him a stack of forms. I signed off, and he said I was good to go.

The wheeled me down to the lobby in a wheelchair and into a waiting cab. We got to the airport with seconds to spare, and we settled in our seats for the flight back to Philadelphia. Tony was quiet. He looked exhausted.

"Guess you didn't get much sleep the last few days," I said.

"And I had to cancel two dates," he said. "It was a living hell."

We sat there for a while not speaking, the sound of the jet engines roaring as we took off. Then, Tony turned his head my way.

"Now that we are in the air, there is something I need to give you," he said, pulling a handwritten letter out of his jacket pocket. "When I told Janine that you had a bad reaction to the anesthesia, she wrote you a letter and asked me to give it to you when you woke up."

"OK," I said.

Tony was still holding on to the letter.

"Your reaction to the anesthesia put us all in a panic. It was unexpected, and scary. And Janine was starting to feel sick. She fought infections like this before and she knew she was in for a rough battle. Mostly though, I think she was afraid."

"Afraid of dying?"

"You would think so, but I'm not so sure that was it. I think she was afraid of something else. I think she was most afraid that she might never get the chance to get to know the man who came to save her life. The man who gave her hope again, the man who became her hero." He looked down at the letter in his hands. "The hero that in the end turned out to be her biological father."

I bolted upright in my seat, my head began to swim. "Tony, what are you saying?"

He spoke slowly and carefully. "The last suite of tests you took needed to establish the degree of donor compatibility in order for Rich to engage his bone marrow transplant and transfusion solution. It was in effect a DNA test, but with much greater reliability and precision."

"So, the odds of me being her father?"

"There are no odds, no chances. Not any more. The tests were so conclusive that there is no margin for error. You are her father. Janine Bateman is your daughter."

"My God, Tony," I managed to say.

"Actually, I think you knew it all along. And I think she did, too."

"Janine knows?"

"She read her chart. She's very bright. She asked one of the med school interns, and he didn't know any better. He told her the test proved conclusively that your DNA was a match."

There it was. Finally. I was really a father. For years I had put the idea out of my mind. I didn't want to dwell on it. It would not be my fate. I would not be that lucky. I would most likely never have a child of my own. But, life had other plans. I was actually the father of a beautiful little girl.

A beautiful little girl who at this moment lay near death in a hospital bed, without her father at her side.

"You waited on purpose until we got on this goddamn plane before you told me," I said. "For Christ-sakes, Tony."

"You have done all you can do for Janine. It's out of your hands now. It's out of all of our hands now. She has to fight this battle herself. Meanwhile, you have one last chance to see your mother while she's still alive, a chance to say goodbye. You want to lose that?"

"No, of course not."

"Well? Who do you choose? Your brain is still in a fog from the anesthesia so I made the decision for you. Hate me if you want."

I stared out the window for a while.

After the initial shock, I started to think about my mother, and my stomach churned. How could I be expected to choose between my mother and my daughter? It was an impossible choice. There was no right answer to this question. Tony had done me a favor and took the decision from me. I slumped in my seat, my head down.

"I don't hate you," I said.

Tony leaned over and handed me the letter. With trembling hands I opened it.

> Skip,
>
> If you are reading this letter, then you are getting better. Thank God! I am so sad to think that you might die trying to save me. Doctor Tony says not to worry because you are strong and you will come back.
>
> And if you are reading this, it also means that I am very sick again and cannot be with you now. But I wanted to

share my thoughts with you.

You probably already know now that I am your biological daughter. I confronted my mom, and she told me the truth. She also admitted to me that she never told you about me. All these years, and she never tried to reach you. You never knew you had a daughter until now. That makes me so sad.

You promised me that I would get better. Even though I know I'm getting sick again, I believe it's just a temporary setback. I will beat this and get better, because you made a promise to me that I would. I will never forget what you have done for me, ever. And when I get better, I want you to know that I will find you. I don't know when or how, but I will. And if I have to, I will get on a plane and fly to Dorchester if that's what it takes. I will never give up looking for you, ever. I promise. And one thing you need to know about me, I always keep my promises, too.

Love, Janine.

The letter fell into my lap. Tears fell from my cheeks onto the letter.

"If she dies, Tony, I will never forgive you."

"If she dies, I will never forgive myself," he said quietly. "I know in my heart I did the right thing, the best thing for you, your mother and your daughter."

We sat without speaking. The clouds sped by outside my window as the plane gained altitude. I wiped my eyes.

"I think you've earned that drink now. God knows I need one," Tony said, pushing the flight attendant call button.

Chapter 9

We landed late, and Tony drove straight to the hospital. My mother was sleeping or zoned out on medication, it was impossible to tell.

Tony pulled some strings and got me into a bed on the same floor. I didn't sleep much. The next day we waited around until finally that evening she was awake. Tony warned me that sometimes patients will rally just before the end. He told me to be prepared.

She recognized me right away. That was a good sign. She smiled.

"Skip," she said. "you look like hell."

"Thanks mom."

"I'm glad you're back."

"How are you feeling, Mom," I asked.

"Not very well," she admitted softly. "I feel very weak."

"The doctors are doing everything they can."

"I know, but I'm very sad."

"Why is that?"

"I don't think I'm going to make it to your baseball game on the Fourth of July."

"We'll see, mom. We'll see."

"Are you okay?" she asked.

"Yes, I'm fine."

"That procedure, how did it go?"

"It went very well."

"I told you," she said. "That girl will be fine. You saved her life."

"That's what the doctors are hoping."

There was a pause, and then she said, "Did the tests come back? Is she your daughter?"

I honestly did not know what to say. I remembered the look on her face when I told her about Kim trying to call. She knew exactly what she did. The pain was all over her face. And now here she was, close to the end. Do I tell her the truth? My mother was hurting so much, I just could not bear to hurt her any more.

"No, she's not. False alarm."

My mother stared at me for what seemed an eternity. Then she smiled and squeezed by hand.

"You're a good son. Every mother's dream."

"I love you, Mom."

"I love you, Skip."

Jimmy and Karen came into the room. Making room for them, I slipped out the door. A few minutes later they came out. Mom was asleep again.

Tony put me back into my room. "Any word about Janine?" I asked.

Tony shook his head. "It's not good. She's fighting for her life. Rich says they're doing everything they can do. It's up to her and your bone marrow cells. She's so weak from the chemo. I just hope we weren't too late."

Tony prescribed a sedative, and I slept for almost eight hours. When I woke, Tony was sitting in the chair next to my bed. I could tell by his face what had happened.

"Your mother passed early this morning."

I nodded. I somehow knew last night that it would be the last time I spoke with her.

"She passed in her sleep. As peaceful a passing as you could hope for."

"She fell asleep when Jimmy and Karen were there."

Tony got up and walked over to the window, sun shining through in his face. "She woke up one last time before the end. I was in the room."

"What did she say?"

"She asked me to keep an eye on you, and to also keep an eye on her new granddaughter."

"What? How did she know? Did you tell her?"

"No, I did not," he said. "I asked her what new granddaughter and she

201

said that you are a wonderful son but, like your father, a terrible liar. She said that you and Janine will need each other. She will need a father, and you will need a daughter to take care of you when your mother is gone. She said it makes her happy, and she can leave now knowing you'll be all right."

That was when I lost it. I sobbed uncontrollably, like never before in my life. Not even when my Dad passed. So much spent up emotion. Everything to do with Kim, and then Janine. And now my Mom. And she was gone, and I felt so alone.

Tony sat patiently in the chair next to me, saying nothing, letting me get it all out. Finally it ended. "Any word about Janine?" I asked.

"No news," he said. He looked over and saw me grimace. "Look, Skip, she's in a battle for her life right now. And every day she hangs on is one more day for your cells to multiple and get in the fight. She's tough. She's a fighter and she's making it happen. She's beating the odds." He smiled. "She's a chip off the old block. I'm very encouraged. Keep the faith."

I slept that night in my apartment in my own bed. It felt like I had been away a year. I had a restless sleep, full of dreams. The next morning I got up and walked out onto the balcony overlooking the river. The dizziness was almost gone, but I was very weak.

The Delaware River flowed passively by as it always did, never ending. A constant flow that never changed. As I stood there looking over the railing, I heard the door open from Tony's apartment. He stood there for a moment, sizing me up.

"Skip, I just talked to Rick Hostler."

"Is she going to make it?"

Tony came up, leaned on the railing and looked out over the river. "It was a very bad infection. It resisted everything they threw at it. She just got weaker and weaker. They did everything they could. They ran out of options. It was up to her. All they could do was wait and hope that your cells would multiple fast enough to fight it for her. But she got them so late in the game. So late."

Not both of them, I thought. Please God, not both of them.

"Rich slept in a chair by her bed last night. This morning, he woke up and looked over, afraid at what he might see. What he saw was Janine, her eyes open and looking back at him. And smiling."

"You mean?"

"She did it, Skip. She did it. The fever broke. She beat the infection. She's going to make it."

I looked back out over the Delaware River, endlessly flowing to the sea. Same as it ever was. But it looked different now. Today really was a new day. The first day of the rest of my life.

"Rich asked her how she was feeling, and she said she was feeling better. And then, she said asked him why he was sleeping in the chair? Why didn't he go home last night? He told her he was worried about her. And you know what she said?"

"What?"

"She told him that he shouldn't have worried about her because her father promised her she would get better, and he never breaks his promises."

We stood there for a while. The sounds of the wind and the river and the street below filling the background of my mind.

"I'm so proud of her," I said.

"Be proud of you, too," Tony said. "If it wasn't for you, she would be gone. You saved her."

"I want to see her."

"Funny you should say that. Rich said that he thought a visit from you would be better than any medicine. How are you feeling? You probably feel very tired."

"Yes, I am. But I'll make it. I want to fly back. I can stay out there until she's recovered."

"That is not a good idea," Tony said. "A short visit would be great, but too much stimulation is not good right now. Listen, you are feeling a little better, but she is nowhere close to 100 percent, nowhere near 10 percent. She just came through the fight of her life. It's going to take some time. She is very weak and needs rest, and no excitement, just a quick visit, in and out. Really, Skip. And no confrontations with Kim, that will stress her out. She does not need stress. That would be the worst thing for her. And the worst thing for you, too."

"I understand."

"She will not rest if you are there by her side 24 hours a day either," he continued. "Remember, she just discovered her real father. She's probably so excited she could burst. She will wear herself out. Just don't tax her strength. Make it quick, give her encouragement, give her hope. Something to dream about. She will be weak, but now I think your visit could be a huge boost for her."

"I don't think Kim will get a boost," I said. "She doesn't want me around."

"I heard. Too bad. It's her loss," Tony said.

"I guess."

"I don't guess, I know. You would be the best thing to ever happen in her life. She'll never know. But, then again I remember the words of a wise old man who always says, never say never. Life can be a funny thing sometimes."

"Indeed it can."

"By the way, there was an open seat on tomorrow morning's United flight to LA. I went ahead and booked it for you. But remember, in and out!"

The next day, Tony dropped me off at Philadelphia International Airport. Later that afternoon I got out of a cab in front of Cedars Sinai Medical Center. I was already exhausted.

As I stood in the lobby the thought came to me that Kim would probably be here. She didn't want to see me, and I didn't want another emotional scene. I felt so tired, I couldn't take another confrontation. She would just have to understand that things had changed. Nothing in heaven or on earth was going to keep me away from my daughter. And if she didn't like it, well it was just too damn bad.

I was directed up to the same nurse who had shooed Janine out of my room a week ago.

"Mr. McCann, how are you feeling?" she asked.

"Better. I'm here to see Janine."

She nodded and made a notation in a book. "She is still weak, but she's doing very well considering what she's been through." She led me down the hall, dressed me in a gown and motioned to a door.

I opened the door and stepped inside the sterile white room with its harsh overhead fluorescent lighting and a wall of beeping instruments and screens. The room was empty, except for a sick little girl in the bed. I heard a soft voice.

"Skip?"

Janine had a look of surprise on her face, her eyes wide with shock, her mouth open. She reached her hands out to me, the tubes and wires in her arms and chest dangling like a forlorn robot. Her bald head was uncovered. Dark circles under her eyes. Pale as moonlight. She looked barely alive, much worse than the last time I saw her. I was stunned at how weak she looked.

206

I quickly walked over and sat down on the edge of the bed and took her in my arms. She buried her face in my neck, and I could feel warm tears running down inside my shirt.

"You came back for me," she said, looking up into my eyes.

"Of course I did, you silly girl," I said, taking my hand and wiping her cheek. "I just happened to be in the neighborhood, and I thought I would save you a trip to Dorchester. Airfare is crazy expensive in the summer. Now, tell me. How are you feeling?"

"I'm feeling better," she said.

"How are my bone marrow cells working out?"

"Dr. Rich says they are a perfect match. He says that I got them just in time. He says they saved my life."

"I'm glad I could help."

"I was so worried about you, Skip," she said. "Dr. Tony said you were strong, but he looked so upset that day he came in. He was worried, but he didn't want me to know. But I knew."

"Tony brought me back. He is a great doctor and an even better friend."

"I was asking him a lot of questions about you. We talked a long time about when you were growing up," she said. "He told my mom and me about when his parents died, and your family took him in, and how you shared your bedroom with him."

"Did he tell you that I snore?" I said. "Don't believe him."

207

"No, he didn't," she said with a laugh, a little color coming to her cheeks. "But he did say that when he lost his parents, he thought it was the end for him. He didn't know what to do. He didn't think he could go on. But you gave him a home and you made him your brother. He said he would not be where he was today if you had not been there for him. He said that I probably wanted to know more about you, which of course I do. And he didn't know what anyone might have told me about you, but he just wanted me to know the truth about what kind of man my father really is."

"I'm glad to see you smiling," I said.

"I need to ask you something," Janine said softly. "I know this must be a shock to you, finding out you have a daughter after all these years.

"Yes. To be honest, it's quite a shock," I said. "And probably a shock for you too."

"I wouldn't call it a shock. I would call it my fairy tale dream."

It was my turn to smile.

"Listen, Skip" she said. "Dr. Tony told me that you aren't married anymore and that you don't have any kids. I guess that's by your own choice. I was thinking, maybe you like it that way, not being tied down to anyone. So, I don't know how you feel about all this, having me for a daughter. I keep worrying that maybe it's not really what you want. I will understand if that's how you feel. But I just want you to know how I feel."

She reached out and took my hand. "My legal father was never much of a real father to me. I think somehow he knew I was not his real child. I don't know for sure, but looking back now it seems likely. He never wanted to spend time with me, he didn't want me around, and it hurt me so much. Thank God for my mother. She is my world. Anyway, now I find out that you are my real father. And I had an instant connection with you the first time I met you. This feels so right to me. Doctor Tony says you're the greatest guy in the world, and he says you will be the greatest dad of all time. I feel so lucky. I never really had a father to love. And, it's all I ever wanted, for my whole life. I just hope that you want it, too. I promise I will be the best daughter I can, if you want me. I really hope you want me."

"Let's get something straight right now," I said "so that you understand completely how I feel about this whole thing. Okay?"

"Okay," she said, trembling.

"Finding out that you, Janine, are my daughter," I began, "has made me the happiest man in the world. And just like you will try to be the best daughter you can, I will try to be the best father I can, because you deserve nothing but the best. If finding a father to love you is your fairy tale dream, then I can tell you, your dream has come true."

Her eyes began to water. She hugged me tightly. "Thank you, thank you," she said through tears.

We hugged and she cried for a while, then she leaned back and gave a tired sigh. I took a long look at her, lying there in the bed. I was feeling weak, but she was totally spent. In just the few minutes I had been there, it seemed as if she had used up all of her energy. I did not realize until that moment just how fragile she was, and how close to death she had come. Now I understood why Tony was so insistent that my presence might make the recovery process longer. She needed uninterrupted rest. And she would not get that with me dropping in every five minutes. I knew what had to be done, and it was the hardest thing in the world for me to do. I had to leave.

"Now, I need to go," I said. "And you need to rest and regain your strength. You won't be able to do that if I keep coming by and bothering you every day."

"No," she said, grabbing my arms tightly and not letting go. "Please don't leave. I'll be okay."

"No, you won't. Now, I mean it. You need to rest and get better. You need to eat good food and build up your strength. The doctors say it should only be a few weeks. When you get out of here, we will be spending a lot of time together, and you will need your energy. We are going to do so many things together, you and me, and I just can't wait. You've got an amazing life waiting for you outside this hospital, and I plan on being a big part of it. We are going to make up for lost time. Get well quickly so we can enjoy it."

"I just hate that it took so long for us to meet," she said, staring off into the distance behind me. "All those years, and you never knew. I never knew."

"What's done is done. Forget about the past."

"But what my mother did was wrong."

"Listen to me for a minute," I said, "and forgive me for speaking like a Dad. When you have lived as long as I have, you'll come to understand that you don't level judgment on a person if you have never walked their path. It's easy sometimes to look backward and second guess a decision. But that's not fair. You weren't there and you will never know. And although I regret the fact that it took this long for us to find each other, I understand why your mom did what she did. She did it for you. And she did it out of love. She found herself in a horrible situation with no right answer. She was afraid, and she was hurting. She made a painful and terribly difficult choice that put her own dreams aside so that you would not grow up the same way she had to."

Janine looked down and nodded, saying nothing.

"Will you do me a favor?" I asked. "This world can be a cold place. There's not a lot of real love out there. When you find it, you need to grab hold and never let go. When you have a person who loves you with all her heart, who will give up everything she has for you, Janine, it's a rare special gift. A gift you should never, ever take for granted. Your mom is that person, and you are blessed. So, next time you see your mom, tell her that you love her, for EVERYTHING she has done for you. And she's done a lot. She's going through hell right now. I think she needs to hear that as often as she can."

"I love you, Mommy," she said, looking over my shoulder.

I turned my head. At some point Kim had slipped in and was standing quietly by the door.

It was time for me to go. I got up and gave Janine my card. "That's my cell number. Don't call me from here. Rest up, get stronger, get better. The time will go fast. Call me when they say you can leave, when you're back to full health. I'll be waiting everyday."

"I'll call. I promise."

I kissed her on the forehead and squeezed her hand one last time, and got up quickly, turning to the door. I didn't want Janine to see the tears streaming down my face. I walked past Kim without meeting her eyes, and through the door into the hallway before my willpower gave out. Leaving her in that room was without a doubt the hardest thing I ever had to do. But now I understood that it was the best thing, the only thing. I quickened my pace. I needed to get away before I changed by mind.

"Skip," Kim called out behind me. She had followed me out.

I kept walking toward the elevator, stripping off my gown as I went, wiping my eyes and tossing it on the floor. The hallway was spinning. I had a preplanned speech for Kim expecting that I would have to face her, but my mind was too wound up in what I had seen and what I was feeling for Janine to get into another emotional tug of war. I just could not deal with it.

"Skip," she called again. I heard her coming down the hallway after me.

I got to the elevator and pushed the button. The door opened immediately and I quickly stepped inside, hitting the Lobby button as I entered.

As I turned, I saw Kim about 15 feet away. I put up my hands in front of me as to say 'stop.' She did.

"Not now Kim, this is not a good time. And just for the record, you may want to think I drove away from you, but that's not what happened. And you know it. If you want to continue to believe that I abandoned you, if it makes you feel better about yourself, then go right ahead. I don't care anymore. But know this, I will never drive away from that little girl in the hospital bed, that girl who I just learned is my daughter. Never! And you will just have to deal with it."

Kim's face turned ashen. She looked in terrible pain, like I had just stabbed her in heart.

"I was going to ask about your mother," she said, slowly. "Tony told us she is very sick."

"She was very sick, but not anymore. She is finally at peace. I fly back tonight. The funeral is tomorrow."

I saw Kim cover her mouth and shut her eyes.

I was punching the elevator buttons. Nothing was happening.

"I'm so sorry Skip," she said. She was starting to lose it. "Sorry for everything. Everything. And I just want you to know one thing..."

The elevator door closed. I couldn't hear what she was saying. It didn't matter anymore, anyway.

We buried my mother in the plot next to my dad on a Tuesday morning in June.

My mother was always a funeral critic. She never missed a Dorchester funeral, as she knew practically everyone in town. She would judge the success of the event by the turnout, the decorations and flowers and by the quality and quantity of food at the wake. Decorations were a must, but not too many pictures. It could get out of hand. Flowers were very important, but too many and especially the large expensive arrangements could be very gaudy. Good simple food, Dorchester food and lots of it. She especially loved sweets. We had Main Street Cafe cater the affair, and as a special nod to mom I had her favorite sweets, Sunrise Bakery sugar cookies and their legendary cinnamon sticky buns. We had a select few family pictures. The flowers were a bit on the gaudy side, but something tells me that in this case, she wouldn't have minded. Almost the entire town turned out for the funeral, including at least a hundred former students. It ended up being a happy occasion, with a lot of funny stories and remembrances from her friends. I think she would have been pleased. A 'B plus,' maybe even an 'A.'

I had to get back to work. I missed it, and I needed the distraction. But I was still tired and very sore. After about a week of bed rest and Mrs. Lee's egg drop soup, I felt well enough to get back to my life. I boarded a flight to Milwaukee to join the team midway through their 11-day NL Central road trip. The Phillies went 7 and 4. Maybe this was the year for these guys. They still had the Mets to catch up with. It would take an unbelievable Philly winning streak coupled with an unbelievable Met losing streak for that to happen. It was a long shot. With the Phillies, everything was a long shot.

Fortunately, my job is not physically challenging. A lot walking, that's about it. Getting back to work was good therapy for me. Doing what I loved kept my mind off the loss of my mother. Tony's meds were keeping the pain at bay. I was slowly regaining my strength. Each day I felt a little stronger. Tony kept me updated on Janine's recovery. She was doing well.

I thought a lot about the reunion game coming up. I was going to try to go out on the field and play. I wanted very much to play, a feeling I hadn't experienced in a long time. But I was nervous. Tony was right, I was a lot weaker. My stamina was low, and I had to rest often. And besides the question of my strength, I was way out of practice. I could get by in the field as long as every ball was hit right at me, but I hadn't hit off live pitching in years. I knew from experience how easy it was to lose your timing at the plate when you don't hit on a regular basis. Flying home at the end of the trip on the team plane, I sat next to one of the hitting coaches. I told him my story. He said when I got a little stronger I could come on down to the clubhouse one day before the team showed up and we would go out on the big field at Citizens Bank Park and take some batting practice.

On our approach into South Philadelphia, the pilot announced a power blackout in New Jersey. From the Delaware River east to the ocean, and for 50

215

miles north and south there was no electricity. As the plane banked and landed in South Philly, it was strangely dark on the Jersey side.

One of the other media guys drove me home. We stayed on the Pennsylvania side up to the Clinton Heights bridge. Crossing the bridge was an eerie experience. The normally well-lit turnpike was blackness. It got very dangerous when we got off at Route 130. No signals or lights except for the state police flashers. It was after midnight, but the traffic was still moving at a crawl. It was a mess getting back to my place. The state police and the Dorchester police directed traffic at all the intersections. The neighborhoods were dark until we came to my building. The lights were on. There were lights in my entrance and the elevator seemed to work fine.

In my apartment, the lights came right on. I flipped on the TV but there was just static. A few minutes later there was a knock at the door. It was Tony.

"Welcome back," he said, carrying a TV coaxial cable.

"What's going on?"

"Half of New Jersey has no power," he said.

"Why do we have power?"

"When I renovated the building, I found a generator in a room on the roof. It was old, but I had it repaired. I was worried that if the power went out, Jonny's family might lose a lot of food in the walk in boxes." He slid my TV around and fastened one end of the cable to the back, and the other to a jack in the wall. "Now I bet you're glad I had those guys install a TV antenna." He grabbed the remote and set up the TV to grab the over-the-air signal, and the screen came to life.

"Just local channels," he said, "no ESPN or Hallmark Channel. No "Doctor Quinn, Medicine Woman." He flipped over to a local station for the news.

> *Utility company officials now confirm that the initial cause of the statewide power outage originated in Dorchester, New Jersey at a local neighborhood electrical substation. Early reports from the scene suggest that this was not an accident. The substation was damaged in an apparent act of sabotage. Congressman Warren McSorley said he could not rule out a terrorist attack.*

"Terrorists? In Dorchester?" I said.

"Who knew," Tony said. "It seems like such a nice town."

"For crying out loud Tony."

"No crying, Skip. It means the terrorists have won."

"Where is this substation?"

"It's over on Chestnut, right behind Jimmy's house."

"Oh shit," I said.

I had no bars on the cellphone, and the house phone was down. I only slept for a few hours, and when I woke up the next morning I drove over to

217

Jimmy's house. I wasn't sure if I could walk it yet. The street was blocked, so I had to park around the corner.

As I turned and walked up Jimmy's street, I got some strange looks from the neighbors. I soon found out why. Three TV station vans and a slew of people waited on the front lawn of the old house. I stood on the sidewalk with some other gawkers and watched as Gene brought out a pitcher of lemonade and started charging fifty cents a glass to the reporters.

Some of the cameramen were lounging out by the trucks. I recognized one of them from the station that carries the Phillies games.

"What's going on?" I asked, looking up at the house.

"This is where the terrorist lives," he said, motioning over toward Jimmy's house. "The one who tried to bring down the northeast electrical grid."

"No shit."

"Yeah. His wife and kids are in there but there's no sign of him."

"How do you know this guy's a terrorist?"

"Neighbor saw him and some other terrorists shooting arrows into that electrical substation."

"Maybe he's just pissed at the electric company?"

"I dunno," he said, scratching his chin. "Never thought of that."

"Hey, Uncle Skip," Gene called, walking over with a pitcher and plastic cups. "Want a lemonade?"

"Sure, bud," I said fishing around in my pocket for some change.

"For you, it's on the house," he said, handing it to me with a smile.

"How about me?" the cameraman next to me asked.

"Fifty cents a cup," he said in a very business-like tone. "And if you want ice, it's five dollars."

"Ouch," he said.

"Uncle Tony came by this morning with ice from the restaurant," Gene said, lowering his voice. "He told me to jack up the price for ice because nobody has any and these leeches can afford it."

"What's your mom doing?"

"She's inside with Aunt Susie," he said turning to a new TV van that just pulled up.

I went into the house.

"Where's Jimmy?" I asked.

"Your guess is as good as mine," Karen said, sipping a glass of lemonade. "Buster called him from the cop shop and tipped him off. They all bolted. I told him not to listen to Max, but he never learns."

"They're probably at a bar that has electricity," Susie said.

"So, what happened?"

"Max told him that his electrician friend said the substation was to blame. They went over there around midnight after Sullivan's and starting lobbing arrows into the place. Guess one of them found the mark. In their condition it's a wonder they didn't shoot somebody in the ass."

"This is turning into a national story," I said. "The politicians are calling it the work of a terrorist cell."

"If the terrorist cells are as clueless as Jimmy and Max, we have nothing to worry about," she said with a laugh. "In the meantime, the entire region is down. Wonder what's up with that? One substation shouldn't cause the entire grid to fail."

"Maybe the power company is as inept as the terrorists," Susie said.

The power outage was a windfall for Best Food in Town and Sullivan's, as they were the only businesses in operation. Best Food hired four drivers to deliver and Sullivan's was standing room only as the only place in town with a cold beer. The Phillies shut down the Cubs that night, behind a five-hit seven inning performance by the old man, Jamie Moyer. The power was finally back on when I got back to the apartment. I got an email from an unknown Yahoo address. The subject line read, "Pop's favorite place for bratwurst, noon" and that could only be one place on earth.

The next day I went over the bridge to the Pennsylvania side and got off in Bristol, a small blue collar town on the Pennsylvania side of the river south of Clinton Heights. My father was born and raised there, and on certain occasions he would find himself back in one of his old watering holes. One of his favorites was a Moose Lodge about a block from the river. It opened at noon for members and old friends like my dad. Only Jimmy, Max, and Wayne were at the bar.

"Knew you'd remember this place," Jimmy said.

"We fished the old man out of here enough times," I said. "So, what's new?"

"Not much," Max said, hitting his Rock. "We're just the subject of a nationwide manhunt. Other than that. . . ."

"Reminds me of your last paternity lawsuit," I said.

"How are you feeling?" Jimmy asked.

"Slowly getting my strength back. I still have some pain in my back. It's manageable. Tony says it will be sore for a while."

"Dr. Tony's a good doctor," Wayne said. "When I had the chicken pox, he made me better."

"I'm to start light workouts this week," I said. "So tell me, what happened out in the back yard the other night?"

"We were drinking down at Sullivan's," Jimmy confessed, "and Max told us that his electrician friend told him the substation behind the house was not providing the proper voltage to the house. The more we drank, the better the idea sounded to put the transformer out of its misery. I had some old arrows that belonged to Pop in the cellar. One thing led to another and then, POW. There was an explosion, and the lights went out."

"All over New Jersey," Wayne added.

"I never knew that the plumber's union was a front for a terrorist cell," I said.

"Yeah, well leave it to the slimy politicians to get involved," Max said. "Hell, I'm not even in the union and they're after me, too."

"Karen told me that your neighbor, Mrs. Bowden, saw you out there shooting arrows," I said.

"Mrs. Bowden is blind, deaf, and senile," Jimmy said. "But she nailed us on this one."

"So, what's next for you terrorists? An attempt on the White House?"

"Max's uncle, the lawyer, is meeting us here. And then we're going in."

"In the meantime, your wife and kids are worried sick about you."

"Are you kidding?" Jimmy said. "They're making bank on lemonade and cookie sales to the TV reporters. They want to know if we can stretch it out for a few weeks."

"I wouldn't do that," I said.

"While we're waiting, how about a sandwich with the world's best bratwurst?" Jimmy said.

The bartender was wiping down the counter. "Are those Brats still as good as I remember?" I asked.

"Sure are," he replied. "We buy them from some guy in a pickup truck. Says they're made from a secret recipe by Amish farmers."

We were all chowing down on the world's best bratwurst when Max's uncle showed up. I had never met Max's famous attorney uncle, Martin Hirsch, but I would have guessed it was him as soon as he breezed through the door.

Black slicked hair, glistening wet with product and wearing a tailored Italian suit.

"Okay, looks like we are all here," Marty said, pulling up a stool. "Who are you?" he asked.

"I'm Jimmy's brother."

"Oh. Okay." Marty paused and looked at Jimmy. "You guys are all over the local news. It's a wonder nobody turned you in."

"News travels slowly to Bristol," Jimmy said.

"Well, that's good. Okay, here's the deal. You have to turn yourselves in."

"I promised Buster that he could bring us in," Jimmy said.

"No problem. He should meet us somewhere inside the Dorchester city limits, near the edge of town."

"How about WDCR?" I asked.

"A radio station?" Marty asked? "Perfect! Can we do a quick interview there?"

"I'm sure Murray will be fine with that," I said. "How is that going to help?"

"I want to shut up the television reporters and politicians."

That's smart, I thought. "This thing has really gotten blown out of proportion."

"There is something odd about how it all went down," Marty said. "The

223

entire grid should not have failed because one substation blew up. I've been asking around, and I've been getting the silent treatment."

"Nobody knows why?" Jimmy asked.

"Or nobody wants to talk?" Max said.

"Bingo," Marty said. "I was contacted a few months ago by a guy in middle management at West Jersey Power. He was pissed because he wasn't getting promoted. Wanted to sue. Kind of an asshole, so I understand why no one liked him. Anyway, he let on to me about some crazy inside deal he had uncovered, something about new equipment. Anyway, I called him up this morning, and he shut me down right away. When I asked why, he told me that he had just gotten a promotion and a big raise and he couldn't talk about it."

"They bought him off," Max said.

"That's what I think. I need to make some calls. West Jersey linemen. I represented a guy high up in their union, he'll get me some names. We'll get to the bottom of this." Marty stood up and smoothed out a wrinkle in his jacket. "Okay, I'll follow you over to that radio station."

Thirty minutes later I was standing in the hallway at WDCR while Murray White interviewed Jimmy. Marty was in the room, coaching Jimmy on the answers. When they were finished, we met in the lobby.

"Okay," Marty said. "Jimmy, call your cop friend."

"Thanks, Marty," Murray said, shaking his hand. "This is a great scoop for me. I won't forget it."

"Glad for the help," Marty said. "This is great damage control. We need to diffuse this terrorism thing the politicians are pushing. Scum sucking bottom feeders looking for something sensational to use to get re-elected. The television reporters are just as bad. Especially that bitch, Josie Jacobs."

Jimmy was talking to Buster on the phone. Then he looked up at Marty. "Really, you don't say. All right, see you in a couple of minutes."

"What's up?"

"Buster says that reporter Josie Jacobs will be at the police station," Jimmy said.

"Great!" Marty said. He reached into his bag and pulled out three tee shirts, handing them to Jimmy, Max and Wayne. "Go put these on. I want you to be wearing them when the cameras are rolling."

Jimmy held up his shirt. It read "Martin Hirsch Attorney at Law" on the front, with a big red phone number. He looked at Max's uncle.

"A little self-promotion for the television cameras, that's all," Marty said.

Wayne's shirt had a picture of a cat on the front, with the caption, "I LOVE KITTENS."

"Everybody loves kittens," Marty explained, "except for terrorists. It will portray you guys as sympathetic."

Max's shirt read "Run for the Nuns 5K."

"That was a charity run for the St. Agnes Catholic orphanage," Marty

225

said. "Makes you look religious and philanthropic."

"Were the nuns hot?" Max asked.

"Never mind about the nuns. That thing's got you in enough trouble as it is," Marty said, pointing a finger at Max's groin. "Now, go put the shirts on."

The three put on the shirts. A few minutes later, Buster pulled into the radio station parking lot in the Dorchester Police Department Suburban.

"Don't forget," Marty reminded. "You say nothing about this incident to anyone. You will remain silent. I will speak for you as your attorney."

Buster came over, shaking his head. "Jesus, Jimmy. It's a freak show down there."

"What do you mean?"

"That reporter must have been waiting around the corner," he said. "I told the chief, and he told me to come get you. As I was leaving, her news van was pulling in. I think she slipped the chief an envelope."

"What does she want?" I asked.

"She wants to be on hand with cameras rolling when we bring in the terrorists," Buster said. "She did a report on home grown terrorism, and she wants to show that it can even happen here in Dorchester."

A few minutes later, the trio properly dressed and handcuffed in the back of Buster's Suburban police vehicle, we started toward the police station. I called Karen, and she met us out front.

Josie Jacobs looked to be in her mid forties. She had been the 5:30 p. m.

226

anchor, but was replaced a few years ago by a newer, younger female newscaster. Now, she did on-the-street and feature stories. The cameras were rolling, and she had staked out a clear spot at the booking desk when Buster escorted the boys in.

"Do you deny that you are part of a homegrown terrorist cell," she shouted at Jimmy as he came in first. Jimmy gave her a dismissive look and walked right on by.

"Was your goal taking down the northeast power grid?" she said, sticking a microphone in Max's face. He stopped, looked her up and down, and gave her a raised eyebrow of interest, then followed Jimmy to the booking desk.

"Are you connected with other, uh, kittens?" she suddenly stopped shouting and just stared as Wayne walked up to her. Her mouth dropped open. The viewers at home on the live feed saw Wayne's tee shirt. Wayne leaned his over toward her, his angelic face and golden locks amplified by the TV lights.

"You're Josie Jacobs," he said excitedly. "Wow, Josie Jacobs! You are my favorite TV news person. I watch you all the time. You're even prettier in real life than you look on the TV at Sullivan's."

Josie Jacobs said nothing. She just stared, open-mouthed at Wayne.

"Can I get your autograph?" Wayne asked.

Her eyes widened, grinning stupidly. She started looking around, confused.

227

"My clients have no statements at this time," Marty said, rushing up and yanking Wayne along past the TV cameras and up to the booking desk. "I will be releasing a statement as soon as the police finish their paperwork."

The television lights switched off. The camera man turned to go out the door.

"Wait a minute," Josie Jacobs said, coming back to reality. "We're waiting for the statement. And get me the name of the kitten man!"

It took about an hour to do the paperwork, and then Jimmy, Max, and Wayne were taken to their deluxe accommodations in the Dorchester jail. Their arraignment was scheduled for the next day at the Burlington County courthouse in Mount Holly. They were the only occupants in the suite. The Dorchester jail was not much more than a holding cell for the occasional drunk and disorderly. The sergeant ordered take out from Lee's Best Food, and they settled in for the night with their hot and sour soup and General Tso's chicken. Marty delivered his statement on the steps of the police station, calling the entire incident an overreaction by the media and the politicians. He dismissed the terrorism claim, called it ridiculous and said that the real reason the grid went down would be revealed in due time.

The next morning, Tony and I had breakfast on his terrace overlooking the river. I filled him on the previous day's events. Tony was quiet.

"What's on your mind?" I asked.

"Fourth of July," he said.

"It's just a game, Tony."

"Not anymore." He grabbed another piece of fruit from the plate. "Guess who's coming in to watch the game?"

"Pamela Anderson?"

"Think twice as beautiful."

"Hugh Hefner's twin girlfriends?"

"How about the most incredible, beautiful goddess of them all."

"You don't mean it, Tony."

"Yes. Angelina told my collections girl that she is definitely coming back to visit her mother. And they will be at the Fourth of July game. According to my office manager she is available."

"Available for what?"

"Available for me."

"Oh, God," I said. "You better get to the supermarket and pick up some Old Spice."

"Seriously now, Skip," Tony said, "you know how I feel about Angelina. There is no one else. I have waited twenty years for this very opportunity. It's my one chance to get her back. I thought it would be no big deal, but now that I know she's coming, I am in full panic mode."

"Just relax already, will ya? You'll be fine. The pressure's on her this time."

"And then there's Kristen."

229

"The nurse?"

"Yes. We've been seeing a lot of each other. I really like her, Skip. What if she catches wind of this thing with Angelina?"

"Is she coming to the game?"

"I don't think so. She has to work."

"Lucky break there," I said. "One crisis at a time. Now, on a less serious note, any word about Janine?"

"Funny you should mention Janine. I spoke to her yesterday afternoon. Three-way conference call with her and Rich."

"How's she doing?"

"So far, so good," he said. "Rich said she could be discharged any day. She still needs to come in for outpatient for a while. They'll do a series of scans when she is discharged."

We sat for a moment, neither of us speaking. My coffee was cold.

"I've been wondering if I should have stayed out in LA for a while," I said.

"You made the right decision. She needed rest, and you might have been an impediment. Kim has been confiding in Rich lately. It's as if he's her shrink. She told him that the DNA results have forced to the surface some old issues that never should have been allowed to go this long without resolution."

"What do you mean?"

"First, she and Janine are still at odds over the fact that nothing was ever said about the possibility of you being her father. Second, Kim finally decided to tell her husband about the DNA tests. Then, he dropped his own bombshell. He told her that he knew the whole time that Janine was not his biological daughter. He found out a year after she was born. He must have had suspicions and apparently had a DNA test performed without her knowledge. That's why he separated and never really warmed up to Janine. He knew she wasn't his."

"Damn."

"He stayed married because he thought a divorce and the revelation that his wife had a child out of wedlock would hurt his political chances in his district. It was all for show."

"What a sad situation."

"Sad for everybody," Tony said, "including you. Let them get through the next couple of weeks. Janine told me yesterday that she was formally accepted by the University of Pennsylvania. Amazing, she's so young. I was prepared to pull some strings with admissions, but there was no need. Her GPA and test scores were off the charts. She's planning to come east next month for a campus visit."

"I am looking forward to that," I said.

Tony stared absently over the river at the Clinton Heights waterfront. "By the way," he said, "with Jimmy and with you now listed as questionable, I think we may be in trouble for Fourth of July."

"I told you, I'll be there. I will take the field. Not sure how long I'll last but I will be there,"

"Even with you on the field, we may not have enough guys to field a team. Will Jimmy be out of jail by then?"

"Marty says he expects the judge will grant them bail."

"Do they have bail money?" Tony asked. "If not, let me know."

Shortly after noon I got a call from Karen.

"Do you know anything about lawn mowers?" she asked.

Fifteen minutes later I was in the old garage, squatting beside an ancient push mower.

"You flooded it, that's all," I said.

"Jimmy didn't cut the grass before he was incarcerated," Karen said. "It's getting high."

"How about if you let me do the grass for you," I said.

"I can do it."

"I know you can," I said. "But, you know what? It's been a long time since I mowed the grass here at the house. A real long time. I think I would like the chance to do it again. For old time sake. Besides, I need the exercise."

"Are you sure?"

"Absolutely."

It took over a dozen pulls, but finally the old mower caught. I started the back and forth pattern that I had done so many times as a kid. The roar of the engine and the smell of the engine and the fresh cut grass was like a tonic for my jumbled thoughts. I took my time. It really wasn't a big lawn. I used to be able to do the whole thing in about twenty minutes. Forty minutes and a couple of rest breaks later, the lawn looked great and despite my fatigue I felt better.

I put the mower away. Karen motioned me up to the front porch. She had made lemonade. We sat in the white wicker chairs while the kids ran around the yard.

"You're not feeling well, are you?" Karen asked.

"I'm fine, really."

"You don't look fine."

"Thanks."

"You know what I mean," she said. "You're exhausted. You were out of breath. I never should have let you do that lawn."

"Actually, I feel a lot better now that I did it," I said. "The procedure left me very weak, but I'm getting stronger every day. This was a good thing for me. I needed the fresh air and the exercise. And the lemonade."

"I hope you're right," she said.

"I thought maybe Jimmy would be home today," I said as I wiped the sweat from my forehead and took a long pull from my glass.

"Bad news," she said. "That stupid grandstanding Congressman McSorely showed up at the arraignment this morning and made a speech on the steps of the courthouse. The judge would not grant bail. Marty petitioned them to reconsider based on a review of the Dorchester police investigation. Buster expects that will be done on Monday. The arraignment is set for next Thursday."

"July 3rd?"

"Yeah. But here's what's worse," she said. "They're holding them down at the county jail in Mount Holly. It's a real jail with barbed wire fences and criminals. Not a Motel Six like Dorchester's."

"Damn."

"Marty says he is sure they will get bail, but he can't say when. He thinks the judge may stall because of the political pressure and news coverage. If it wasn't for the pressure from the Congressman, they would have been out by now. He says not to worry."

"He's right, Karen," I said. "It's a mess, but they'll get out. Don't worry about it."

"Easy for you to say not to worry," she said. "You're not the one with two little kids at home asking where their daddy is."

Chapter 10

A three-game home stand with the Braves started July 2nd. I was worried about Jimmy, and it was looking more and more each day that we would not have enough guys to field a team on the Fourth of July.

My first practice back with the team was a shock. I was exhausted after warm ups. My first throw during infield practice bounced twice before reaching first base. I had to take a break and rest in the dugout after only a few minutes. This wasn't good.

I was also anxious about whether I could get back my swing after all these years away from baseball. I considered the Phillies coach and his offer for some live batting practice before a game. He said to come by around noon. When I walked into the clubhouse he told me to find an empty locker and get changed.

I was alone in the clubhouse well before the regular team would report. Although I have been in every National League clubhouse and nearly every American League one, it was still very surreal to be dressing there. I stood there for a while in the empty room, looking at the lockers and imagining what it would be like. What might have been? How far might I have made it if I hadn't made that awkward slide into second base at Dedeaux Field. How far might I had made it if I had tried again? I daydreamed a little. It was bittersweet.

I dressed and sat down on the bench, lacing up my new cleats, now showing some dirt from the practices. When I finished, I allowed myself a few more minutes to dream a little more, and then I grabbed my bat bag and walked out the tunnel to the dugout.

"Over here, Skip," the coach called out from the cage. "Stretch out a little before you get in."

I stretched. A few of the younger players as well as one new call up from the Triple A minor league team were rotating in and out of the cage. They didn't recognize me at first, but then one of the guys I had interviewed after a four-for-four night at the plate came over.

"Skip, you taking some swings?"

"Yeah," I said. "I'm playing in a high school twentieth anniversary game, and the coach offered to help me shake the rust off."

"Twenty years? Wow, that's a long time."

"You said it."

As I looked around at the guys cycling in and out of the batting cage, I realized that most of them were in their very early twenties. They were giving me very skeptical looks. I suppose the fact that I had been out of high school for twenty years seemed to blow their minds. And that I was here on the field, hoping to hit a baseball. They crowded along the backstop when I stepped into the cage.

"Easy swings, establish your timing first, then you can ramp it up," the coach said.

"Don't have a heart attack out there," somebody shouted out.

I missed the first two pitches. "Lead with your hands," the coach shouted to me.

I got a piece of the third pitch. The fourth was a ground ball down the first base line. The fifth pitch I smoked into the gap.

"Woo, look at that," somebody called out behind me.

I connected with the other five pitches, and then rotated out of the cage. Some of the guys came over and gave me their encouragement. It had been long time, and it felt good. I was back in my element. I was where I belonged. Whatever doubts I had about timing were now gone. I knew I could still swing the bat. It always came down to timing.

But, I was getting tired.

When I cycled in again, I brought with me the confidence I had as a twenty-one year old. I was on fire. Hitting had always come easy to me, and I could drive the ball a long way in college. I started pounding them out into the outfield. But on my third pass through, I started to drift. My swing was noticeably weaker and I was having a hard time concentrating. I was exhausted. The coach pulled me aside.

"Are you okay," he asked?

"Yeah, just a little tired."

He gave me a skeptical look. "You have some skills, Skip," he said, shaking my hand. "You swing well, especially for someone who hasn't done anything for a while. Did you say you played in college?"

"USC," I said. "Had a full ride. I made the MLB draft twice, but I turned it down to finish school. But I blew out my ACL my senior year. After recovery I knew it would be a tough road to the pros, so I decided to move to the press room."

"Too bad," he said. "It would have been a tough road, but you might have made it. You've got good hands. We can't teach that. It's something you're born with. Lead with your hands, and take your hands to the ball. Always trust your hands and you'll be fine."

The Braves were a real test for the Phillies, as they were the class of the division. The road to the pennant ran through Atlanta. The Phillies looked surprisingly good that night, and by the fifth inning they had an 8-1 lead. The hitting practice had made me very tired, and I was thinking about packing up early when my cell phone went off. I did not recognize the number. But something told me to answer it.

"Hi, it's Janine," came the voice over the phone. She sounded excited. She sounded strong.

I felt my heart race. But even more, I felt relief. "It's great to hear from you," I said. "Are you out?"

"I was discharged this morning."

"How are you feeling?"

"Stronger every day, once I got over the infection," she said. "How's your back?"

"Better. It doesn't hurt as much."

"Good. You'll need it for your big baseball game coming up."

"How did you know about our game?"

"Dr. Tony told me. He said you're the star of the team, and that they need you to be well or they won't win."

"Everyone needs to play well or we won't win. Even Tony."

"Today, my mom and me, we finally had a talk. A real talk."

"Oh?" I said.

"About you."

"I see."

"She told me everything from the beginning. She said that you were her best friend in college. And that she fell in love with you. When it came time to say goodbye to you, she didn't want to leave you so she stayed the night. That's where I came from. Then afterward, you left her and my other dad, Roger proposed. She found out she was pregnant, but she was told that you were engaged, and she didn't know what to do so she decided to try to forget about you and marry him."

"I'm glad you guys talked," I said.

"Me too. I think I understand a little better now why she did what she did."

"Good," I said.

"Can I ask you a personal question?"

"Sure."

"It's none of my business really. If you don't want to answer, I will understand."

"Go ahead."

"This has nothing to do with you and me."

"Janine, ask away," I said.

"My mom told me that she fell in love with you, but then you left her."

"I guess that's your mom's way of looking at it."

"I'm trying to understand. I wanted to hear your side. How do you see it?"

There was an uncomfortable silence between us as I searched for the words.

"Like I said, if you don't want. . . " she started.

"No, I do want to answer that. First, tell me. Is your mom home right now?"

"No, she went out to run some errands. That's why I'm calling you now.

I thought it would be easier."

"Ok. When your mom left the house, did you say goodbye to her?"

"Of course."

"Do you think she'll be back later, or is she gone forever?"

There was a pause. "It's not forever. She'll be back in a couple of hours."

"I never thought when I said goodbye to your mother that morning that it would be goodbye forever, either. I was physically leaving, driving my car home, but in my mind, I wasn't leaving her behind, far from it. We were just friends in college, but after that last night things had changed. The very last thing I said to her was that I would be calling her in a month when I got home. We didn't have cell phones back then. We couldn't be in constant contact as we are today. And when I got home, the first thing I did was try to reach her, but I couldn't. And then I found out she was married. I was in shock. I thought I knew her so well, I never thought she would do that without at least letting me know. But, then I started thinking that maybe I was wrong about her all along. What I thought was this fantastic experience was not so fantastic to her. And that when I left, she changed her mind and went back to her boyfriend."

"I see," she said.

"Janine, put yourself in my position. What would you have thought? The reality was that she was gone, married to another man. I had to try and forget her, and get on with my life."

"But you were engaged. She thought you didn't want her," she said.

"She was told that I was engaged, but I wasn't. She had no way of knowing, and she did what she had to do. I understand that now, and I don't hold that against her. I might have made the same choice if I were her."

"So, you weren't engaged to someone else?"

"No, I wasn't. I wanted to see her again. It never happened. She had disappeared. So it was over."

"Did you did love her?"

"Love is a very complicated emotion, Janine. And I don't throw that word around lightly. But, looking back at our friendship and everything that happened, and remembering how terrible I felt when I found out she was married and out of my life, I would say that yes, I was in love with your mother."

"Do you still love her?"

I had to take a deep breath. "I think I know where you're going with this," I said. "That was a long time ago. But now it's over. Your mom made it very clear to me that she has no interest whatsoever in having any contact with me. Once upon a time she may have loved me, but she does not love me anymore. It sounds to me like she's afraid of being hurt again. And I understand how she feels. It takes a long time to get over someone you love when you don't think they'll love you back. She is moving on, so I am moving on, and I am not going to dwell on what will never be. That's no way to live your life. It was a great friendship and something I will always remember.

"My mother told me things today about herself and how she feels that I never had any idea about. And yes, she desperately wants to get past this and start a new life. But, you're wrong about one thing. She does still love you. She denies it. She's so scared she won't even think about it. I can hear it in her voice. But one day, I think she will be honest with herself and stop being afraid. Anyway, enough about my mom. That's not why I called. I called to talk about you and me. I know practically nothing about you, except that you're my biological father and you saved my life. It's wonderful and exciting and a little scary, but I'm so happy. I'm not even sure what I should call you?"

"Call me whatever you are comfortable with. How about for now you just call me Skip. As I said, all my friends call me Skip."

"It's a start," she said. "Okay, Skip. You can call me Janine. Or, Angel. I like that. That's what my mom calls me. Either one."

We talked on about her recovery and mine. We compared likes and dislikes. She wanted to know everything about me and I wanted to know everything about her. There was so much to learn. So much lost time. She would be in Philadelphia in a few weeks to visit Penn and wanted to see me. The time flew. We promised to talk tomorrow night at the same time. When we finally hung up, the Press box was empty and the janitors were sweeping up and turning out the lights. We had talked for over two hours.

On July 3rd, the day before the game we had our last practice. We hoped to have more than seven players.

Tony had personally called on both Wes Kaminsky and Flash Gordon
that week. Wes had at first said he was not coming to Dorchester for the Fourth
of July. Tony talked with him for quite a while, and at the end he said he would
see what he could do. Tony seemed discouraged. I asked about Flash. Tony
said he was taking off the gloves. We needed his speed in center field. It was
time for serious arm twisting.

I was sitting next to Karen in the gallery behind the defendants' chairs
at ten in the Burlington County courthouse. I looked around but could not find
the congressman who had made the impassioned speech on the news the other
night. Josie Jacobs was seated in the back of the room, but there were no
cameras. Jimmy, Max, and Wayne were led in and seated in front of me.
Jimmy gave us a wink. Marty was whispering something to him when Judge
Dorothy McGuire was introduced and took her chair.

The county prosecutor stood. "May I approach the bench, your honor?"
he asked.

She nodded. He and Marty walked up and began to talk. The judge
looked confused and threw her hands into the air.

"Court will recess for thirty minutes," she said, banging her gavel.
"Attorneys in my chambers right now."

As they got up and went into the judge's chamber, Jimmy turned around
to Karen. "How are the kids?" he asked.

"Fine," she answered. "They're at archery practice."

"Listen, Karen," Jimmy started.

"You listen," she shot back. "This little stunt of yours could put you in prison. Your children saw your picture on the television and now they think their father is going to jail forever. They were sobbing. I can't believe you are so stupid."

"I'm sorry, Karen. Marty says they may drop the charges."

"You better hope you get prison. If they let you go, I may kill you myself."

A few minutes later, the judge and the attorneys came back into the court room.

"In the matter of the State of New Jersey versus McCann, Hirsch, and Towne," the judge began, "the charge being brought by the state is one single count of criminal mischief against James McCann. No charges are being filed against Mr. Hirsch and Mr. Towne. James McCann, how do you plead?"

Marty whispered to Jimmy. He stood up. "Guilty, your honor."

"Very well," she said. "You are hereby sentenced to time served and 100 hours of community service. This case is dismissed." The gavel came down.

The court room was buzzing.

I collared Marty in the aisle. "What the hell just happened?" I asked.

"After the last court room episode," he began, "I decided to take a chance. I remember that manager who had talked to me, saying that the company had bought electrical gear that would turn out to be illegal. So I reached out to the attorney for West Jersey Electric. I told him that if this went to trial, I would be calling witnesses who work inside the electric company to testify about certain electrical components that mysteriously failed, including where they came from. Next day I got a call from the prosecutor. They wanted this to go away. It was a lucky break."

"I'll say. I wonder what the real story is."

"I wonder too," Marty said. "Must be big, or they wouldn't have called Congressman McSorely and told him to stay away. And something tells me that West Jersey Power would be very unhappy were Jimmy to file a civil lawsuit over the excess electrical charges he has had to pay. This ain't over yet."

Jimmy shook Marty's hand and turned to Karen. She looked madder than I had ever seen her in the 20 years she and Jimmy had been married. Then, I saw a tear form in the corner of one eye. She softened.

"I love you," Jimmy said tentatively, reaching over to hug her.

She hesitated, shaking her head. Then, she leaned in and they embraced. "I love you too," she said. "But, I still may kill you on the way home. Don't hold it against me."

"I won't," Jimmy said, smiling.

Josie Jacobs walked up, pushing past Jimmy and Max to get to Wayne.

"I knew you were innocent," she told him.

"Really? That's very nice. Thank you," he said. "How did you know?"

"Your shirt," she said. "No terrorist would wear a shirt that says 'I Love Kittens.' Terrorists hate kittens. I think they even eat them."

"No," Wayne said, his face a grimace. "That's so cruel."

"I know," she said. "Say, now that you are free, I would love the chance to talk. Are you hungry? We can get lunch?"

"I'm starving. The county jail food isn't very good."

"Great," she said, locking an arm in his. "I know this nice little place just a short walk away. It's very quiet."

"I'm hungry, too," Max said, stepping in.

"Right," she said. "There's a Burger King a couple of blocks away. Try the Whopper." She turned back to Wayne. "Come on, Kitten Man."

I dropped Jimmy and Karen off at their place. I was just getting out of my car back at the apartment, trying to decide if I wanted to step into Sullivan's for a hot dog when my cell phone went off.

"Hi, it's Kelli."

I was having trouble placing the voice with a face when she added, "I sold you some baseball cleats, remember?"

I did. "Oh, sure. Kelli, how did you make out?"

"I got the job," she said. "I wanted to thank you again for getting me the interview."

"Well, Steve is a great manager. He's tough, and but he's really good. The Mets have a good TV product."

"I'm an assistant producer, so I'm running all over the place. And, I just love it."

"Good for you," I said. "I know Steve is partial to USC grads, but he would not have hired you if he didn't think you could do the job."

"Thanks. The whole thing is so surreal. Last month I was selling shoes and today I'm working at Shea Stadium. My dad has been bringing me to games since I could barely walk. It's a dream come true."

"So, let's see," I said. "You've got the Dodgers in town this weekend."

"Yes," she said. "That's the other reason I'm calling. Steve told me that you hit a home run off Brad Cole when you guys played in high school."

"Twenty years ago."

"And I remember when you bought the cleats you said you needed them for a twentieth anniversary game. I remember because I was surprised. You didn't look that old."

"Well, thanks. I guess."

"I don't mean that you're old. It's just that you looked younger. That's a better way to say it. Anyway, I saw on the rosters that Brad Cole will not be here on July 4th. I asked Steve about it and he said that Cole was excused for a private commitment that day in his hometown. So, are you playing against him in your game?"

"Yes."

"Oh my God. For real?"

"For real. It will be interesting."

"That would make an incredible story," she said. "And I guess the next time we play is early September, here at Shea. I want to hear all about it. And I want to buy you a beer, to say thanks for being kind."

"I'll take you up on that beer. And maybe a sandwich from Mama's of Corona."

"You know about Mama's?"

"I've eaten in all the ballparks, so I guess I'm an expert. You'll be one too."

"Ok then, it's a date," she said. "Good luck in your game."

Tony and I got to the field early for our final practice. We were stretching out our arms along the third base line. He was unusually quiet. Lost in his thoughts. A lot on his mind, I supposed.

"Here comes somebody," Tony said, as a blue Honda Accord pulled into the baseball field parking lot.

"It's got North Carolina plates," I said.

Wes Kaminsky got out, reached into the back seat and pulled out a glove. He took a moment to look around the field, and then walked down to the backstop.

"Skip, Tony," he said coming around the fence. "Good to see you."

"Good to see you, Wes," Tony said. "Thanks for coming back for the game."

"Well, it took a little persuading, but I'm glad I could come," he said, still looking around and taking it all in. "We had some good times here, didn't we?"

"Hey, Wes," Jimmy called, walking over and shaking his hand. Wes, who was Jimmy's age, was in the class below ours. The two were the co-captains the year after I graduated. "Just get in today?"

"Yeah, last minute decision. I drove straight through," Wes said. "Dropped my wife off at my mom's house. The boys are staying with my in-laws. We live just outside of Charlotte."

"Ready for some baseball?" Tony asked.

"Absolutely. I have twin boys in American Legion Ball. I'm one of the coaches."

"Good," I said. "We're little shaky. It will be nice to have another player who is still connected with the game."

"My boys told me I have to get a Brad Cole autograph," Wes said, laughing. "I told them I'll just be happy if he doesn't bean me in the ass." He paused and looked around. "I don't see John Stone out here."

"He'll be here tomorrow," Tony said. "But I don't think we see him on the field."

"After the shot he took, I wouldn't either," he said. "That was scary enough to watch."

Wes warmed up with Jimmy, and then started taking fly balls in the outfield. He still had it. That was good because we needed him.

"Where's Flash?" Woody said, walking in from first. "Without him we don't have enough guys. And we need somebody fast in centerfield."

"He told me last night he was coming," Tony said. "He was catching a flight up this morning and renting a car at the airport." Tony looked at his watch.

"Maybe he made some stops along the way," Woody said.

"Maybe," I said.

With that, a black Cadillac Escalade roared into the parking lot, sending up a curtain of dust.

"That must be Flash," I said.

"Hey, Skip, don't go anywhere," Tony said, grabbing my arm. "I don't know how this is going to turn out."

"What do you mean?"

"To get Flash to come up, I had to do something slightly unethical."

"How unethical?"

Tony looked down. "I abused my doctor privilege."

"What did you do?"

"I called him up while he was on the air. Before he could hang up, I told him to go to the

studio fax request machine listed on the website. I faxed him an official medical request form. It was asking for a blood test to confirm his DNA in the case of a 16-year-old girl who had found herself pregnant and with gonorrhea. She claimed that he was the father and that he had picked her up at his Saturday night dance party at a club downtown."

"What?" I said. "Who is this girl?"

"There is no girl," he said. "It was just to get him on a plane to Dorchester.

"Oh no, Tony."

The car door opened, and a man wearing a shiny sequin satin black jacket that with "Power 99" on the back jumped out. He wore a white fedora and a bright orange polyester jogging suit.

He must have weighed at least three hundred pounds. He was enormous. And he looked angry.

"He said he was flying up to kill me." Tony said.

"Tony," I said, putting a hand on his shoulder, "You are a dead man."

Flash lumbered up to us. "Tony Adamo, you son of a bitch."

"Hey, Flash," I said, stepping in between them. "Thanks for coming. Glad you could make it."

Flash moved past me right to Tony. He towered over him. He leaned over and got right in Tony's face.

"I got on the plane today with a plan," Flash said. "They wouldn't have let me on with a gun. So I decided that when I got here, I would get a baseball bat and smash your head in."

"Listen, Flash," Tony started.

Flash waved him off. "So, I'm sitting in first class, steaming fucking mad. I'm sitting next to this guy. Was coming up to see his son. Plays minor league ball for Reading. Anyway, he asks me why I look so angry. I tell him. He listens, straight face, shaking his head. I get to the part where you said if I didn't come, you would fax that medical paper to my number one radio competitor, as well as every dance club, every church and every woman's organization in Tampa, including the fucking Girl Scouts."

I looked at Tony. "Really?"

"Really really," he said, looking down.

"Anyway, when I said the Girl Scouts, this guy starts to tremble and shake. Then he busts out laughing so damn loud, the flight attendants had to come and try to calm him down. The fucker must have laughed for ten minutes while I sat there, totally embarrassed. Then, he ordered two shots from the bar. He says to me, 'Dude, do you know how lucky you are? To have somebody who want you so bad that they would risk it all to get you on a plane home? You are blessed, brother. You are blessed. You're going to play that game, and I'm coming to watch. And after the game I want to shake that doctor's hand.'

We drank our shots, then he ordered another. And another. The more I drank, the more sense it made. He was right. So, here I am."

He reached out his hand. Tony took it. Then he pulled Tony in and gave him a big bear hug.

"You are one crazy mother fucker," he said to Tony.

"Welcome home, Flash," I said.

He took off his mirrored shades. "God, Skip, this field has not changed in twenty years. It's great to be back! I can't wait to get out there."

The other members of the team stared in amazement. And shock. The high school kids came over and introduced themselves. Flash talked music with one of them. He told them he worked for a hip hop station in Tampa.

I looked over at Tony. He stared back at me with his mouth open. "OH. MY. GOD," was all he could say.

Two hours later Tony said, "OH. MY. GOD. WE SUCK!" He was sweaty and dirty from hitting balls to the team.

"We just need some work, that's all," I said sitting in the dugout next to him. Everyone else had left. We were the only ones left at the field.

"We could work for a year and we would still suck. We are going to get our asses kicked tomorrow," Tony said, looking at me. "It will be the biggest disgrace in the history of Dorchester."

"Wow, that would be something. Dorchester has excelled in being a disgrace. It will take a supreme effort for us to top that list."

"We're not that terrible on the ground," he continued. "Not bad up the middle, especially when you are in there. But we're weak on the corners. Flash is so damn big, his ass covers most of center field. He doesn't run, he trots like a pregnant Clydesdale. And the outfielders can't even reach the cutoff in the air. What happened to those boys?"

"They got old."

"So did you, and you're not even a month out of a bone marrow harvest, but you can still field and throw."

"They're doing their best, Tony."

"I know," he said, exhaling loudly and slumping back against the concrete block wall.

"I was starting to think of us as the boys of summer again," I said.

"We're more like the lost boys of summer," he said.

We sat for a while in the dugout without speaking. The sun was setting over the river behind the wooden scoreboard in left, painting the old field in a warm hazy orange glow. The mosquitos were beginning to make their appearance and a few early lighting bugs were dancing around the backstop. The bats had come out of the woods in the gathering twilight, swooping over the field for their dinner.

"Come on," I said, giving him a pat on the shoulder. "You didn't really think we could take those guys again, did you?"

255

He took a moment. Looked out over the field where we had scored our greatest sports triumph.

"Yeah," he finally answered. "I did."

"Twenty years ago, everything went our way. It was luck beyond belief. We were good, don't get me wrong. But they were great. They played like shit that day and it was a lucky self-defense full count panic swing I made that launched the home run. This time, I just hope we stay close. Like Rocky, remember? He didn't have to win the fight with Apollo Creed. He just needed to go the distance. That's what we have to do. We won the big game when it counted. As long as we don't embarrass ourselves tomorrow and get 'ten runned.' We just need to go the distance."

"That would be fine with me," Tony said. "It might not be fine with the citizens of Dorchester who are depending on us to win."

"It's just an exhibition game."

"Not anymore." Tony put his head in hands. "I found out at the hospital yesterday that a group of individuals in Clinton Heights have been offering outrageous odds on the outcome of the game."

"Yeah, I heard that," I said.

"Did you hear that nearly everybody in Dorchester has a wager on this game?" he said, looking over at me. "Some people took money from their 401Ks or got cash advances on their credit cards. I was told by a prominent Clinton Heights city official that Dorchester fans have ponied up almost

$50,000 so far. That's a lot of money for a not so affluent community like this one to lose."

"What happened to no pressure. Just an exhibition game?" I said. "This is not good."

"There's something else I need to talk to you about. Something more important than the game tomorrow," he said.

My body tensed up like a steel spring. "What is it."

"I got a call from Rich Hostler while we were practicing. I just listened to the voicemail. Before they discharged Janine, Rich ran a series of scans."

My heart sank. "What is it?"

"He found cancer cells. The chemo didn't get it all."

"Oh my God, Tony," I said, throwing back my head and flopping back agains't the concrete block wall. "So what do they do? Does Janine go back to the hospital?"

"The short answer is most likely yes, but not right away," Tony said.

"Why not now?"

"Her body needs to recover from the last set of treatments before attempting another round. As it was, Rich couldn't do as strong a solution as he wanted because she was so weak from the previous chemotherapy. The last one nearly took her as is. Rich is recommending they wait until the next scans in October before doing anything."

"Then they'll do the bone marrow transplant again?" I asked.

"It all depends on what they find come October, Tony said. "Another round of chemo will be very hard on her. They'll see how strong she is, and how much the cancer has spread."

I looked at Tony. I always knew when he was holding back.

"You don't think she's going to make it," I said.

He looked over at me. "I'm hoping and praying for a miracle, Skip."

I was stunned. We sat for a long time in the dugout without speaking.

"Does Janine know?" I finally asked.

"Janine does not know and Kim does not want her to know anything yet. She's feeling better than she has in two years. She's excited about college in the fall, and about spending time with her dad," he said, looking me in the eye. "She's feeling great right now, and a happy, positive attitude is paramount when it comes to fighting a disease like cancer. Allow her to enjoy life for a little while. Be the dad she always wanted, and let her live her dream while she can. Kim says it will break her heart when she learns the truth."

"Her heart will not be the only one that's broken," I said.

Chapter 11

From year to year, as far back as I remember, the Fourth of July was always the same. Sticky, hot and humid. Every Fourth of July parade was sweltering, participants struggling to reach the end before succumbing to heat stroke. The unmerciful rays of the sun toasting anyone not fortunate enough to be under some type of shade. After nightfall, the temperature would dip slightly, and the fireworks display would be enjoyed by reclining in a camp chair in the hazy humid summer evening overlooking the river. This year was no different.

Both Clinton Heights and Dorchester had their own morning parades. The Clinton Heights parade was the envy of the Delaware Valley, with floats, marching bands, state legislators and other dignitaries. Residents would line the streets under the careful watch of the smartly uniformed city police department with VIP seating in special designated areas. Marching bands and colorful floats would garner polite applause. The entire event looked like a choreographed show straight from Main Street in Walt Disney World.

The parade was hosted and funded by the Clinton Heights Founders Club,
a fraternal organization made up of the most important of the city's male
residents. The Clinton Heights Founders Club Auxiliary, made up of the wives
of the founders had a float that led off the spectacle. Some 30 invited high
school and college bands, the best in the Commonwealth of Pennsylvania,
would march, interspersed with various civic and business organization floats,
tossing wrapped candies to the cheering children along the route. In the finale
keynote spot, the grand marshal of the event, a well-known area celebrity
would ride atop the Founders float right on the heels of the Clinton Heights
official city council float. That signaled the end of the event. The parade
viewers would then exit the streets in an orderly fashion and prepare for their
own private fireworks parties in McMansions dotted along the bluff.

Across the river in Dorchester, things were different. The town's annual
Fourth of July parade was more of a raucous street party than a solemn event.
Groups of families and friends would spill over into the street. Public drinking
ordinances were ignored for one day. Laughter and screams were heard amid
the strained sounds of the rag tag marching bands trying their best to stay on
key in oppressive July heat. It was pure fun. This was Dorchester – blue collar
folks celebrating the birth of their nation in the way that suited them best. This
was the one time, even more than Christmas, when people who grew up in
Dorchester would come home. The morning parade, afternoon fair and

carnival, as well as the evening fireworks presentation, made it THE homecoming event of the year.

People in Dorchester liked to sleep in on their day off, and Fourth of July would be a long day. The parade organizers queued up in Tony's vacant lot behind the apartment around ten, and the parade would begin an hour later. It would already be hot, so adult refreshments would be on hand for the parched. The parade route stretched up from the river at Front Street down Main Street and the downtown area and past city hall before turning out to the school. The Dorchester High School marching band would lead the procession followed in a very loose order by the town EMTs and fire department vehicles, Boy Scouts, Girl Scouts, 4H Clubs and other organizations. The Delaware Valley Hobo Band would precede Miss Dorchester, who rode in a convertible emblazoned with magnetic signs advertising Bob Fare Chrysler Dodge. Then the police vehicles would drive by followed by the mayor in his convertible Cadillac, which he had gotten a fair deal on from Bob Fare Chrysler Dodge.

At this point, the crowds along the sidewalks would fall into the streets and begin to march behind the parade, following them up and all the way to the high school fields. The football field would be filled with food and craft vendors and carnival rides, all the picnic tables the city possessed, and a long line of food vendors stretched the length of the field. In the adjoining soccer field, a traveling circus, complete with big top tents and exotic camels and elephants, would urge visitors to come inside. This would benefit the

Dorchester Rotary Club, the only non-veterans fraternal organization in the town.

Even though food and drink were available, many city residents would bring folding tables and grills, set up in the big parking lot bordering the fields like a huge stadium tailgate party. People would drift back and forth from the carnival to the circus and back to the tailgaters. Folding chairs out, it was time to reminisce about old time Dorchester and catch up on what had happened over the past twelve months. This would normally go on until dusk, and the first fireworks would light off around 9:15 p.m. When the Dorchester fifteen minute warm up show was finished, at 9:30 p.m, the main event, the Clinton Heights City fireworks extravaganza would start, lasting exactly thirty minutes and thrilling crowds on both sides of the river.

This year, however, there was the little matter of the baseball game. Behind the football fields bordering the river, the high school baseball field was raked and lined, ready for the big contest. After having done the traditional walk down to the school, Tony and I were standing at the old chain link fence looking in.

"Looks like it's all ready," I said.

"Yes, the city boys did well," he answered, surveying the infield. "They did a nice job with the ruts over by third base."

"All ready to make history."

With a slow grin forming on his knotted face, Tony said, "Yeah."

Tony pulled an envelope from his pocket and handed it to me. "Got this last night. Courier from Nick Danno. Ground rules for the game."

I opened the letter on official stationery from the City of Clinton Heights Mayor's office.

> *The following are additional ground rules we would like to agree upon for the 20th Anniversary Fourth of July Baseball Game between Clinton High School and Dorchester High School Classes of 1988.*
>
> *1) This exhibition game will played according to 1988 NJSAIA field rules, with any exceptions noted here. Specific ground rules pertaining to the actual baseball field will be discussed by the umpires prior to the game.*
>
> *2) The game will last four complete innings regardless of score. The "ten run rule" will not be in effect. Using four full innings will allow both teams, starters and substitutes, the opportunity for at least one at bat.*
>
> *3) After the game, we ask that both teams remain on the field for a presentation by Congressman Torrey and postgame pictures from various newspaper and TV media outlets.*
>
> *4) We are pleased to have Clinton High School alumnus Brad Cole playing with us today. Brad is under contract with the Los Angeles Dodgers and has obtained special*

dispensation to participate. His role will most likely be limited. We ask that your players treat Brad Cole with appropriate respect and avoid physical contact that might jeopardize his ability to continue to play professional sports. Brad also asks that the players on your team please refrain from asking for pictures or autographs during the game. He will try to sign as many autographs for your players and their families as he can in the brief time he will have after the game.

"Four innings," I said. "I don't know if that's a good thing. And no ten-run rule either."

"I saw that," Tony said, frowning. "And plenty of photo ops after the game with political dignitaries for a complete media slam dunk."

"No physical contact with Brad? Does he think we're going to hurt him?"

"That also means no hugs."

"And no autographs or pictures."

Tony looked at me and let out a laugh. "What an asshole," he said, shaking his head.

We had three hours to kill before the team was to meet at the field, so we walked back through the carnival. It was already hot and I was thirsty. Every year, the Dorchester volunteer fire company would offer a barbecue and pig roast. They would bring in this old wizened piney and his two sons from somewhere in the swamps of Jersey. The guy knew how to cook barbecue, and he had the most amazing homemade sauce for his chicken, ribs and pulled pork. Continuing with Dorchester Fourth of July tradition, I got a barbecued pulled pork sandwich from the fire company stand and a cold beer. Tony said he wasn't hungry and that he didn't want alcohol to dull his senses for the game. I told him he may feel differently about the sharpness of his senses by the third inning. He reconsidered and bought a beer for himself.

"Hey, guys!" It was Wayne. And walking along next to him was a woman who could have stepped right from the pages of the *Sports Illustrated* Swimsuit Edition. Blonde hair cascading down over her smooth white shoulders, a red and white and very tiny bikini top working double overtime to keep her very impressive chest somewhat in control. Blue jean shorts that could not be cut any smaller surrounded her well defined derrière.

"This is Sasha," Wayne said. "Remember, the girl from Russia who emailed me."

Tony's mouth hung open. My mouth hung open. We were probably drooling, but we never would have known.

"This is Skip and Tony," Wayne said.

"Hi, Skeep, hi, Tonee," Sasha said, with a thick accent and a wide smile.

"It's great to have you here," Tony said, beginning to regain control. "You are a wonderful ambassador for Russia."

"Wayne was so nice to help me come here." She looked around at the carnival and the crowds. "Happy Birthday, America!" she said, putting her arms up in the air with excitement and spinning around.

"How do you like America?" I asked.

"It is so wonderful. I love it!" she said. "I have wanted to come to America all my life, and now thanks to Wayne, I'm here." She turned and gave Wayne a huge hug.

"Oh, look," Wayne said. "There's Max. Remember at the bowling alley when he said nothing about Sasha was real. I want to show him so he can see for himself." They walked off toward the circus.

Tony and I looked at each other for a moment, speechless. Then Tony said, "I noticed at least two things on her that looked very real."

"And you are a trained medical doctor," I added. "You know about this stuff."

We continued past the other food and craft vendors and back through the parking lot, stopping at the different tailgate parties. This always took a long time because we knew so many people. And this year everyone was excited about baseball. Most of them had bets riding on the game; that made me very uneasy. The parking lot overlooked the ball fields and the river, and it was the perfect viewing place for the fireworks. A lot of people had come back this year, and a surprising number had come specifically for the baseball game. I had almost forgotten how big a deal that one win against Clinton Heights had been to this town. It was everything.

As we made our way through the parking area, I spied Dorchester's oldest resident, Chet Williams. He and his wife Delores lived around the corner from us on Sixth Street for as long as I can remember.

"Mr. Williams," I greeted him. "Skip McCann."

"Skip," he said. "Good seeing you again. Hey there, Tony."

"How's it going, Mr. Williams?"

"I woke up this morning, so it's a good day. Better than the alternative. What the hell, I just turned ninety, and I still walk a mile every day."

"That's great," I said.

"Now if I could just get Tony here to slip me some Viagra, he would really make my day," he laughed.

"Oh stop that, you rascal," his wife Delores said, walking over.

"The secret of a happy marriage, Skip. Marry a young hot girl."

Delores was eighty-eight.

"You know it, Mr. Williams," Tony said. "How long have you two been married?"

"We'll celebrate our fortieth anniversary in September, if I can keep him away from the Viagra," Delores said.

"Forty years?" I asked.

"Chet was a long time bachelor. He was fifty when we got married," she said.

"I knew I wanted Delores when she was in high school with me, but she went and married herself a salesman when she was eighteen," Chet said. "He sold rubbers."

"He was a tire salesman," she corrected him and gave him a swat on the arm.

"Whatever. Anyway, she moved back to Dorchester in, when was it, 1967? Yeah, 1967, the summer of love. Oh, boy, was it ever! We got together and married the next year. I wanted to make an honest woman out of her."

"My parents were married in 1967," I said.

"Must have been something in the water that year," Chet said.

"Are you boys thirsty?" Delores asked. "Maybe a cup of my famous Singapore Punch?"

"No, no," Chet said, shaking his head. "These boys need to be sharp for the big game."

"That's right, Mr. Williams," Tony said. "Thanks anyway."

"Well, then you can stop back up after your baseball game," Delores said. "I have enough here for half the town."

"I hope you put it to those Clinton Heights boys," Chet said. "I've got my social security check riding on Dorchester."

"We'll do our best," Tony said, looking over at me with a pained expression on his face.

At four, we started back to the baseball field. We talked to a lot of other people who had bet money on the game. Much more than I was comfortable with. There was enough pressure without thinking of all the people who had money they really couldn't afford to lose.

The team was assembling, and some of the guys were throwing around a ball, loosening up. As we approached the backstop, a short woman with dark leathery skin who looked in her late forties popped out from behind a porta potty. She had dark frizzy hair and was almost as round as she was tall. Her clothing, far too youthful for someone her age was tight fitting, and it showed off every love handle. As soon as she opened her mouth, I knew who she was.

"Hey, Tony, remember me?"

Tony didn't at first. He stared, a questioning look on his face. And then, the horror struck him.

It was Angelina.

"Hi, Angelina," Tony said, his voice suddenly weak and trembling. "Wow. What a surprise!" He looked over at me in terror.

"I came back for the Fourth of July party and to see you play your game."

"That's really great."

"Anyway, after the game let's get together. We've got a lot to catch up on."

"Oh yeah," Tony said nervously. He grabbed my arm. "No time, running late. Come on, Skip, we need to get on the field."

"See you later, Tony," she said, blowing him a kiss and shaking her ample derrière.

Tony literally sprinted through the gate onto the field and straight into the dugout, looking for a nice hiding spot. I followed him in.

"Looks like you have plans after the game," I said, smiling.

"OH, MY GOD," he said. "What the hell happened, Skip? What the hell happened?"

"She grew up."

"Did she ever."

"Maybe you two kids can get in that Porsche of yours and go parking out by the turnpike bridge?"

"I don't think she'll fit in the Porsche," he said.

"Maybe you'll need to buy a Hummer. Or an F-350 pickup truck with an extended bed."

"All these years I've saved myself for her. Oh my God. My dreams. They're shattered!" Tony said, slumping down onto the dugout bench. He was breathing heavy. I thought he might be hyperventilating. "Damn it, I think I've got a fever. Where's my medical bag? I'll bet my blood pressure is 200 over 110! I need a drink."

"She's got you hotter than a red assed monkey in heat," I said, laughing.

Tony looked at me in horror. He took a long drink from a water bottle and started to choke. I patted him on the back.

"Tony," I said, getting down right in his face. "Get a grip brother. We have a big game coming up and we need you to focus. And trust me, you have nothing to fear from Angelina. You could outrun her if you have to."

Slowly the look of fear and pain on his face was replaced with a grin, and then a wide smile. He exhaled loudly and started to laugh.

"A red assed monkey in heat?" he said between laughs. "Where in the hell did you come up with that?"

"National Geographic Magazine. It got me through puberty."

"I'm feeling better now," he said, taking a deep cleansing breath. "I needed that laugh. Thanks, Skip."

"All part of the friendly service," I said. "You can handle this."

"If you say so. I'm not so sure I could handle that, though."

We walked out of the dugout and onto the infield. Behind first base I saw Big John, playing catch with his son. Junior and his high school teammates had been a big help, practicing and scrimmaging with the boys. Tony had gotten the kids team tee shirts with the words "TRAINING STAFF" on the backs.

"Hey, Big John, great to see you," I said coming up and shaking his hand.

"Thanks, Skip. My boy has been pestering the heck out of me to come on down and make an appearance, so here I am."

"I found his original glove and bat in the attic," John Jr. said. "The bat is huge! I don't know how he every got around with it."

"I remember that bat," I said. "It was a monster. I remember we nicknamed it Goliath."

"I was in shape back then, son," Big John said with a grin. "Say, Skip, does the offer still stand for me to ride the pine in the dugout? I would love to do that again, hang with the team and be with the guys."

"If you're going to sit in the team dugout, you are going to need this," Tony said walking up. He handed Big John a brand new team baseball jersey with his name monogrammed on the back.

John was speechless. He carefully unfolded the jersey and held it up.

"Number 19," John Jr. said. "It's my number too."

"Tony, this is a real nice surprise," John said, carefully unfolding the shirt. "Thank you."

"We may not play well, but at least we'll look good," Tony said.

The silence was broken by the blast from a bus horn, scattering children playing in the parking area. I had expected the Clinton Heights team to bring their own cars since they were just over the river from us. Instead, a gleaming luxury motor coach pulled into the baseball parking lot, plowing over the temporary no parking signs and pulled up on the grass directly behind the visitors' dugout. The doors opened and the players ran out and onto the field, lining up in the outfield in left. Running with them was a smaller man who looked and acted like a drill sergeant. He blew a whistle and the group began warm up drills.

"They look like the Hitler youth," Tony said.

"I'm getting tired just watching them," I said.

As the teams warmed up, a stretch limousine pulled in, past the bus on the grass. The driver rushed around to open the door, and out stepped Brad Cole dressed and ready for the game. Instantly he was surrounded by kids with pads and baseballs asking for his autograph. Without a word or even a nod, he brushed by them and into the visitors' dugout. A tall solidly built man in a Clinton Heights police department uniform walked behind him, taking up position at the dugout door and refusing access to anyone not part of the official Clinton Heights baseball team delegation.

"Should we go over? Maybe say hi and ask for a picture?" Tony asked with a raised eyebrow.

"No. Looks like he's in pregame mode," I said. Cole was sitting on the dugout, head resting back against the block wall. He had a mean look of concentration on his face as he just stared out at the center field flag. No one approached him or spoke to him.

"For Chris-sakes, it's an exhibition game," Tony said.

"I don't think Brad feels that way," I said.

The rest of the Dorchester team straggled in and started warming up near John and his son in right field. John got a lot of high fives. Tony and I started stretching and throwing with them.

"Freakin' hot," Jimmy said, walking up and wiping his brow with a sleeve. He had been warming up over behind the dugout. Jimmy always had a strong arm and as a left hander did well for the over-35 team. I hoped he might be able to keep the Clinton Bombers in check. But that would also depend on the defense, and that was not a sure thing.

"Look it those guys," Billy Harper said in a low voice. He gestured over toward the dugout at Cole with his face mask. "Damn, there he is."

We stared for a while at the left field workouts and warm ups. Brad Cole was pacing in the dugout like a caged tiger. It was intimidating.

Jimmy finally broke the ice. "Besides Cole, I see a couple of studs. Those two next to third base were on that over-35 Pennsylvania all-star team. The guy out by the wall has a gun for an arm. But the rest look human. If we play well, we're in this one."

I looked over toward the Clinton Heights side of the field where a video crew was setting up equipment. Tony had asked the local high school AV club to video for us, but I wondered who this crew was. That's when one of the crew gave me a wave. I walked over to the low fence past third base.

"Kelli?" I asked.

"Hi, Skip," she said with a smile. The last time I saw her she was wearing the oversized sporting goods uniform shirt which wasn't very flattering. Today, she was wearing a cut off orange sleeveless Mets shirt which showed off her flat stomach, along with tight blue shorts. Her long blonde hair was sticking out the back of her Mets baseball cap. Quite a difference from the referee outfit. She was very fit. She looked incredible.

"What are you doing here?" I asked.

"Steve thought this story about your high school reunion game would be great color for tonight's broadcast, so I volunteered to bring a crew down and get some video."

"I'm surprised you found the field."

"We got lost," she said laughing. "This is a beautiful little town. A nice slice of Americana on the Fourth of July."

"You're not staying for the whole game, are you?"

"No, probably just a couple of innings. Some shots of Brad Cole at third and maybe hitting a couple of home runs."

"God, I hope not," I said. "I just hope we keep it close."

"Are you feeling alright?" she asked.

"Yeah, why do you ask?"

"You look tired."

"It's a hot day."

"Well, at least you look stylish," she said, smiling. "I love your cleats."

I looked down at the baseball shoes she sold me. "Yeah, best looking shoes on the field."

"Well, good luck Skip." She leaned over and gave me a hug, and a quick kiss on the cheek.

"Now, you've got the ball," she added. "Make it happen."

I paused for a moment and let that comment sink in. I smiled at her.

"Thanks," I said.

The rest of the team came in from warmups and we all posed in front of the dugout for the official team picture. Jimmy looked over toward the other dugout. "Look, there's Danno."

Clinton Heights Mayor Nick Danno walked over to us. "Well, well, if it isn't the pride of Dorchester!" he said with his politician's grin. "It's a fine afternoon for baseball." His new Clinton Heights uniform was tucked in, his tight white baseball pants pulled up over his large belly.

"Are we going to see you at second base, Mayor?" Tony asked.

"Oh, maybe for an inning," he said looking over at Cole in the dugout. "I think I pulled something in my back in my last workout. Don't want to aggravate it. We're not as young as we used to be," he said, giving me a fake punch on the arm. "You got the amended rules?" he asked.

"Yes, we got them," Tony said. "No problem here."

"Good, good," Danno said, nodding his head. "And good news for you. The Dodgers organization has asked that Cole not pitch today. They're concerned about his arm."

"That's fine with us," I said.

"Well, good luck," Danno said. "And I hope there are no hard feelings after the game."

"Why would there be?" I said.

"Oh, you know how some people get, especially when they lose money."

"Yes, I know," Tony said. "Hope there are no hard feelings on your side, either."

Danno nodded, gave a condescending smile, and walked back to his dugout.

Jimmy looked at me. "Did you get load of those pants?" he asked. "Pulled up almost to his nipples. That waistband is stretched so tight he'll take out half the dugout if it snaps."

The laughter broke the tension. The umpires were on the field and the teams returned to their dugouts.

"OK, guys," Tony said, getting everyone's attention. "The day we have been practicing for is here. The lineup is posted on the wall although we have exactly nine players." He looked over at John. "Nice to see Big John in here with us." The guys murmured their approval. "Thanks, John. Just so you know, John would rather sit this one out, but I think I speak for all of us when I say it's great to see Big John back in a Dorchester Wildcats uniform."

The guys clapped and cheered.

"Skipper, any last words?" Tony said looking at me.

I wasn't prepared for a speech, and I didn't think we needed one. But there was one thing I wanted everyone to know. "Twenty years ago on this very field, we did something that had never been done before and hasn't been done since. We beat Clinton Heights High School baseball team. No one can ever take that away from us. Today's game was their idea. They would love to try to save face from that one loss all those years ago. So, as I see it, the pressure is on them. They are the ones who need to win, not us. So, let's just go out and have a good time. I think it's a gift that we can all be here again and go out on the field as a team after all these years. Do your best and have fun. No matter what happens today, no matter what the score, we still beat these chumps in the game that mattered. Today is just a wonderful chance to relive our past. A chance for us to have fun together and play a game we love one more time. Let's keep it light."

There was silence. Then, Tony said, "Fuck that, I want to kick their asses." The bench erupted in shouts of approval.

The umpires were gathered around home plate. Tony and I went out with our lineup card. The amended rules had irritated him, and he had been shooting dirty looks over at the Clinton Heights dugout ever since they arrived. Nick Danno's dismissive attitude and presumption of victory had rubbed Tony the wrong way. Tony had that look in his eyes. His Italian was getting up, and that was never a good thing.

Cole and Danno represented Clinton Heights at the home plate meeting, just as they had in '88.

"I've been waiting a long time for this chance," Danno said. "Twenty years." He looked at Cole. "Time to set things right."

"Just one small thing you may have forgotten," Tony said. "You actually have to win."

Nick gave a belly laugh. "I don't think that will be a problem, do you, Brad?"

Cole had been staring me down, like a boxer in the ring before the opening bell. With Nick's quip, he broke his stare and snorted. "Ha, not from what I see out here."

"That's probably what you thought twenty years ago," I said, staring back at him.

He looked around. "I almost forgot how shitty this little town field is."

"You're right, Brad," Tony jumped in. "It is a shitty little field. But imagine how nice it could be with a $20,000 donation to the school baseball program. Care for a friendly wager?"

Cole looked at Tony in disbelief; after a moment of speechlessness, he leaned in. "And the Clinton Heights High School field could use new urinals and toilets. Twenty large would do nicely. And your name will be on a bronze plaque hung over the shitters, giving you all the credit. I accept."

They shook hands. The umpires went over the ground rules. We walked back to the dugout.

"Are you crazy?" I said.

"You know better than to ask me that question," Tony said.

Chapter 12

"Ladies and gentlemen, welcome to Dorchester All Wars Memorial Field," came the booming radio voice of Murray White over the public address speakers. White was broadcasting the game live on 1340 AM WDCR and doing local on field announcements. "This is the twentieth anniversary Cross River Series baseball game between Clinton High School and Dorchester High School class of 1988."

One by one, the Clinton High School players were announced, and applause greeted each player as he took a spot along third base line. When Brad Cole was introduced, a surge of cheers came from both sides of the field. Halfway to the line, Cole stopped and tipped his cap toward the Clinton side of the field and didn't even glance at the Dorchester side.

When the Dorchester team was announced, each player received boisterous yells and screams as they filed in along the first base chalk. I was surprised at the reception I got. After all, it had been twenty years. But this town never forgot. The biggest ovation though was for Tony. Everyone knew Dr. Tony, and everyone loved him.

Miss Dorchester came out to home plate and sang the national anthem. Murray's voice rang over the P.A. "And now, ladies and gentlemen, please welcome your Dorchester Wildcats."

We took the field, and Woody started warming us up, throwing some infield balls from first. The whole introduction thing was surreal, and for a time I was caught in a fog of memory of the last time I was on this field in uniform, at the 1988 Cross River game. The biggest game of my life. And here I was ready for a repeat. The last game ended in the most incredible win I was ever part of. We were underdogs that game. The odds were stacked even more against us today. I was getting nervous, the tension growing. I fought hard to take my own advice to the team - keep it light and have fun.

Tony took the final warm-up throw from Harper behind the plate and flipped it to Larkin at third. He tossed it to me. I walked to the mound and put the ball in Jimmy's glove. "No pressure, but you've got eight old ballplayers behind you in the field who are already worn out just from the warmups."

"Well, then," Jimmy said, "I guess I'll just have to strike them all out."

"Good plan," I said giving him a pat on the back with my glove. "Let's get started."

Jimmy's being a southpaw was a real advantage. Most of the Clinton lineup was right handed, and Jimmy had one hell of a curve that could bite the outside corner. He struck out the first batter on three pitches. A roar came from the Dorchester bleachers.

"All right, Jimmy," Tony called out. "Just do that same thing eleven more times."

The second batter got under the first pitch. It carried into center field. My heart rose into my throat. Luckily not so Flash Gordon only had to take a few steps to get under the ball and he pulled it in. Two down.

The third batter was the best hitter on the field besides Brad Cole. He worked the count. At 2-2 he reached for an outside fastball and drove it into the ground hard at second, right at Tony. He fielded it cleanly and threw to Woody at first for the third out.

We got a nice round of applause from the home crowd as we jogged back to the dugout. Jimmy got high-fives from the team.

"Nice pick up at second, Doc," I said to Tony.

"Yep, one for the highlight reel," he said, taking a seat on the bench.

Our leadoff batter, Billy Harper walked to the plate. Tony was batting the three over-35 league players first in the order. Then Jimmy, me and Tony, with Wes, Woody and Flash in the seven, eight and nine spots. The Clinton pitcher was originally the right fielder on the '88 team, and he threw hard. Billy went down on three pitches. So did Larkin and Marshall.

"Struck out the side," Tony said as we ran back out on the field for the start of the second inning. "Not good."

"We've got time," I said.

Brad Cole was batting cleanup and walked to the plate amid cheers and applause. Jimmy threw the first pitch in the dirt and the second one outside for a ball. Count was 2-0.

"C'mon, Jimmy, we got your back," Woody shouted from first.

Jimmy's next pitch was not where he wanted it. It was in tight and hard to get around on,

but this was not an over-35 league player. This was future Hall of Fame Los Angeles Dodgers third baseman Brad Cole, with a .303 lifetime batting average and 457 career home runs. He turned on it with ease, caught all of it, and the ball sailed down the line and over the left field fence. Cole tipped his hat to the Clinton side as he rounded third and stepped on home plate. 1-0, Clinton Heights.

I knew better than to say anything to Jimmy. All the pressure was from Cole. Now he could relax. Jimmy struck out the next two batters. The fourth batter in the inning hit a liner at third just out of the reach of Larkin, but I thought he was leaning to pull and was shading that side. I made a backhand grab in the hold and fired as hard as I could to first. My throws did not have the zip that they had before the procedure, but the batter was not fast, and I got him by a step.

"The old man still has it," Jimmy said, with a pat on the back.

"Even a blind squirrel finds a nut sometimes," I laughed. "Now we need some runs."

Jimmy led off. He batted from the left side, the only one on our team. The big pitcher knew him from the over-35 leagues and was being careful, pitching the corners but missing. Jimmy laid off a low 3-1 fastball and drew the walk.

As I came to the plate, the catcher ran out to the mound. Cole walked in from third. I heard Cole say, "Just throw a goddamn strike. He won't get it out of the infield. Just don't walk anybody else."

I could imagine what was going through the big pitcher's mind. Calamity! A walk, and in the presence of the star, Brad Cole, and then admonished to throw strikes. I knew what was coming. He needed to get up early on me. A fastball was coming first pitch.

I was always a good fastball hitter. Jimmy had buzzed me with some good ones during our final practice. But this was my first real game batting situation in many years, and I could feel myself shaking. Then I remembered how I felt in the cage at Citizens Bank Park. I could hit this guy, I thought; he's nothing special. I figured I had at least one good at bat in me before I got tired. I remembered the coach's words: "You've got good hands, trust your hands, hands to the ball."

The big pitcher tucked and fired a blazing fastball at the letters over the outside part of the plate, and I was ready for it. It was moving faster than I thought, and I was late but I kept my head down and got all of it. I took off running and watched the ball sail out over the right fielder's head. It kept going

284

and going until it landed a couple of feet behind the fence for a home run.

There was an eruption of screams and shouts from the Dorchester side of the field as I rounded the bases. I felt numb and my brain was in the clouds. As I approached third base, I tipped my cap to Kelli, who was grinning and making the round tripper wave with her hand. Jimmy high fived me at home plate. The old scoreboard in left read "HOME 2 VISITORS 1."

Cole walked to the mound and stuck out his hand. The big pitcher gave him the ball. Cole then looked at the dugout and jerked with his thumb. A smaller, wiry man ran out to the mound and started warming up.

"Guess they're getting their substitutions in," I said to Tony, as he loosened up in the on-deck circle.

"I think it's more like Brad Cole having a tantrum," Tony said. Cole was staring at our dugout and at Tony in the circle. Tony put down the bat and with his hands flashed ten digits, twice. Okay, $20,000. Cole smiled an evil smile and shook his head.

"Don't tease the bear," I said.

"This may be my last chance," he said walking up to the box.

This pitcher was not a hard thrower, but a master of junk. Sliders, curves, sinkers and changes. Tony got on one and drove it down the third base line. Cole fielded it smoothly and with a rifle shot fired it across to first. As Tony crossed the bag behind the throw, he heard the first baseman howl in pain from the force of the ball into his glove.

285

Kaminsky struck out on a called third strike. Woody looked at two balls, then two strikes. He finally swung on a slider low and outside. The ball went straight to ground and rolled up the first base line like a bunt. Woody stretched it out and ran harder than he had in 20 years, but there wasn't much speed there and the catcher made a barehanded pickup, throwing him out easily at first.

I picked up my glove and started toward short. I saw Tony run over toward first. Woody was stumbling back to the dugout, with a face that bore a gray pasty pallor. Tony grabbed an arm as he came into the dugout and helped him sit down. Woody pulled over a trash can and promptly threw up in it.

"I don't know what's happening," Woody said, out of breath. "I'm really dizzy, and my chest hurts."

"Shut up, lean your head back," Tony snapped. He had his bag out and stethoscope in hand.

"Am I gonna die?"

Tony was listening to his stethoscope while checking Woody's pulse. "What did you eat today?"

"I had a 1/4-pound chili dog from the carnival stand."

Tony removed the stethoscope and gave him a long, pathetic stare.

"But it was all beef," Woody pleaded.

"What did you have to drink?"

"About six cups of coffee this morning. Then I was feeling a little jumpy so I had three or four beers at the carnival."

Tony grabbed his bag and replaced his stuff. "Your heart rate is setting new records but your heart sounds fine, unbelievably. I'm sure your blood pressure is through the roof. Coffee and alcohol are diuretics. I think you're just dehydrated."

He motioned to one of the high school kids helping out. "Get him some water, call over the EMTs. If he starts to pass out, lay him down and maybe they can hook him up with some fluids. You don't need the ER, but you need to rest for a while. You're not used to the exertion, and the heat is putting you over the top. As of now, you are out of the game."

We had only nine players. This would mean a forfeit. And with us in the lead. Tony walked the length of the dugout toward the field entrance. Everyone knew where he was going.

"Tony, wait." Big John was walking down the dugout. "I'm available. I don't want this to end in a forfeit."

Tony took a long look at John and shook his head. "John, you don't need to do this. I think we showed something today. It will probably make the Clinton Heights boys more angry that we forfeited with a lead."

"No, I want to do this. I really do," John said.

Tony looked at me. It had been twenty years ago that John had taken a fastball to the head right here, and his life had never been the same. He had been afraid to get back in the game, who wouldn't be after that? But right now, John wanted to do this. Maybe he needed to do this. In front of his friends and family. And his son.

I nodded my head yes.

Tony looked up. Closed his eyes. "Ok, John, take right field. Wes, we need you at first."

The team was in shock heading out to the field. John settled in and made some warm up throws to Flash.

"He looks pretty good, considering," I said to Tony as he jogged out on the field from delivering the lineup change.

"This is a very big jump into a very cold lake for him," Tony said, looking out to right. "You just don't walk out here after twenty years of not touching a glove, I don't care who you are."

"Would it make you feel better to know that John and his son have been down here at the field shagging fly balls the last three nights?"

"Really?"

"Really really. The kid even put him in the batting cage. Jimmy said he took some good cuts."

"Well," Tony said, "let's just hope to God we end this before he gets up again. I don't want to see him in a batter's box, not after what he went through. I don't want to take any chances. We're out of bench players."

Jimmy got up on the first batter 0-2. He laid off Jimmy's third pitch low and outside. Jimmy came back and challenged him with a fastball that strayed a little over the plate. He drove it deep to right near the foul line. Big John went back, circled under it, and made what looked like a routine catch.

"You feel better now?" I said to Tony as the ball came back to the infield.

Tony was smiling. "Yes, I do. That was BIG, Skip. That broke the ice. I think we're going to be okay."

The second batter, number nine in the order, swung and missed a nasty curve for a third strike. Now, with the top of the order up, the leadoff batter smashed a rocket on Jimmy's first pitch. It screamed back to his right. Jimmy stuck out his glove and the ball deflected off and rolled toward third. He sprinted over, barehanded it and threw the runner out at first.

"Nice stop," I said, as we jogged back to the dugout. "Self-defense."

"Whatever gets it done," he said.

John came into the dugout amidst a hail of cheers and a high five from his son.

"You still got it, Pop," Junior said.

"Now, let's add some more. Put it to them, guys," Tony said,

Flash Gordon led off the bottom of the third. He was always a pretty good contact hitter but never had much power. However, in the twenty years since high school he had gained well over a a hundred fifty pounds. He guessed right on a 2-1 count and ripped a slow curve out toward left centerfield. The bench erupted. But the centerfielder ran like the Flash of old and made a spectacular diving catch to rob him of a base hit.

Top of the order Billy Harper swung on the first pitch and punched a ball through the gap for a base hit. Third baseman Kyle Larkin quickly got down in the count. The pitcher was crafty and was not giving him anything to swing at. With the count evened at 2-2, Larkin reached for a pitch on the corner and drove it right at the second baseman. He flipped to the shortstop who threw it to first for a very clean double play.

"Not the way I wanted that inning to go," I said, looking at Tony on the bench next to me.

"We've still got the lead."

"Are you comfortable with a one-run lead over these guys?"

"Skip, I'm ecstatic about a one-run lead over these guys," he said. "I was expecting to be down twenty to nothing at this point, with the Dorchester bleachers empty and the guys looking for any excuse to get out of here. The fact that we are competitive, actually leading them. Man, it's like a dream come true."

"You expected to lose and yet you bet Brad Cole $20,000 we'd win"?

"He got my Italian up," he said gathering up his glove and standing up. "Hey, look who is throwing a tantrum."

From the Clinton Heights dugout came the sound of Brad Cole ripping his teammates. It was loud and it was laced with profanities. Some of the parents on the Clinton Heights bleachers were holding their hands over their kids' ears.

Jimmy was standing next to me. "Not pretty," he said, nodding over at the dugout.

"No," I said.

"Listen, Skip, I think you should get ready to come in."

"You mean pitch?"

"Yeah."

"What are you talking about?" I said. "You're mowing them down."

"First time through the order it's easy to keep them off balance. But, these guys are really good. I've used up all my tricks. They will be ready for me. Besides, I'm really gassed. I've thrown as hard as I can for three innings. The most I throw in the league in an inning or maybe two, and not this hard. And it's so hot, I'm broiling like a goddamn steak out there. My arm feels like a limp noodle."

"Jimmy, maybe I can throw to a batter or two if you get hurt, but I'm not ready for this."

"You're ready; you've always been ready. You're my big brother. You were always the star. You can do anything."

I didn't know what to say. Jimmy was my younger brother. I had never thought about what it might be like to grow up as my brother. He never said much about stuff like that. He was worried; it must have just slipped out.

I looked at him and shook my head. "Not this time, Bro. My time has passed. Today, it's your show. Just one more inning Jimmy, one more inning. You've got this."

Tony ran back on the field from the Clinton dugout. "I was over there

291

asking what substitutions they wanted to make since this was the last inning. Remember they said that they want to play everybody, and they've got ten guys who haven't left the bench."

"Did they give you their subs?" I asked.

"They told me to go fuck myself," he said, with wide eyes of amazement.

Jimmy and I laughed out loud. I slapped him on the back. "Go get them, little brother," I said.

Jimmy's first pitch to the leadoff batter sailed out deep to center. I turned, hoping that Flash could make a routine play, but the Flash of today never had a prayer of getting to this one. It rolled to the fence. By the time Flash rumbled out to get it, the runner was rounding second. Flash picked it up and fired, throwing behind the runner and he easily pulled into third with a standup triple.

Jimmy took the throw back at the mound, head down. Not good, I thought.

The next batter watched three balls go by. He swung on the 3-0 count and sent a fastball over the plate sailing out high over the centerfield fence for a home run, and giving them a 3-2 lead. The Clinton Heights bench was now all cheers, hugs and laughter. Cole was chest bumping Nick Danno, hooting and hollering. He grabbed his bat and swaggered onto the field.

"Time blue," Jimmy said to the umpire, who held up his hands. Jimmy motioned me over.

"I'm done," he said, shaking his head. "I'm out of gas. I need the hook."

"Listen Jimmy, there is absolutely no way I can take the mound," I said. "I

292

haven't told anyone, but that procedure I had in LA left me weak as a kitten. I have zero stamina. I'm already exhausted. I'm running on pure adrenaline. Now, we're only one run down. You may be tired, but you're the best hope we've got. At least with you on the mound we have a chance to keep this close."

Tony walked up. "Once you get past Cole, you'll handle them. I say, walk him. That'll piss him off so much he'll explode."

"Hey," Cole called out from the plate. "I've got autographs to sign. Get your asses in gear so I can collect my 20,000 and get out of this shithole."

"On second thought," Tony said. "Don't walk him. Bean him."

Jimmy was staring at Cole. That last outburst had gotten him angry. He nodded. "Ok, let's do it." We took our places on the field.

Jimmy started Brad Cole with a sharp curveball, inside at the hands. He turned on it perfectly and it shot out like a cannon toward the left field line. Being inside to start, the ball curved foul by a few feet.

"Hey, Brad, put a hole in that piece of shit scoreboard out there," came a call that sounded like Nick Danno from the dugout. The old painted plywood scoreboard had been there since before we played here. It stood about six feet inside the left field line.

"Good idea," Cole said laughing. "Then I'll sign it for them. I'll put an arrow at the hole and write on it 'Brad Cole was here.'"

A howl of laughter came from the dugout. Jimmy threw his next pitch, another curve, the same thing as the first pitch. Cole again turned and delivered, trying to hit the scoreboard. The ball sailed foul down the line, missing by a couple of feet.

Jimmy took a deep breath and walked back on to the mound. Cole stepped out of the box.

"Yo, Twinkie," he started, "I know you're not going to throw anything over the plate. I guess you're too much of a pussy. So, either just intentionally walk me, or stop this chickenshit inside crap and show me what you got. If you've got any balls left, that is."

My blood ran cold. I knew what Jimmy was thinking. It was what any one of us would have been thinking. Jimmy was going to throw at him.

Jimmy stepped onto the rubber and right into his wind up. He turned and fired the hardest fastball he had thrown all day.

The pitch was up, out of the zone about shoulder high. It was inside, but it wasn't thrown right at Cole as I had thought he might. It was not a good pitch to hit, but Cole was cocky and impatient and he went for it. Jimmy's fastball would have blown by every other batter on the field, but this was Brad Cole. He pulled in and took a vicious cut. The bat made a loud crack and the ball disappeared into the sky.

I looked up. The ball was nowhere to be found. I had lost it. I looked left, right. I turned and looked to the outfield. The fielders were all motionless, staring into the sky. Not a sound from either side.

Now, I began to worry. Was it over top of me? I looked again, but the sun was coming in at the same angle, and I was momentarily blinded. Where was it?

"MINE," came Jimmy's voice, a few feet in front of me. He had one hand out shading the sun, as he got under the monster infield pop fly, and made a one-handed catch between second and third. A roar came from the Dorchester bleachers. People were stomping their feet on the steel treads so hard it was like a wall of noise. The Clinton Heights bleacher viewers were stunned, silent.

"That was really my ball," I said, laughing and giving Jimmy a pat on the shoulder.

"You looked like you were about to wet your pants, so I thought I would just handle it."

"Good call, Bro."

We were still losing, but the tension had evaporated. The moment of truth was past. I heard a crack and saw Brad Cole smash his bat against the side of the concrete dugout. "I HATE this place. It's a fucking toilet," he screamed. The rest of the bench was silent.

We gave up one more run that inning. Wes bobbled one at first and the runner took second. He took third on a long fly to Flash in center and scored when the throw got by Larkin at third. Jimmy got the last batter to pop out to Tony.

I sat in the dugout before the final half inning, feeling very pleased that we would not be blown out by twenty runs. Losing 4-2 to this powerhouse team after all these years, with barely enough bodies to field each position. That's pretty good, I thought.

Tony had other ideas.

"Here we go, guys," he yelled at us. "We are still in this game. Don't be satisfied with yourselves. We are losing and this is our last chance. Everyone we know has money riding on this game. We cannot let them down. We can still win this if you really want it. Well? DO YOU REALLY WANT IT?"

A chorus of yeahs rang the dugout. Winston Marshall grabbed his bat and walked to the plate. Marshall was a sophomore on the '88 team when I was a senior. He had looked the best of all of us at the plate, which is why Tony had batted him third in the order. He patiently watched some junk go by, and then absolutely nailed a 3-1 slider to right center. Both center and right fielders converged, and then neither one having called the ball ran right into each other, the ball skipping by and rolling to the fence. They lay there, stunned and bewildered. The left fielder ran all the way over, got the ball at the wall and fired it in, but Marshall was fast and trotted into third standing up with a triple.

Brad Cole walked over onto the grass toward the dugout. "You and you," he said pointing to two players and jerking with his thumb toward the outfield. They grabbed their gloves and sprinted out as the dazed former right and centerfielders stumbled in.

Jimmy got in the box. Cole yelled out to the pitcher, "Nothing but shit to

296

him, but don't walk him." Don't throw any strikes but don't walk him. With that great advice, the pitcher nibbled at the corners. Jimmy fouled off the only fastball the guy had thrown all day. The count was 3-2.

"Don't you lose him," Cole yelled.

The pitcher took a deep breath and fired. It was the fastball again. The heat had gotten to him and he was gassed. The pitch was low and outside. Ball four.

Jimmy jogged out to the bag as Cole came roaring in to the mound. "Give me the goddamn ball, you shithead." The pitcher dropped the ball in his hand and walked to the dugout. "You,
Malvern, take third," he said. "I guess I gotta do this myself."

"I thought the Dodgers didn't want him to pitch," I said to Tony who was standing next to me on deck.

"I don't think the Dodgers know what he's doing," Tony replied. "Oh boy, this is getting interesting."

"Do we have a steel helmet?" I asked.

"No, but you've got good medical insurance, and you had your will updated last year. You'll be fine."

"Thanks, I needed that. By the way, there's nobody out and you're after me. I hope he's not thinking about that $20,000 bet of yours."

"I think we are both screwed," Tony said. He gave me a slap on the backside. "Look alive in there."

297

Cole threw two or three warm up pitches and then waved off the catcher. "C'mon let's get this over with," he snarled.

I stepped up to the plate, and the field started to spin. I was fading. I stepped back out, and took a few swings. Then I took a deep breath and stepped back in. He fired almost immediately. I was expecting fastball but not that fast. It blew by me before I could even start my swing. Strike one.

There was no hesitation, no sign from the catcher. Cole tucked and fired. Another fast ball. Strike two.

I backed out of the box, took a couple more practice swings and stepped back in. Cole was all business. He reared and fired.

I was as ready as I would ever be. I gambled that he was going for the kill. I figured I had one good swing left in me. I started it ridiculously early and I was still way behind. But I got a piece of the ball, and my weak swing lifted a pop fly to shallow right field. The ball drifted out right behind the first baseman, too far in for the right fielder to make a play. It hit the grass inches inside the line. The first baseman took off after it and picked it up in the outfield grass, turning and then hesitating. Jimmy had rounded second and was heading for third. I came around first and advanced toward second, watching the play. The first baseman fired across the diamond and hit the third baseman with a perfect strike, well before Jimmy could get there. But, Jimmy was caught, halfway between the bags. He dodged and weaved but was caught in the rundown. In the flurry of throws, Marshall scored and I snuck into second.

Cole held up one finger. One out. The score was now 4-3, Clinton Heights. Tony came to the plate. Cole gritted his teeth, grinned an evil grin and fired. Fastball, strike one. Another quick pitch. Strike two.

Tony looked out at me at second and made a sign. I could not believe it. He stepped back into the box. When Cole started his motion, I took off for third.

As he reared and fired another heater, Tony squared and bunted. The sheer speed of the ball made it come off the bat harder than Tony probably would have wanted, but it was clean and in off the third base line. The third baseman wasn't thinking bunt and had been playing back but was now charging in. Cole got to the ball first, bare handing it in a move worthy of an ESPN highlight reel. He never turned to first, his eyes following me all the time. The shortstop was stunned. He never made a move to cover 3rd base. Now it was a race between Brad Cole and me to the bag. I had a monster head start, but he was closer and faster. We would arrive at nearly the same time.

I saw him out of the corner of my eye, closing in. I spent the last of my energy and thundered down the base path with everything I had left. I began my slide, well to the outfield side of the bag, trying to stay out of his reach. He stretched, sliding in the dirt toward me with his glove outstretched for the tag. I thought I may have slid too wide, but as I came even with the bag and out past his hand, I pulled my arms back tight to my body and then flipped over to my stomach and grabbed desperately for the base, catching it in one hand and holding on by my fingernails. The momentum carried me around the bag, and I ended up feet toward home plate and facing left field.

"Safe!" shouted the umpire.

"Damn it," Cole howled, getting up and walking back to the mound. I lay there for a few seconds, still in shock that I actually beat the tag. The field was spinning again. I managed to get to my knees, and straightened up. The field stopped spinning. I pulled myself up and stood proudly on third base. Tony gave me the thumbs up from first.

I thought Cole was upset before. He was practically purple with rage now as he stood on the mound. Wes Kaminsky stood in the box and was right up on the plate. Cole tried to throw inside and brush him back, but Wes was not fast enough and the pitch glanced off his ass as tried to spin out of the way.

The Dorchester bleachers were now getting on Cole, lots of boos and hisses. The Clinton Heights side watched in stunned disbelief; the bases were now loaded with only one out. There was no one in our on-deck circle, and then I realized why. This was Woody's spot in the order. That meant Big John was up.

I called time out and walked back to the dugout. I saw Tony running in from second base. John walked onto the field carrying Goliath as I approached.

"John, listen," I began, grabbing him by a thick shoulder. "You don't need to do this. I think we've done better than anybody ever imagined. Only down by a run, loaded bases. We've hung in there. We have nothing left to prove."

300

"No Skip," John said. "For the last twenty years I've wondered if I would ever be brave enough to get back into a batters box. I didn't plan for this to happen, but it did. For some reason, this is God's plan. And he always knows best. So now, the question will once and for all be answered. And with that guy on the mound again."

"One thing's for certain," Tony said looking out at the mound. "He will not be throwing inside. If he hits you, then a run scores and we have a tie game. He will be ashamed to ever show his face across the river again. He'll be throwing fastballs, low and outside and trying to get out of here as fast as he can."

"John, he's even faster at the plate than he looks in the dugout," I said. "Start your swing way early."

He nodded yes, acknowledging our last minute admonitions. Then he looked at Tony and me.

"Thanks, guys," he said. He looked down at the giant bat in his hands. "I really appreciate you trying to build up my confidence. It means a lot. But you know and I know that I don't have a prayer of hitting that ball."

Tony and I just stood there for a moment, speechless.

"That's not true, John," I finally said, grabbing him by his massive shoulders. "He's not unhittable."

"He's way out of my league," John said. "I know that. But that's not the point here. The lesson I need to learn is that I can conquer my fear. I don't have

301

to let it beat me. And when I get into that box, and take my cuts, I will finally prove to myself that with God's help I am bigger than my fears. He has given me the strength. They will not hold me back anymore."

"Listen John," I said, leaning in. "If you don't think you can get around on him, you can always bunt. If I see you square around, I'll break for the plate."

"You think you're fast enough to beat the throw home," Tony asked. "Skip, with all due respect."

"If he squares, I'll make it home. I'll get there."

Tony looked back at John. "Number one John, you are bigger than your fears, and you will prove it to yourself and the world when you step into that box. And number two, you WILL hit that ball.," he said. "Believe it! Now, go chase him home, Big John."

The umpire came over and made a hurry up sign. Tony and I went back to our bases. John stepped into the batter's box.

The roar that came from the Dorchester side of the field was deafening. Everyone in the bleachers, everyone in the dugout, everyone behind the fences was on their feet, screaming and cheering and clapping for Big John.

I looked over at Cole, who was standing behind the mound, and I was startled by the change. He was smiling. His purple furor was gone. He was relaxed and loose. He was no longer out of control. Maybe that wasn't such a good thing.

"Well, well," he said looking in at John. "Long time no see. How's the old noggin?"

John said nothing. He stretched his big bat over the plate and pulled it back.

"I think it's time we end all this fun," Cole said. He went into his windup and threw a blistering fastball low and out over the plate. John started his swing early, but it was late. Swing and a miss, strike one.

"Gonna have to be faster than that, old man," Cole said with a chuckle. The infielders laughed nervously. John edged closer to the plate.

Cole fired again. Another fast ball, about thigh high and over the middle of the plate. Cole didn't need to nibble at the corners. John hadn't hit in a game situation in twenty years. Cole could just rely on his speed.

John tried to square around for a bunt. I was caught off guard and froze on the base path. John never got into position in time, and his attempt was clumsy and off balance. Once again, John missed, well behind the pitch.

The volume of the Dorchester side had dropped. The Clinton Heights stands were beginning to chant COLE, COLE, COLE, and the bench players were all standing at the fence shouting for Cole to put it away.

I wanted to believe so bad that John could do the job, but the truth was he could never get his bat on that fastball. It was just too fast.

Only one out. I considered trying to just steal home. I had done it before. But then I realized that I did not have the greatest weapon of my youth. My speed. Hell, I was having a hard time just standing on third. I was cooked.

But, there was still hope. I looked to the on-deck circle and saw Flash Gordon staring, fixated on the man at the plate. Flash had become a big man, but he still had fast hands. He showed it during his last at bat. He might be able to get around and get a piece of that fast ball if he started early enough. Just a poke, just getting it out of the infield would score a run.

But part of me was happy for John. He had done it. He had gotten back into the baseball box and conquered his fear. Even after strike three, John would be the winner.

John stepped out of the box. I saw him bow his head, saying a prayer. Then, he looked up at Brad Cole and settled into the box. His stance was open. I immediately thought bunt. I took another couple of steps down the line. I would need every step I could get.

Then I saw John move right up on top of home plate. He was hanging over it, crowding the plate. And he was smiling. What the hell? What was he doing, I thought to myself. Did he want to get hit again?

The crowding of the plate and the confident smile was all it took to set Cole off. "You son of a bitch," he said, with narrowing eyes and a sneering grin. He shot a look over at the third baseman, who took a few steps up onto the grass. He was too close to me. I had to retreat back to the bag.

Being on third I had the best look at Cole's hands, and I saw him looking down and adjusting his grip on the ball. He slid his index and middle fingers close up on the left side of the seams. I knew at once what he was going to do.

It was a stupid egotistical move. John was too slow to catch up with the fast ball, even on a bunt. Cole had a certain strike three with one over the middle. But he wanted more. He was going to throw an inside backdoor curve. It would be high, looking to John like it was coming at his head, making him buckle at the knees and fall to the ground. John's fear would take over and strike him down into the dirt, and settle the question once and for all which of them was stronger. Then, the ball would curve in over the back of the plate for a called third strike. Cole would get the strikeout and destroy John and Dorchester once again. I opened my mouth to call another time out when he launched into his windup.

I broke for home. A million scenarios had run through my mind standing on that bag, but now as I labored down the base path, the realization hit me about how this would end. John would duck to avoid the pitch. It would be a strike, for out number two. Then, the catcher would take two steps down the 3rd base line and put an easy tag on the old out of shape baserunner thundering toward home. Instead of winning the game, I would be the third out. And it was too late to stop, I was too far down the line. I was in no mans land. It was over.

As Cole leaned back into his windup, he added a slow twirling body move, twisting his torso to present his backside to the plate and pausing for dramatic effect before continuing his delivery. Instead of a bunt, John pulled his bat back into launch position, and then immediately started into his swing,

305

ridiculously early. The combination of the extra windup flourish and the slower curveball pitch meant that the ball took longer to get to the batter. John's hands were pulling hard through the zone almost before the ball was even released. It started straight for his head, but John did not flinch, not one bit. He was fully committed. The hanging backdoor curve folded back neatly across the plate at exactly the same time as Big John's powerful swing was crossing the zone.

His old companion Goliath, who had set the home run record in 1988 and had spent the last 20 years gathering dust in the attic, had one last hit left in its timber. The ancient ash bat made a sharp thunder crack, like the mighty bats of old we would hear over the radio when we were kids listening as the great Harry Kalas called the Phillies games. The sound of the bat was so piercing and powerful, it stunned the crowd into complete silence, and left them gasping for breath.

Jacked by a swing fueled with twenty years of frustration, pain and emotion, the ball shot off the bat like a missile, sailed into the hazy afternoon sun and disappeared high over the left field scoreboard, over the dirt road behind the fence, over the marsh and cattails and landed with a splash out in the Delaware River.

Chapter 13

There are no words to begin to fully describe the transition from stunned silence to complete and utter pandemonium on the afternoon of the Fourth of July 2008 at the Dorchester High School baseball field after John Stone won the game with his walk-off grand slam home run. The Dorchester bleachers emptied and screaming fans, waving their hands in the air ran onto the field. I crossed the plate amid high fives, followed by Tony and Wes. The players formed a semi-circle as John rounded third. He raised his hands like Rocky, and made a final big jump with both feet onto home plate. We all rushed him, hugs and tears.

Tony grabbed me by the shoulder. "Can you believe this? We did it. Again!"

It seemed as if every person in Dorchester was on that field, and the noise was deafening. The infield was packed with delirious fans who wanted to congratulate their Dorchester Wildcats. No one wanted to leave; we were there a long time.

"Where is the media?" Tony shouted. "They said there would be a congressman."

I looked for the postgame media event organized by Nick Danno. There was no one. The Clinton team bus and Cole's limousine had vanished without a trace, no postgame handshakes, no autographs, nothing.

"Going into hiding before everybody starts wanting to get paid up," I said.

With that, a microphone was shoved in my face. It had a worn WDCR flag on it. "Skip McCann, how does it feel to do it all over again?" Murray White asked.

"Unbelievable, Murray," I croaked out. "I'm speechless."

"I'm not," Tony said leaning in. "From the very start I knew we would win. We showed Clinton Heights that the first time was not a fluke."

"Indeed it was not," Murray said. "That was probably the most incredible finish I have ever seen. Congratulations, guys!"

"And here's to our captain and our manager," Woody said, bottles of Rolling Rock in each of his massive paws. He proceeded to pour one over Tony and the other over me. That started the Rolling Rock shower, and soon we were all drenched with beer. Cameras were flashing and my eyes started to burn from the beer.

A high pitched voice cried out.

"Hey, Tony, congratulations."

It was Angelina. She bulldozed through the players to reach Tony, and before he could organize a defense, she grabbed him around the waist and pulled him in for a hug and a kiss.

"Thanks, Angelina," Tony said in a shaking voice.

"I love a man in a uniform," she said, in a husky, come hither voice. "Tonight is going be your lucky night."

At that moment, Kristen came up behind Tony, pulled him around and gave him a kiss on the lips and a big hug, and she got soaked in another Rolling Rock shower.

"Wow, what a game!" she said.

"I didn't think you were coming," Tony said. "I thought you were working."

"I got off early. Everybody from the hospital was going to be here. They were calling it the rematch of the century. I knew I had to come. You guys were awesome!"

Angelina was taking all this in. She looked at Kristen.

"Hi, my name is Angelina," she said. "I was Tony's girlfriend in high school."

"High school? Wow, that must have been a long time ago," Kristen said, looking back at Tony. "I'm his new girlfriend."

"You look very young," Angelina said, frowning.

"Yeah, well I guess he's got this thing for women half his age," Kristen said laughing as she hugged Tony again.

The look on Angelina's face was one of pure disgust. "I'll see you around, Tony," she said and backed away, disappearing into the crowd.

Tony started to come around. "Thanks," he said to Kristen. "And, to set the record straight, you're not half my age."

"Close enough."

"Anyway, I'm glad you were here to see history in the making," Tony said, looking over at me. "And I have to say very modestly that it was my managerial skills that won this game. And now where are we going? The hell with Disney World, we're going to Dorchester!" That got a round of applause from the crowd.

"Hey, Skip." Kelli ran up to me through the crowd and gave me a hug. She squeezed her body against me and wouldn't let go. It felt very good.

"I thought you were leaving early," I said.

"The camera guys wouldn't leave. They said they had to stay to the end. What a finish! Unbelievable!"

"I'm in shock, Kelli. I just can't believe it."

"Believe it, Skip, believe it. You made it happen," she said, grabbing my arm. "And I had no idea how good you really are. You have mad skills. And great shoes."

"Not bad for an old man?"

"I told you, you are not old," she said, pushing her index finger into my chest. "You are in your prime."

"In my prime," I repeated. "I like the sound of that."

"Picture time!" Karen called out, grabbing me by the arm and pulling me over to Jimmy, who was drinking from little green bottles with Max, Wayne, and Sasha.

"To the Dorchester Wildcats of 1988," my brother said, toasting us with his beer bottle.

"And to a day this town will never forget," I said, clinking his bottle.

"Honestly Skip, I never dreamed it would end up like this."

"I don't think anybody did," I said. "Say, by the way. Does that 35 and over baseball team you play on need any more guys? I might know a shortstop who would be interested in joining up."

Jimmy grabbed my shoulders and locked me up in a bear hug. "Hell yeah there's a spot for you. There's always a spot for you, bro. Hot damn, the McCann brothers are back!" he shouted at the top of his lungs.

"Look here and smile," Karen shouted, snapping a picture of Jimmy and me.

"Great game, Skip," Max said.

"Big John said he wasn't an athlete anymore," Wayne said. "But he was wrong."

"That's right, Wayne," I said. "He had it in him all the time."

"Wayne cried when that man hit ball into river," Sasha said, pulling Wayne in for a hug.

"So did I," Max said. "I had a hundred bucks on Clinton Heights. I could have made eight hundred if I had bet on Dorchester. But hell, it was worth it to see Brad Cole run to his limo and speed out of here in a cloud of dust."

A group of firefighters had come on to the field, and they hoisted Big John up on their shoulders. A voice called out over the crowd.

"Hey, John, you want this?"

A wet soggy firefighter tossed John a wet, soggy baseball. He caught it with one hand, and took a good long look.

"We just fished it out of the river. Thought you might want it," the young man said, toweling off.

"The cover's half torn off from the pounding you gave it," someone else shouted.

There was a roar from the firefighters, and they started carrying him back to the football field. We all fell in line. We marched around the field, getting doused with more beer and then back over to the parking lot where the tailgating was now going on in full fury. It was a mob scene, and everyone came over and had to tell me what they were going to do with their new found riches from their baseball game bet. Kelli and I had at least three of Delores Williams' Singapore punch drinks. Wherever we went, people passed us drinks and offered toasts. We toasted the Dorchester 1988 baseball team at every car and then the 1982 Little League team, and then we started toasting everything else from motherhood to the founding fathers and things started to get hazy. I faintly remember seeing the fireworks out over the river. I had no idea how I got home.

I woke up around noon the next morning still dressed in my baseball uniform with the worst hangover I think I ever had. I staggered into the kitchen and popped some aspirins and then walked out onto the terrace. I heard the other door slide open, and Tony walked out. He was still wearing his baseball shirt, but had changed into shorts. He looked rough.

"You look like total shit, Skip," he said, clapping a hand on my shoulder.

"You don't look much better," I said. I looked at his uniform shirt. "What happened to the buttons?" I asked.

"Kristen wanted me to leave my uniform top on last night." He looked down at the shirt. "And then, when she tore it off she ripped out the buttons. She's a savage. Now I need to get this fixed at the tailor."

"Winning nookie is sweet."

"It certainly is. And you almost got some winning nookie yourself."

"I don't remember much about last night. I hope I didn't do something I will regret."

"Unfortunately, you did not. Sometimes you need to cut loose and let it all hang out. It would be good for you. No, I was talking about that girl, Kelli."

"What happened?"

"What happened?" Tony said. "She was all over you; that's what happened. She was talking to Kristen while we were toasting the team. She has

313

the serious hots for you. I'll bet you would have woken up in that bed of yours with her beside you this morning if those asshole Mets camera guys didn't drag her off, kicking and screaming during the fireworks."

I thought about that for a moment. "Maybe it was for the best," I said. "I hardly know her. She's young."

"How young?"

"Twenty-three."

"Ouch, that is young, even for me," Tony said. "But damn, she looked really good in those shorts."

I heard Tony's phone getting a text. He pulled it out and looked at it. "It's your daughter. I gave her my cell number. She knew we had the game yesterday. She's been trying to reach you, but you're not answering."

"I'm not sure where my phone is," I said. "I think it's in my equipment bag."

"Karen loaded it up with Jimmy's stuff. By the way, when you get your bag, make sure you thank her for bringing you home last night."

"I wondered how I got here."

"Your daughter wanted to know how we did. I sent her this picture. Karen sent it to me."

The picture was of Tony and me smiling broadly, surrounded by the rest of the team, all toasting our success. Kristen was hanging all over Tony and Kelli had me locked up in a tight squeeze..

314

"After I sent her this text, she asked about the 'two drunk bimbos with the wet tee shirts' who were hanging on us."

Maybe it was because we were so physically and emotionally exhausted, or maybe it was the residual euphoria from the game, but just I started laughing. Then Tony started laughing and we couldn't stop. We stood there on the terrace laughing uncontrollably. Finally, he regained his composure.

"I texted her, 'To the victors go the spoils.'" Tony said.

"Oh, I'll bet that went over big. What did she say?"

She wanted to know if the blonde hanging on you was your girlfriend."

"And you said?"

"I told her no, but that she was just one of a hundred women who lined up for the opportunity to take you home and compromise your morals after the game. She didn't text me back. A few minutes later, I texted that amazingly enough, despite their best efforts, not one of the town's young women were successful in debauching your integrity. Your dignity was still intact. Then, you want to know what she texted back?"

"What?"

"I'll let you read it." He showed me the text on his phone.

"Good. She's too young for him and besides she looks like a ho."

We started laughing again, and this time we both had to sit down in the deck chairs. My head was pounding, my lungs and throat were burning. After a long while, our laughing died down to involuntary whimpers.

315

"The girl is looking out for her old man," Tony said, nodding his head.

I smiled. A warm feeling was spreading across my heart. My daughter was looking out for me.

I said a silent prayer to God that he would look out for her.

I spent a long time in the shower that morning, the steamy hot water loosening up my tired muscles. The fog in my head was clearing, and I was starting to come back to life. It was mid afternoon, another hot humid day. Tony said he had decided for medical reasons against taking a walk and instead he drove me over to Jimmy's house.

"So, how are we feeling this morning?" Karen said as she let us in. "Actually, it's afternoon," she added, looking at her watch.

"My eyes are open, and my brain is running at about thirty percent," I said.

"I'm surprised you're even awake," she said, giving me the once over. "In all the time I've known you, yesterday was the first time I have ever seen you so drunk you couldn't walk. I had to load you and Jimmy in the minivan. You weigh a ton."

"Sorry about that. Thanks for taking me home. It doesn't happen much, but when it does I make it count."

"That was quite a honey you had with you yesterday," she said, giving me a quizzical look. "Very cute. Where have you been hiding her?"

"She works for the Mets TV operation. They wanted some footage of Brad Cole for the broadcast. I didn't even know she was coming."

"She certainly liked you. She couldn't keep her hands off you. Actually, she was a really nice kid. She hung out with us for a while before her coworkers made her leave. A little young, Skip. That's just my opinion."

"He would date older women, but there are none around that are his age," Tony said.

I gave Tony a nod. "Where's the man of the house?"

"He's helping Wayne clean up the fire company stand at the field. Speaking of honeys, how

about Sasha? That is an incredible story."

"Only Wayne would find the one real person in an ocean of spam," I said. "She seems nice, and God knows she improves the appearance of Dorchester, especially in that red bikini."

"I guess it was a pretty good day for everybody," Tony said.

"A lot of people made a lot of money," I said.

"It was probably the greatest day ever for almost everybody in Dorchester," Karen said. "I think we were due."

My bag was still in the van. I found my phone and the multiple texts from Janine along with other congratulatory texts and messages. And, there was also a phone message from Kelli. I texted back to Janine that I had finally found my phone and asked her to call me when she got the chance. I listened to Kelli's message: "Skip, it's Kelli. Just wanted to say how much fun I had yesterday at your game and meeting all your friends and family. It was great. When you

317

wake up and if you're not too hung over, give me a call. I hope to see you soon."

Although Sullivan's was open, I could not handle the sight, smell or taste of another beer, so Tony and I went over to the Main Street Cafe across from the bakery. It was crowded, a lot of people in for the Fourth of July event. I was embarrassed as Tony and I were greeted with a round of applause when we walked in. Everyone wanted to talk to us about the game and most were thanking us for their winnings.

"Skip, Tony." It was Murray White.

"Hey, Murray," I said. Tony and I got up and shook his hand.

"That baseball game," he said, "will go down in history as the greatest game ever played in Dorchester. I have never seen such an emotionally charged sporting event in all my years of covering sports here. You boys are this town's heroes! And, I made myself $4,000."

The other tables around us chimed in. It was overwhelming.

"Monday morning, I want both of you to come over to the station. You have to go on the air with me. Everyone wants to hear from you."

One of the most important days of my life came a couple of weeks later on a warm late July Saturday morning, I was feeling a lot better, almost back to normal. Tony, Kristen, and I were having a late breakfast in the sunshine on the terrace. Kristen stayed over more often these days.

"What are you two doing today?" I asked.

"We are going tubing this afternoon down the Delaware," Kristen said. "Why don't you come with us? I'll invite my friend Ally. You'll like her. She's fun, and she's cute."

"Another time, perhaps," I said. "I already have a date for today."

"You do?" Kristen said.

"Skip's date is with his daughter, Janine," Tony said.

"She flew in Thursday. She's staying with family friends in Bryn Mawr. She did the tour at Penn yesterday and loves it. She can't wait to start school next month. I'm meeting her at the ballpark today. Got field box tickets. The Giants are in town."

"You've been talking to her a lot lately."

"Just about every other day. And for an hour at a time. She says she's feeling great."

"That's a good sign," Tony said. "A very good sign."

"This will be the first time I've actually seen her since LA. Anyway, I asked her if she would like to see a baseball game and she got very excited."

"Speaking of baseball, guess what I got in the mail yesterday," Tony said.

"An autographed baseball from Brad Cole?"

"Better than a baseball." He slid over an envelope with no return address. Inside there was no card or letter, just a check for 20,000 dollars made out to the Dorchester Baseball Association signed by Brad Cole.

319

"An autographed check. Damn! He made good," I said.

"This will go a long way to fix up the old field," Tony said. "I already met with the baseball association. They know exactly what they want."

"Did everybody get paid from their bets?"

"Just about everybody," Tony said. "I thought they would try to weasel their way out of it. Too much money at stake, and it would have turned ugly. A lot of old Clinton Heights money is now in the wallets of the fine people of Dorchester."

A knock came from the door. Kristen was halfway to the kitchen for more coffee and she returned with a familiar face.

It was Janine.

The photos she sent to me had showed a marked improvement from the sick little girl in the bandana and Hello Kitty slippers. Seeing her now in person for the first time, I was stunned. Gone were the dark circles under her eyes, the haggard look, and the pale complexion. I've always heard about the resilience of youth, but here it was standing right in front of me. She still looked thin, but amazingly young and healthy. It was hard to imagine that she still had cancer cells inside her body.

I was also startled at how much she resembled her mother. Her hair, which had fallen out from the chemotherapy was now growing back. I could see the short dark straight strands starting to peek out from under her San Francisco Giants cap. But it was her tee shirt that stopped me cold. It was my old

Dorchester baseball shirt, the one Kim was wearing when I pulled out of the apartment complex at USC all those years ago.

Tony got up and gave her a big hug. I hugged her and kissed her on the forehead.

"You look fantastic, Janine," I said.

"I feel fantastic. Better than ever, thanks to you."

I swallowed hard to keep my composure. Keep it together, Skip, I thought to myself.

"I thought we were meeting at the ballpark?" I said.

"I know I told you that, but it's such a nice day, and I've heard so much about Dorchester that I asked my friends to drive me over."

"I haven't seen one of those shirts for a long time," Tony said, looking at the old baseball shirt.

Janine looked up at me, hesitating.

"Me neither," I said with a smile. "Nice to see it's getting some use again."

Tony took Janine on a tour. First the apartments, then the second floor billing offices and finally his private practice and the urgent care facility, which was open and seeing patients. Tony introduced Janine to his staff as his niece. She asked him if she could intern at his practice this fall. Tony laughed and answered, "Yes, but only if you start calling me "Uncle Tony."

We said our goodbyes as Kristen and Tony got ready to leave for their day on the river. As we climbed into my car for the drive to Philadelphia, Janine asked, "Can you show me the baseball field?"

"You mean the high school field?"

"Yes. The place where you played the Fourth of July game."

"That was quite a game."

"I saw some pictures. Uncle Tony sent me a clipping from your weekly newspaper," she said. "There was a picture of you and Tony and some other guys pouring beer all over yourselves and celebrating. I hung it on my wall."

We pulled up to the field and walked down onto the baseball diamond. She was holding on to her shirt. She was so thin that the shirt swam on her. She squeezed it hard around her tiny waist as she looked around the field.

"I remember that shirt," I said.

"Mom said you would." She looked down at the shirt, smoothing out some wrinkles. "She told me that you gave her it to her when you left California."

"Actually as I recall, she just put it on and kept it," I said with a laugh.

She smiled. "I remember seeing this shirt in her closet. She never wore it, and it wasn't like anything else she had so I was always curious. I always wondered where Dorchester was and what the connection could be. I asked her once and she brushed me off. I assumed it was from sometime in her past. As I was packing my suitcase for this trip, she came in and said that there was something very special to her that she would like me to have. She told me the story about the shirt. I didn't want to take it, but she insisted. 'Skip gave it to me,' she said 'and asked me not to give it away.' But in this case, she felt you

322

wouldn't mind."

I turned and looked out over the river. "How is she doing, with you leaving and all?"

"She's handling it, but I can tell it's getting real hard. I told her she should come with me. Move east, start a new life. I told her she should see you, Skip. Get to know you again. She says she can't do that now. She burned her bridge. And now it's time to move on. She told me about the terrible way she treated you at the hospital. She felt really bad afterward. She wouldn't say any more."

"I hope she finds what she's looking for," I said.

We walked around the infield. I showed her where Tony and I played our positions. We walked to the outfield fence and I showed her where Big John's ball landed in the river. Then we started walking back to the parking lot. It was warming up with a gentle breeze was coming across the river, and the trees with their thick summer foliage rippled in the morning stillness.

"Dorchester is beautiful," she said. "Everything is so green. California is always brown."

"I remember thinking the same thing when I came back after college."

"This town is like something out of a magazine."

"It's my home," I said.

"I grew up in San Francisco. Concrete and steel and lots of cars. This is like heaven."

We walked around the fields and back to the car.

"I know you're a California girl, but have you ever had an authentic Philly cheesesteak?"

"I don't think so," she said. "I'm sort of a vegan."

I started laughing. "Then let's forget that idea."

"No," she said, grabbing my shoulder. "I want to try one."

"You sure?"

"Is it good?"

"Are you kidding? It's great."

"If you say it's great, then I want to try it," she said.

Where do you take someone to try her very first Philly cheesesteak? So many great variations. In the end I stayed traditional and took her to Tony Luke's in South Philly. We parked and walked up to the street side counter.

"Two Whiz wit," I told the order guy.

"I thought we were getting cheesesteaks?" Janine asked.

"That's how you say cheesesteak in Philly," I said.

"Oh."

When the sandwiches came, we sat at a picnic table on the sidewalk, overlooking the not so scenic I-95 overpass at Oregon Avenue. She looked at the gooey mass of fresh chipped steak, fried onions and cheese whiz with some skepticism. All it took was one bite. "Oh, God, this is awesome!" she said, taking a huge bite, globs of it running down her face.

"They've got one at the ballpark too, but you don't get the full South Philly

324

ambience."

After lunch we rolled over to Citizens Bank Park. I gave her a tour of the press area and introduced her as my daughter to the other reporters and broadcasters. Then we went to the field behind the cage and watched the Giants taking batting practice.

"Is that Barry Bonds?" she asked, pointing to the guy in the cage, who hit one over the wall.

"No, that's the catcher, Bengie Molina. Barry Bonds is retired. He was a lot bigger."

"He's hitting the balls over the fence."

"You're wearing a Giants hat," I said. "I didn't know that you are a baseball fan"

"I've seen it on television, but I've only been to one game in my life," she said. "Two years ago. I remember Barry Bonds hit a home run that day. That's where I bought this hat."

We watched some of the other players take their turns in the cage. She was quiet for a while. The she leaned against me.

"I went with a friend of mine. Her Dad took us to the game. He had box seats." She paused for a moment. "I was so jealous."

"Because they had box seats?"

"No," she said, "because she had a dad who took her places like baseball games, and I never ever saw my dad. He never wanted me around."

"Well," I said, "if it means anything, I want you around."

"It means everything," she said, putting her head against my shoulder.

We walked over to our seats which were on the field next to the dugout. The players saw me and came over, making a fuss over her. She loved it. In the sixth inning, I felt a very large presence behind me. It was the team mascot, the Philly Phanatic who climbed up onto the dugout roof, stuck out his tongue, and held out a hand to Janine. She climbed up and danced with him as the song "Wild Thing" came over the PA. The crowd was clapping and cheering. The Phanatic reached around, pulled out a Phillies hat, and held it out to Janine. She flipped her Giants cap to me and put the Phillies cap on her head. The crowd went wild. The wide smile on her face when she climbed back down to our seats made my heart almost burst with joy.

"I'm hungry," I said. "What would you like?"

"Do they have sushi?" She asked.

I stared at her for a minute, and she burst out laughing. "I'm kidding."

We settled on nachos. "Ooh, plastic cheese," she said with delight. "My mom is very picky about eating healthy food. Lots of fruits and vegetables. But she has one weakness. Sometimes when we're out, like at a street fair at the pier, we'll get nachos with this same kind of cheese sauce. That's what she calls this, plastic cheese. She loves it. It's her guilty pleasure."

"Plastic cheese? How about that," I said, smiling.

The Giants came from behind to beat the Phillies 5-4, and she was ecstatic.

After the game, I dropped her off at her friend's place in Bryn Mawr.

"Thank you for an awesome day today," she said. "I had more fun today than I have had in like, forever. Getting to spend the whole day with you was something I have been looking forward to for a long time. I just wish my mom could have been here, too. She needs to have a good day."

"I'm glad you had fun. This was a great day for me too."

"I'm so happy to be coming to Penn this semester. I need the change. It's a new beginning. And most of all I'm glad that you are here. It's like a dream. You made me feel so special today. You're the best dad in the world. I'm so lucky."

"We are both very lucky," I said.

I choked up a little as I said that, her cancer coming back to mind. I had made a promise to my little girl that she would get well. A promise I might not be able to keep. It was breaking my heart.

She looked at me with those big brown eyes, and then she leaned over and put her arms around my neck. We hugged each other there in the car, holding tightly to each other. I could not help but wonder how many more hugs I might be able to get before the cancer came back. I resolved to get as many as I could.

"You better get going," I finally said. "Have a good flight home tomorrow. And don't forget to text me that you landed safely. You know how I worry about you."

She laughed. She reached over and touched my cheek.

"I love you, Daddy," she said softly.

"I love you too, Angel."

In mid August, Janine moved into her apartment in University City. I was on the road with the team for eight days in Chicago, where I got my "Chicago Dog," and in Washington, DC, where I enjoyed a "half-smoke" dog at Ben's Chili Bowl. I caught up with Janine again the next weekend.

For someone so small and thin, she had an unbelievable appetite. She put me to shame. Each morning, Janine, Tony and I would grab breakfast out, and then we'd play tourist. Janine wanted to see everything about Philly. Saturday we did Penn's Landing and explored the funky scene on South Street. Sunday we went to the Philadelphia Zoo, a place I had not been to since my sixth grade class trip and then we wandered around Boathouse Row in Fairmount Park in the afternoon.

"Are you having fun?" she asked, as we walked along the Schuylkill River.

"Absolutely."

"I mean, you've probably seen all this a million times. I hope it's not too boring.

"Yes, I have seen this before," I said. "But today I'm seeing it through new eyes."

Each night she would come to the ballpark with me, hanging out in the press room and wandering around the stadium, trying any new food she had never been able to get in San Fransisco. She was so full of energy, full of life.

And the Phillies were suddenly red hot. This was not the Phillies season I was used to seeing. Normally at this time they were running on fumes, losing ground and talking about next year. But now they were winning a lot of games and making up a lot of ground on the Mets. At the end of the month we were at Shea Stadium. We were only two games back in the standings. This would decide the season.

I had talked to Kelli a couple of times in the past few weeks. This would be the first time I had seen her since Fourth of July. She was wearing a tight black Mets polo and a pair of very snug gray slacks. Her blonde hair was down and parted to the side. She gave me a big hug as I walked into the press room and then said, "Come with me."

We went around the hall and down the television production suite. "In here," she said, pointing to a small editing booth. It was barely big enough for the two of us. We sat on the small swivel stools so close that our bodies were close together. As she leaned across me to access the editing controls, I could feel the warmth of her body and smell the perfume on her neck.

"Ready?" she asked.

"For what?"

She clicked the mouse and up on the monitor came the Dorchester baseball field.

"The guys filmed Brad Cole, but then they just kept going," she said. "They really got into the game. Let's jump ahead."

The next scene was me at in the batter's box. I swung, and the ball sailed over the fence.

"Wow," I said. "You got that?"

"We got practically the whole game," she said. "I've had so much fun editing this."

She clicked the mouse again and advanced to the last at bat. Big John connected, and the ball sailed into the river.

"I heard later that he had been hit by a Brad Cole pitch in high school and that he was hospitalized. Took a lot of guts to get back in that box again."

"A great ending to the story," I said.

She got up and pulled a disc from the machine. "Here," she said. "I hope you enjoy it."

"Kelli," I started, "I don't know what to say. I mean, thank you so much. This really means a lot to me."

"How about lunch," she asked.

We walked down to the first level concourse behind home plate to a little stand called "Mama's Italian Specialties of Corona." I ordered the hot roast turkey and mozzarella sandwich.

"How do you know about that?" she asked.

"I've been coming to Shea for ten years," I said.

"Ten years ago, I was in seventh grade," she said, looking at the menu board.

The sandwiches came out. We stopped for a couple of beers and made our way back to the press room, grabbing a quiet table in the back.

She did most of the talking. A lot about her life, growing up in Brooklyn and going to college. We compared some notes about USC in 1992 when I graduated and in 2005 when she graduated. She loved her job with the Mets, and she kept thanking me for the introduction. She loved Dorchester and the game and the tailgate parties, and she said she didn't speak to the camera guys all the way back to New York when they made her leave.

The game was about to start, and she had to get back to the production room. I walked her to the press room door.

"Skip," she said, "after the game would you like to go out and get a drink or something? This is a three-game series, so you're staying at the Hilton, right?"

"Actually I have to leave right after the game today," I said. "My brother Jimmy and his wife are going out of town, and I told them I would watch their kids. But I would really like a raincheck, if you're interested."

"I'm very interested," she said.

"Let's stay in touch, Kelli. And, thanks for the video, and the beer." I gave her a quick hug and she kissed me on the cheek. I watched her walk down the hallway.

I hoped she didn't feel bad. I felt bad about lying to her; I didn't really have to go back to Dorchester that night. I had been thinking about her and feeling a little awkward. The age thing had been bothering me. I knew where this was going. She was attractive, actually very attractive and I would have had no trouble sliding in to bed with her. Five years ago, hell, one year ago I would have met her after the game and we most likely would have ended up waking up together in my hotel room. It would not have been the first time that had happened. Now things were different. While we talked, or rather while she talked over lunch, I thought how similar the conversation was to those I had been having with Janine. She just seemed so young, and I had trouble connecting conversationally as well as emotionally if that makes any sense. Perhaps I just needed more time to get to know her. For the first time in my life, I felt that maybe a beautiful young woman might be just too young for me.

After the game, I took a cab to Penn Station where I caught a train back to Trenton. Then I went home to Dorchester. I would file my stories from the apartment. As I got into my bed alone that night, I had very mixed emotions, but no regrets.

Chapter 14

On September 28th, the unthinkable happened. The Philadelphia Phillies won the National League East Championship.

Their first playoff opponent were the Milwaukee Brewers. Time to pay the piper. Time for the dream season to end. It did not. The Phillies dispatched the Brewers 3 games to 1.

On to the National League Championship, and the Los Angeles Dodgers. Surely, this would be the end of the Cinderella season. They had come so far, and now it would be time to say goodbye. It was not. They beat the Dodgers 4 games to 1. And now, only one hurdle left. The World Series. The pinnacle of baseball. The golden dream of every player.

It was October 28th, after a two day rain delay. The time was 9:58 PM. The Phillies had only won one World Series in their entire one hundred twenty-five year existence. They had lost more games than any other professional baseball team in history. But they had gone an unbelievable 25-4 over the last month. Pitcher Brad Lidge had successfully closed his last forty-six games. They were due, but once again, they were the Phillies. They had always found a way to lose. It was the Phillies way.

The 9th inning, two out. Lidge stared down Eric Hinske, turned and fired his bread and butter slider, and it was all over. The team I had a feeling about during spring training had won the World Series, 4 games to 1.

Only a Phillies fan, with hopes and dreams battered and broken over years and years of futility, can understand the emotions that went through my head as Brad Lidge sank to his knees on the mound amid the rush of players. Shock and disbelief were my first emotions. Was it really the third out? Would the umpire reverse his call? Maybe the commissioner of baseball would step onto the field and nullify the win? But that did not happen. Then the joy, the euphoria, the release of years and years of emotion culminated in one gut wrenching screaming cry in unison from the almost forty-six thousand people in the ballpark, blasting into the cold South Philly night sky. As second baseman Chase Utley would most eloquently put it later, My Philadelphia Phillies were world "fucking" champions.

The Press box was out of control. Down the elevators we went to the clubhouse. TV lights blazed as I was getting drenched with champagne along with the players, I thought back to the Fourth of July game and the Rolling Rock victory shower on the old Dorchester high school field. I saw the look in these players' eyes. All those practices, all those swings and misses and road trips and slumps. From tee ball to Little League to Babe Ruth League to American Legion ball to high school and college ball and through four levels of minor league baseball. All those games of catch with their dads. They had worked their entire lives to get to this one moment in time. A moment they would never forget. And as a sportswriter who covered nearly every game from spring training to the World Series, a season I would never forget. A year I could never forget.

My phone went off. It was Jimmy. He, Tony, and the boys had watched the finale on the little 19-inch set above the bar with a packed house at Sullivan's, and now they were laughing their asses off watching me get soaked on the TV. A couple of days later on a beautiful sunny 60 degree Halloween afternoon, I got Tony onto a flatbed truck with some of the players and management in front of a million screaming Phillies fans for the big ticker tape parade. It wound down Broad Street to Pattison Avenue and Citizens Bank Park for the mother of all victory parties.

We left straight from the ballpark, exhausted and headed to the Dorchester High School football field. The Friday night football game was the big town event each week during the fall, and Tony and I tried not to miss it. The Wildcats had a pretty good team that was headed to the playoffs.

Tony parked his car in the lot and then told me to walk over with him to the baseball field next door. The sun was just under the horizon, and what leaves that were left on the big red maples surrounding the field glowed scarlet in the light of dusk. The Baseball Association repairs were very evident. Even in the fading light, the old field looked great. Tony showed me a huge bronze plaque on the side of the newly refurbished restrooms, around behind the snack bar. The plaque featured an etching of Brad Cole and a dedication of the new toilet facilities to a wonderful benefactor who showed a keen interest in the sanitary conditions of Dorchester.

"That plaque must have cost the Association a bundle," I said in disbelief.

"It didn't cost them anything," Tony said. "I paid for it with the money I won from my other bet."

We walked back in the darkness to the lights of the football field. Tony was the team doctor; he was there for every game and so they let us roam the sidelines.

"My phone keeps turning off," I said, looking at my dark screen. "Ever since that champagne shower in the clubhouse the other day. I probably need a new one."

"Did Janine make it to the parade?"

"I think so. I left passes for her and her friend to sit in the newspaper VIP section. In all the confusion I didn't look when we went by the stands."

"She aced her anatomy exam," Tony said.

"Yeah, she told me. She said it's nice having an uncle who is a doctor as her tutor."

"All part of the friendly service," Tony said, smiling. "I've got to tell you,

Skip. I'm really getting into this 'uncle' thing."

"Speaking of Janine, I think she was at Penn yesterday getting those follow up scans," I said.

"That's right," Tony said. "Rich flew in from LA. It will take a few days to go over them. I'll give him a call tomorrow."

I looked quietly onto the field. My mind was elsewhere. Tony squeezed my shoulder. "Positive thoughts, Skip. Don't give up," he said.

Up in the stands, someone was standing and waving at us.

"Here comes trouble," I said.

"I just heard from my Uncle Marty, the lawyer," Max said as we walked over. "The utility company has offered a big settlement to Jimmy for the electrical transformer problem."

"Why are they offering to pay Jimmy when it was Jimmy who brought down the whole grid?" I asked.

"Because the grid circuit breakers were defective. That's what the whole thing was about. They had just been replaced in a very expensive retrofit ordered personally by the president of the utility company, unanimously approved by the board. There was nothing wrong with the original circuit protectors, but the board insisted they be replaced. The new ones were shit, imported from China, and sold by a company that made millions on the deal. A company that is almost wholly owned by, guess who?"

"The utility company president and board members," Tony said.

"You're pretty smart, college boy," Max said. "My uncle followed up on that call from the purchasing manager who was pissed about the whole thing. He got one of the bad circuit breakers from a lineman, a former client, who showed him that it was cheap junk. The utility company does not want this to go public; they prefer to make restitution to Jimmy and sweep the whole thing under the rug."

"Unbelievable," I said. "I hope this pays Jimmy back for the extra electrical charges."

"It will be that and more. A lot more," Max said.

"Only in America," Tony said.

There was a time out on the field. A Dorchester player was down. The trainer looked over and motioned for Tony to come onto the field. He knelt down beside the boy and motioned to the EMTs. They lifted the player onto a stretcher and carried him over to the sideline behind the benches.

As I walked over, Tony was shining a little pen light in his eyes. The boy was groggy but awake and was talking slow. "I think you're okay, Brian, but we're going to just make sure and check for concussion over at Clinton Heights. The emergency van will be here in a couple of minutes."

The boy looked over to the side where the cheerleaders were lined up. One cheerleader, a petite blonde with big eyes was clutching her pom poms close and looking back with a worried expression.

"Is that your girlfriend?" Tony said, smiling.

"I wish," the boy said. "I think she likes me, but I'm afraid to ask her out."

Tony looked at me. He had that look. "Excuse me for a minute," he said, and walked over toward the cheerleaders. He talked to the girl for a moment and together they walked back. She put her pom poms down and knelt down next to the boy. She took his hand and held it in hers.

"Are you okay, Brian?" she asked.

"I think I'm dreaming," he confessed.

She looked up at Tony, and he nodded back.

"You were so brave out there. When you didn't get up, I was really worried. Doctor Tony said they're taking you to the hospital."

"Everything is spinning," he said with wide eyes.

"Oh," she said with a sad look. "I wish there was something I could do."

"I think he'll be fine," Tony said. "He took one heck of a hit. Big strong guy like him, he'll be up and around tomorrow, no problem."

The EMTs came over with their gurney.

"Maybe," she started, "maybe if you're feeling okay, maybe we can hang out this weekend?"

"Yes, absolutely yes," the boy said as they put him on the gurney.

"Call me," she said, giving his hand a final squeeze. "Please?"

"I definitely will," he said with a grin from ear to ear.

Tony and I walked alongside as they loaded him into the back of the van. "I'm going over in my car," he said.

"I'll get Max to drop me off."

"Dr. Tony," came a distraught voice from the back of the van. "Dr. Tony?"

"I'm coming over," Tony said. "I'll meet you in the emergency room."

"Dr. Tony, she said to call her, but I don't have her phone number. What if it's unlisted?"

Tony smiled. "I'm her family doctor. I have the number. No worries, Brian. You're covered."

The boy relaxed back in the gurney, a dreamy look on his face. "Thanks, Doc."

"All part of the friendly service."

After the game, Max dropped me off out in front of my apartment. Even though I hadn't eaten, I wasn't starving, so I thought I would grab something quick from Best Food. Mrs. Lee was standing at the counter speaking in Mandarin with a customer. That was unusual, because almost no one in Dorchester spoke Mandarin, except for Janine. The customer turned her head.

It was Kim Gundersen.

She was wearing jeans and a white oxford shirt with the sleeves rolled up. Her hair was in a short ponytail. She looked at me and smiled.

I stood there, stunned.

"Sorry to drop in unannounced," she said. "I tried to call your cell to warn you I was coming, but it went right to voicemail."

"My phone was submerged," I said, regaining my composure and looking at my phone. "It keeps randomly turning on and off."

"Can we talk?" she asked, a little nervous, looking down at her feet.

"Sure," I said, more than a little nervous.

Kim looked at Mrs. Lee. Mrs. Lee patted Kim on the arm and said something in Mandarin. She pointed to the first booth. We walked over and slid in.

"I did not expect to see you again," I said.

"Is it okay that I'm here? Would you rather I go?"

"No," I said. "Not at all. I'm glad you're here. This is good. We should talk. Thanks for coming over."

"Janine has been asking me to come out and see her. I helped her move in at Penn. I haven't seen her in over two months, I've missed her very much."

"That's understandable."

"Anyway, she's relentless, as you are probably already finding out. And I miss her so much. Plus she had the scans at the Penn Cancer center, so I flew in last night for a long weekend. She asked if I want to go with her to the Phillies parade today." Kim smiled. "It was nuts! We had a blast. The best time I've had in a long while. Janine and me. It was like old times."

"I'm glad you had fun," I said, "Janine misses you terribly. We see each other a lot, but she always talks about you."

"It sounds as if the two of you spend a lot of time together," she said.

341

"Almost every weekend."

"She tells me everything. She likes school, and she loves spending time with you. Wherever you go, she has so much fun. She absolutely loved Six Flags."

"I thought I was going to die on the Scream Machine coaster. I was screaming like a child and she's shouting 'faster, faster.' She's fun to hang with. She's up for anything."

"Anyway, I saw you and Tony on that float with the ballplayers. I've never seen so many crazy people in all my life."

"Philly is unique," I said. "And we don't get the chance to celebrate a World Series win too often. It was very emotional for the players and the fans."

"When you rode by, Janine grabbed my arm and shouted, 'Look, there's Daddy.' It stunned me for a moment because Daddy for me meant Roger, but she was pointing at you."

I heard a buzzing noise. Kim reached into her bag and hit a button on her cell phone.

Mrs. Lee came to the table and brought a bowl of vegetable sesame noodles and two smaller bowls.

"Mmm, this is delicious," Kim said, digging in with her chopsticks. "Janine raves about these. We used to go to a little noodle shop down the street from our apartment. I guess she orders these when she interns here for Tony."

"Janine and Mrs. Lee talk in Mandarin. Mrs. Lee says she's so cute."

"Mrs. Lee really likes you," Kim said. "I told her I was Janine's mother, and she said, 'Skip is the nicest man in town. He is so very kind to Janine. They are so happy together. I wish he would find a nice Chinese girl for a wife.'"

I started choking on my noodles. As I tried to catch my breath, Kim slid my water toward me, and I took a long drink.

"Sorry," she said.

"No, excuse me. Mrs. Lee is great. She's like a mom to Tony and me."

"Oh, and I saw the video of the Fourth of July game. Janine's been talking about it forever. She put in on last night. It reminded me of watching you play at USC all those years ago. You were really good. You still are. Brought back some memories."

"It was an experience I will never forget."

"I imagine it was. It was very emotional. Janine said that when she watches it she almost cries every time that guy John hits the home run."

"She's become a regular townie here in Dorchester," I said. "She volunteers at Tony's clinic when she can and already she knows everybody. She met John for the first time last week. They all love her."

"She loves them too. She's found a home. Here, with you."

"I always wanted to be a father. It's a dream come true."

"Listen Skip, like I said I tried to call you but I couldn't get through. I wanted to talk to you about Janine's medical situation. That's one reason I came out here. I didn't want to tell you over the phone. I wanted to tell you in person, face to face. You know what they found during the scans out in LA when she was released over the summer."

"Yes. The cancer was still inside her," I said.

"Well, she had the followup scans."

My heart was in my throat, and I stiffened up like a board. I didn't think I could bear to hear any more bad medical news about Janine. "Yes, I knew that," I said. "What did they find?"

Kim set down the chopsticks, leaned over the table and looked me straight in the eyes. I saw a tear running down her cheek. My heart stopped.

"What they found," she said, "was nothing."

My brain was not comprehending. I shook my head. "What do you mean, nothing?"

She started to cry. "It's gone," she said. "The cancer is gone. She's cancer free."

"Wait a minute," I interrupted. "Tony told me that in July they found cancer cells in her. The chemo treatment didn't get it all."

"He's right. The scan they did before she was discharged showed that some of the cancer cells had survived the chemo treatments. But she was too weak to do any more chemo, let alone receive another bone marrow harvest, so they decided to let her try to recover some of her strength before they tried again."

344

"So what happened?"

"Rich Hostler flew in to supervise these tests personally. They could find no trace of the cancer cells anywhere in her body. It's gone."

"How can that be," I asked. "Cancer doesn't just disappear."

"Apparently, sometimes, it does," she said. "Rich says that as incredible as it seems, in rare cases, the white blood cells from a bone marrow donor are so powerful, and can multiply so quickly and in such numbers that they can overwhelm weakened cancer cells. That is apparently what happened with Janine. Your cells not only beat her infection, they killed what was left of her cancer, too."

"My God," I said. "A miracle."

"That's what the doctors say. You saved her life, Skip. Not once, but twice. You really are her hero."

It was like a dam releasing millions of gallons of lake water. My whole body emptied out the bad emotion, and I was filled with more happiness than I had ever experienced in my life. My Janine was cancer free. She would live.

I shook with joy. We both had tears in our eyes.

We sat there for a while in silence, both of us absorbed in our thoughts and emotions. Then, Kim slid her noodle bowl aside.

"My marriage to Roger is now over. I mean, it's been over for years but now it's officially over. We signed the papers. It will be announced to the public in a few days after the election. But, before I can start thinking about my

345

future, there is one thing left for me to come to terms with," she said.

"What's that?"

"Us."

"Regarding us, I mean you and me, I don't think there's anything left to discuss," I said. "You made yourself very clear. You want a new start. You want to live separate lives. I understand. I won't be any trouble. When you come to visit or when Janine goes home to be with you in San Francisco I'll back off and stay out of the way. I don't want to get between the two of you. She is your daughter and Janine loves you more than anything. I'm trying to keep my distance and give you your space."

"I remember you told me once that if I ever wanted to talk, no matter what it is you'd be there to listen, right?"

It was like a kick in the teeth. What was I saying? She was trying to reach out to me. I felt like such a fool.

"Yes, you're right, I did," I said. "I'm sorry for saying that. Please, go ahead. Tell me what's on your mind."

"Listen Skip, I survived all these years by building an emotional wall around myself. When I first saw you again at the hotel in Philadelphia, all my old feelings for you came rushing back. I was afraid. There were suddenly cracks in the walls. For years, I was able to survive without you by making you a villain. I convinced myself that you never wanted more than a one-night stand and that when I needed you, you were gone, engaged. I was comfortable with that story because it made me feel good about the decision I made not to find you all those years ago. At that lunch I found out that story wasn't entirely true. In fact, it wasn't true at all. Sometimes it's easier to keep believing a lie than it is to accept the truth. You just get used to it. You get too comfortable. But, I can't do that anymore."

"Why not?"

"Because of Janine," she said. "You and Janine. The one thing I love most in my life is my daughter. And now she is hopelessly in love with you. She has found the man who will always love her, always protect her. When she hurts, you will be there to kiss the boo boo and make it better. Because you are Daddy. The daddy she never had. The daddy she always dreamed about. The daddy she wanted more than anything else in the world. And not just any daddy. You are the greatest daddy in the world. You are her hero. You saved her life. How many daughters can say that about their fathers? She is filled with wonder and love. She is so unbelievably happy. She talks about you constantly. You will forever be a part of her world. And now if I want to be part of her world, then that means I will have to accept the fact that you will be there, too. And in a big way. And that presents a problem." She reached down and took out her cell phone again, hitting the silence button.

"Sorry," she said. "Janine keeps texting me. Anyway, this afternoon we get back from the parade. Janine is gushing about you as usual, how wonderful you are and everything. Then she says for the umpteenth time that it would be great if you and I could get together. Her two favorite people in the world. Her mother and her father. And for the umpteenth time I tell her that can never happen. You just don't understand. She looks at me and says, 'You're right, I don't understand. You loved him and he loved you and then you were split up by things beyond your control, and now you have the chance to try again. Why not?'"

"What did you say?"

"I opened my mouth to argue and no words came out," she said. "My mind was blank. Suddenly all my old excuses wouldn't work anymore. I had no defense. I had nothing to say."

Kim absentmindedly played with her chopsticks. "I told her about when we met in the hospital, about how told me you wanted to be friends again. My wall was starting to fall down, and it scared the hell out of me. I was worried that I was losing control. I was afraid that I would get hurt again, and I had to just get away. I told you that this time, I was the one driving away. Damn it, I really regret saying that, Skip. I'm so sorry for that. It was so stupid. It was so wrong. I wish I could take that back, but I know I can't. I'm really sorry."

"I think we've both said and done things we regret," I said.

She nodded. "And I told her about what I said to you that night before the surgery, that I never wanted to see you again. And that after that, I told her you would probably never want to ever see me again, either."

"What did she say?"

"Janine said 'I know Skip, and I know that if you reach out to him and tell him how you feel, he will at least listen. Maybe he doesn't want you anymore, and I wouldn't blame him if that's how he feels. But, you need to sit down with him and talk to him face to face. You need to give him the chance to say no, face to face, person to person. You won't have any peace until you do.' I thought about it, and about everything that's happened, and how I feel. I really wanted to tell you the good news about Janine's cancer scan. And I wanted to you to know how much it means to me that you saved her life. I decided that she was right. I need to speak my mind, face to face. I need to be honest with myself and with you. About everything. Maybe it will bring some closure to all this. Or maybe something else. So, here I am."

"And here we are, sixteen years later."

She was trembling. "My walls are completely down. I'm wide open. I feel helpless. And I'm scared to death. I have to tell you something. So just let me say this before I lose my courage."

"I'm listening."

"I am jealous of you and Janine. Of the both of you. Jealous of you because my daughter has found someone to love as much as she does me. And I'm jealous of her because the person she found to love her back is the man who stole my heart. The man who became my closest friend. I've never had a friendship like that in all the years since. The man who put his arm around me and calmed my panic attack as we sung "Happy Together" in front of 100,000

349

people on the beach in Santa Monica. The man who made my body melt down when we made love on his apartment balcony. Every time Janine calls me and tells me about how great it is to spend time with you, I realize more and more what I gave up all those years ago. Every time Janine tells me about how much she loves you, there is a pain deep in my heart. And it won't go away.

She leaned back and took a deep breath. "What I'm trying to say is that I would like another chance, Skip. Another chance at you and me, together. What's past is past, and I can't change what happened or how I acted. I've said terrible things and I know I've hurt you so much. But, if you can forget the past and if you still feel anything in your heart for me, even if it's only a tiny little bit, please tell me now. If there is nothing there, then I promise I will give you your space with Janine and never bother you again."

I took a deep breath. "Well," I began, "this has been the most unbelievable, emotional, life changing year I have ever had. I lost my mother and I found my daughter. I got the chance to replay the greatest baseball game of my live. I mean, come on, the Philadelphia Phillies even won the World Series! It's crazy!"

I reached across the table and took her hand. "So, you really want to know what's in my heart? Here it is. It's the same thing that's in yours. We shared so many good times together. We were so close, you and I. It was always so comfortable, so natural to be with you. I've missed that. I missed it when I made the biggest mistake of my life and pulled out of that parking lot in LA all those years ago. And I still miss it today. And the more time I spend with Janine, the more I realize what I lost all those years ago, too. I don't know if too much time has passed for us, or how this is going to end. It's scary. But I hope, I really hope that maybe this time, the story will have a happier ending. Just like it has with Janine."

"I hope so, too," Kim said, squeezing my hand. She had a far off look on her face. "It's kinda ironic, really, when you think about it. The daughter we conceived together all those years ago was the one who brought us back together all these years later."

"Alright, how about we try this over again and we'll see what happens, okay?"

"Yes. Let's do this," she said.

"Let's start from the beginning."

"Ok."

"Hi. What's your name?" I said.

"My name is Kim," she said with a laugh. "You can call me, ah, Kim."

"Nice to meet you, ah-Kim. And I'm Skip. But you can call me 'Johnny Rotten.'"

She laughed. "Okay, Skip."

My phone let out a curious garbled ring tone. It had decided to start working again. I looked at the screen. It was Janine.

"Someone is very curious," I said.

"I told her I was coming here. She gave me directions to your place and gave me specific instructions to wait there outside your door until you showed up. She sent a hundred texts. She's probably dying to know what's happening. I didn't want to answer until after we had talked."

"Maybe we should put her out of her misery," I said. I answered the phone.

"Hey, Janine. How are you?"

"I'm good," Janine said. "What's going on?"

"What a crazy day," I said. "Did you see me in the parade today?"

"Yes! You and Uncle Tony were on that truck with the baseball players. Thanks for the seats. They were great."

"I'm glad you got to see the parade. Knowing the Phillies, it may be 30 years before the next one."

"Are you home?"

"No, actually I just left the Dorchester High School football game. I'm in Best Foods getting some dinner."

"Oh, ok," she said.

"Are you working tomorrow for Uncle Tony?"

"Yes, ten till four."

"Good. Now that baseball is over I have a lot of free time. Maybe tomorrow night we can try that Vietnamese restaurant you heard about in Old City?"

"Sure, that would be great."

352

"Oh, I forgot to tell you, the most amazing thing happened to me tonight," I said. "I came into Best Food and met someone that I went to school with years ago. I was so surprised."

"That's nice. So, you haven't been home yet?"

"No, I came straight here after the game."

"Oh. You should probably go home."

"Yes, I will in a while. Anyway, I never expected to see this girl here at Best Foods. Who would have thought?"

"A girl?"

"Yes, we used to be really good friends. She's really cute, too."

There was silence on the other end of the phone.

"In fact, we're having dinner together right now," I said. "I really like her. I have a very good feeling about this, wish me luck."

"Um, Daddy," she started, "I need to tell you something."

"I want you to say hi to her," I said, leaning over and offering the phone to Kim. "This is my daughter, Janine."

Kim took the phone. "Hi Angel," she said.

I heard a scream from over the phone. Kim pulled it away from her ear and smiled. Kim was listening as Janine went on and on. And then she started laughing. "Okay, thanks for the advice. I love you too. Talk to you soon." She ended the call and handed the phone back to me.

"What did she say to make you laugh?"

"She said not to hurry back. Stay as long as I want. She won't wait up."

"Good advice," I said.

"Well," she said, leaning over the table toward me. "Here we are. We've been properly introduced. What next?"

Mrs. Lee came by and set the check on the table. Then, out of her left pocket she pulled a fortune cookie and gave it to me, and she pulled one out of her right pocket and gave it to Kim.

I looked up at Mrs. Lee. She smiled and gave me a wink and a quick nod of her head, then turned and walked back to the cash register.

"I wonder what my fortune holds?" Kim said, with a smile.

I opened my fortune cookie.

"*Destiny awaits! Speak your heart's utmost desire.*"

I took a deep breath.

"Kim," I said, "it's still early. Now that we were just properly re-introduced, I don't want to have to say goodbye so soon. I'd like to catch up for lost time. Would you like to come up to my place for a while? I've actually got furniture we can sit on this time. And real wine glasses."

She cracked open her cookie and was staring at the fortune. Her face lit up with a wry smile. She tilted her head. "By chance, do you have any sangria at Casa McCann?"

"It just so happens that I've got a jug of the finest Carlo Rossi chilling in the fridge," I said.

"Really?"

"Really."

She looked down and laughed. It was a good laugh. Genuine. The kind you can't fake. The kind that comes from deep inside.

She looked up at me with a smile. "I would like to accept your proposition, with all my heart." She slid her fortune across the table to me.

"Accept the next proposition you hear."

I paid the bill and we walked outside into the chilly Halloween night air, the orange neon light of the Best Food in Town sign casting a warm glow around our shadows on the old cracked sidewalk as we slowly made out way to the corner. Across the street at Sullivan's, the door opened, and I could hear the sounds of the crowd inside and the music from the jukebox blaring a country love song. Kim and I watched as a young couple stepped out. They stopped at the corner and kissed, a young excited kiss delivered with the passion of youth. Then they turned to walk away down the dimly lit deserted Front Street.

I stopped at the corner and turned to face Kim. I traced my fingers down her cheek and gave her chin a gentle squeeze. Then I kissed her softly on the mouth. I felt her hand come up and reach behind my neck, pulling me in for a deeper lingering kiss. When our lips parted, we stood there on the corner for a while, looking into each other's eyes.

"I never dreamed that after all these years we would find ourselves together again. And on a street corner in downtown Dorchester," I said.

"Never say never," she said. "Life can be a funny thing. You used to say that all the time."

We turned and I led her down the sidewalk toward the apartment entrance.

As we approached the elevator, Kim leaned over toward me. "I have a request to make, and I hope you won't be mad at me for asking this."

"What is it?"

"Would you happen to have another Dorchester baseball shirt? I'm afraid I gave the last one away."

52672065R00213

Made in the USA
Middletown, DE
20 November 2017